THE WHITE TOWER

Also by Dorothy Johnston

The Trojan Dog

THE WHITE TOWER

DOROTHY JOHNSTON

Thomas Dunne Books
St. Martin's Minotaur ≋ New York

THOMAS DUNNE BOOKS.
An imprint of St. Martin's Press.

www.thomasdunnebooks.com
www.minotaurbooks.com

Library of Congress Cataloging-in-Publication Data

Johnston, Dorothy, 1948–
    The white tower / Dorothy Johnston.--1st U.S. ed.
        p. cm.
    ISBN-13: 978-0-312-33249-5
    ISBN-10: 0-312-33249-1
    1. Computer games—Fiction. 2. Computer crimes—Australia—Fiction.
I. Title.

PR9619.3.J672 W47 2006
823'.914—dc22

2006046339

First published in Australia by Wakefield Press

First U.S. Edition: August 2006

10 9 8 7 6 5 4 3 2 1

. . . . . .

To my father,
Eric Johnston, 1919-2001

· · · · · ·

Thanks

I'd like to thank the Australia Council for awarding me the grant that enabled me to write this book. Thanks also to friends who read early drafts, made suggestions and argued points with me, to Lois Murphy and Michael Bollen for their thoughtful and insightful editing, to members and retired members of the Federal police for their help, to my family for their patience, and the ACT public libraries for the great service they provide.

The White Tower is a work of fiction. Though real places are used, the characters are entirely imaginary. I do not intend any reflection on actual security arrangements at the Telstra Tower.

Dorothy Johnston

THE WHITE TOWER

One

Grey castle walls rose from sheer cliffs. I felt as though spires of salt water were constantly washing over me, as they washed and worried the sharp rocks at the cliff's base. Intense cold entered my body through my fingernails and ankle joints, and I forgot I was standing in a room in Canberra, staring at a computer screen. Whoever had created the scene in front of me had drawn the walls and rocks as though they were almost one – straight grey smoothness of the walls, more variation of colour in the cliff face – inseparable and yet not quite. I felt that he – for I knew the artist's name – had intended both rocks and walls to rise from the ocean as though the whole of Irish history could be made contingent in the blinking of an eye.

Yet I stared for a long time at the dividing line, as though it was the picture's most important feature. Directly below it was the body of a young man, his blond hair a single spot of brightness on the screen, long enough to cover his face, and flowing over one dark shoulder. He lay on the spray-wet rocks with his left arm bent underneath his head. A single, hurried glance might have left the viewer with the impression that he was asleep, except for the impossible angle of his legs, spired rocks that gave no quarter.

He wore a black shirt that might have been a uniform. I imagined him standing on the castle wall, looking down, or up, in that last moment before he jumped, a person whose decision, or blank despair without decision, had got him that far, to stand above the ocean on the thick waist of an ancient building.

I turned to the woman standing next to me, realising that the grip of cold came from her as well.

I was aware that Moira Howley, the mother of the young man whose computer we were looking at, in fact wasn't looking at it, hadn't looked at it since she'd led me to her son's room and switched it on. While I'd been staring at the screen, she'd been standing with her head down, one hand resting on a black table.

'Is this all Niall left? No note? No other message?'

'No,' Moira said. 'Just this.'

'What about a will?'

Moira did not so much shake her head as her whole body. She turned from the computer to stare out a window at a square of grass. A magpie hopped across it, dragging a tangled piece of string.

'It's a nightmare,' she said softly. Her eyes were swollen, yet suddenly full of pride.

'But you kept it?'

'I've stared at it till I was sure I was going mad. That's why I phoned you.'

'What did the police say?'

'A suicide note,' Moira said, finally looking at me. 'That was *their* conclusion.'

'Did you attend the hearing?'

'I couldn't. Bernard did.'

'But you –'

'The coroner said he was satisfied that Niall had taken his own life.'

I didn't know why my questions were making Moira impatient. She looked top-heavy and yet frail, a house of cards that was about to topple over, a house a child had made and then forgotten, that the first breeze from an open door might send scattering. Part of it was winter clothes too thick for a September morning, a morning people were celebrating all over Canberra, throwing off jumpers, getting out of doors.

Her only son had killed himself on the night of the winter solstice, and she shivered in remembrance. Her brown woollen cardigan had wide lapels and sagging hip-length pockets. A long skirt, colour of mustard that had been in the fridge too long, was designed to be worn with boots, yet Moira had on thick white socks and a pair of dark blue clogs. When she'd brushed her hand against mine, it felt like I'd put my hand in a freezer.

After my mother died, I'd wrapped myself in layer after layer, and trembled underneath them.

'I want someone who can find out what my son was doing.' Moira's breath strained as though she, and her words, moved forward in spasms. 'Who were these people he sat up half the night playing that game with? What did they do to him?'

'Didn't the police follow that trail?'

'Not that *I* know of,' Moira said dismissively. She smiled. 'It's all right. Sandra. God knows, I've spent enough time working myself up to this. I have cousins called Mahoney. Did you – ?' She bit her lip without finishing her question, but I realised that my Irish surname was the reason she'd picked it from the phone book. 'How about I make some tea?'

I smiled back encouragingly. 'While you're making it, I'll copy this.'

Moira left me alone in her son's room and I copied the castle scene, not quite sure why I was being so careful, since I intended asking her if I could take the computer home, so that my partner, Ivan Semyonov, could go through the hard drive.

I closed the image file. All that remained was the single icon Niall had chosen to leave on the screen. The white tower.

Moira didn't return, and I found my own way back to the front of the house.

I didn't have to hesitate over where to sit because there were only two unmatching chairs squatting in front of a television set. The room reminded me more than anything of a flat my girlfriend Lois and I had rented when we'd first moved out of home. Fully furnished, the newspaper ad had said, and you couldn't complain, Lois had pointed out, because it wasn't actually missing any of the essentials. Two plates and coffee mugs, two forks and spoons. Two beds with identically sagging mattresses, and these unwholesome, vinyl-covered chairs.

I chose the one facing away from the door.

Moira appeared, weighted down with clothes, carrying a tea tray. She told me she'd been home alone when the police had come to inform her of Niall's death. Her husband, Bernard, had already left for work. There'd been two of them, a woman in uniform and a detective in a dark grey suit. They'd stood there and words had come out of their mouths and after the first few her mind had shut down.

'It's still like that.'

The policewoman had sat with Moira while the man phoned Bernard at work, and he'd gone to identify Niall's body.

'I've been unable to focus. Remember even simple things.'

'Have you seen a counsellor?'

She nodded indifferently.

I asked her for a photograph of Niall, and an address book, notebook, something with his friends' phone numbers, then watched the back of her head as she left the room. Her hair was uncombed, uncared for, an ingrown nest. She came back carrying a medium-sized envelope between her thumb and forefinger.

'It was taken on Niall's birthday.'

'What about the phone numbers?'

Moira cleared her throat. 'You see, Bernard and I think Niall must have destroyed everything, you know in preparation –'

'What about bank or cheque books? Financial statements?'

'We closed Niall's account. The bank gave us a final statement.'

'Could I see it please?'

Moira looked as though she was about to ask me why. She left the room again, and came back with a single folded sheet of paper. I sensed she didn't want me looking at the photo, even at her son's last bank statement, in front of her. I put the statement in the envelope, saying, 'I'll return them next time I see you.'

'Niall was very tidy,' she told me, hesitating, then with more determination: 'I never had to nag him. He was always neat. And quiet. He hardly spoke to us those last few weeks. We hardly saw him. He'd come home from work, go into his room. He didn't even want to eat with us. Bernard said he was angry with me. With us. For prying. For trying to control his life. Bernard said we should leave him alone, not pester him, that we had to let him go. Well, Niall had made that clear to us himself – very clear that he was only coming back home for a few weeks, till he found somewhere else to live. Bernard said we should make sure he understood that he was welcome at home, but not put any pressure on him to stay.'

'Where had your son been living?'

'With Natalie. His girlfriend Natalie.'

'They broke up?'

'Yes.'

'Was Niall upset?'

'Well, yes, but it was his decision. He left her.'

'And that night?'

'He came home. Well, before that, he phoned me from work to tell me he was meeting a friend for a drink. I wasn't to keep dinner for him. I was so grateful that he'd phoned, so pleased. You see, half the time he didn't come home, but I'd cook dinner anyway, cook something he liked. He'd turn up at ten o'clock or later, and head straight to his room. And he didn't go to bed either. I'd see his light on. He sat there playing that game. I don't know when he slept.'

'That night?' I repeated.

'Oh yes. Well, he phoned from work. He sounded different. He even called me Mum. Usually he didn't call me anything. I said that was fine. I tried not to gush. I said I'd see him later.'

'Did you?'

'That's the terrible thing. He *did* come home. It was seven, shortly after seven. Bernard and I were in the living room. We don't have central heating or anything. We only heat one room in the evenings. Niall didn't come in. He went straight to his room. I wanted to go after him, but Bernard said no – if he wanted to say hello to us, or get something to eat, he would. I should leave him alone. So I didn't go. I just sat there, even though I felt it wasn't right. And after about half an hour, I heard his footsteps in the corridor, and then the front door. He went out, and – and that was it. I never saw him again.'

I put out my hand. Moira let me take hers and I patted it awkwardly.

'I'll have to talk to Natalie. And to the friend Niall met that night. Who was it?'

'Eamonn. Niall worked with him at the hospital.'

'Could you make me a list? Friends, work colleagues, anybody your son talked about or saw, anyone you remember phoning him here in those last few weeks.'

Moira looked puzzled and I sighed inwardly. She didn't realise that, for me, any investigative work meant going over the traces bit by bit, turning over every stone. Most of my work, since Ivan and I set

up our consultancy, had involved standard white collar crime. It hadn't
been difficult. Most people who commit crimes using computers also
commit elementary errors. But this was different. We weren't talking
about cheating an ATM, or skimming a few thousand bucks from
social security.

We agreed that I would find out what I could about the MUD, and
that Moira would pay my standard hourly rate. I said goodbye and
left, tucking the envelope into my shoulder bag.

. . .

As soon as I'd driven round the corner, I pulled up and ripped it open.

Niall Howley had been a nice-looking young man, small and neatly
made. He faced the camera with his shoulders back and arms relaxed by
his sides. I turned over the photograph. On the back was the date,
9/1/1997, and underneath it '24 today'. As a birthday snapshot, it had
nothing of the strain of an adult son posing for his parents, performing
a ritual years ago outgrown. The Howley's garden, where I presumed
the shot was taken, was in full summer leaf. Niall's last birthday, though
his mother could not possibly have known it then.

Moira. The name had a pleasant ring to my ear. Had Niall called his
mother by her first name?

I've sometimes wondered, watching my son Peter with his friends, or
running across the high school oval with his dog, whether anyone
would ever pick him for mine. Peter has his father's brown hair and
eyes. His nose and chin, all the cast of his face and body are his father's.
Studying Niall's photograph, I wondered the same about him and his
mother. Moira was middle-aged, burdened with sorrow, but even imagining a younger Moira, shoulders back, looking briskly at the world, it
was hard to see what features she had shared with her son.

I started up the car again, remembering the dry ice of her hand, her
lumpy body and stiff yet pleading words, the whole so tense and brittle
that the lightest kiss of wind might bring it to the ground.

My first investigation involving a death. But instead of dwelling on
this, my thoughts, as I negotiated the afternoon traffic on Northbourne
Avenue, returned to my own family, Peter and my baby daughter
Katya, and the business Katya's father, Ivan, and I were trying to run.

Ivan and I had had great hopes when we'd started. We'd moved his computers and fax machine into my house while my ex-husband, Derek, and I were working out our divorce. Peter lived with me most of the time, spending Wednesday nights and part of every weekend with his dad. It was during the year Derek had been away that I'd met Ivan, who was – what? Lover, business partner, the father of my daughter.

We'd had cases and we'd solved them. A few public service fiddles. Enough to keep us from chucking it in. I'm not knocking the fraud stuff. That and Ivan's stints as a techie at the Australian National University had paid our bills. Ivan's six month contract with the ANU was the most job security either of us had enjoyed in quite a while.

Then there was Katya, our woolly-headed baby. There's an irony in having borne two children who physically owe a great deal to their different fathers, and practically nothing to me. Getting pregnant had been an accident. When I'd found out, Ivan and I had both been against going ahead with it. Peter had desperately wanted a baby brother or sister when he was younger, but had grown used to being an only child. Unhappy in my marriage to Derek, I hadn't wanted a second child and, in my mid-thirties, was determined to make a career for myself.

But the night before I was due to keep my appointment for a termination, I announced to Ivan that I'd changed my mind. He fought me tooth and nail for forty-eight hours, then gave in with bad grace. Now he was in love with Katya as I'd never seen him in love with anyone before.

TWO

'I've got the job,' I announced, watching Ivan fill the doorway with our daughter in his arms.

He glanced at me over the top of Katya's head. 'That's good.' Pleased, yet holding something back.

I kissed him and felt the cold of the coming night on his black hair and beard. I took Katya from him, rubbed my chin over her dark fuzz which might one day grow unruly as her father's. She had the smell of a baby who all day has been looked after by other people. I didn't like it. I wanted straight away to bath her, hold her naked against me.

'I rang the creche to see if they had a full-time place for a few weeks and they said no way, which was nice.'

Ivan made a face. 'Very accommodating.' He dumped the bag with Katya's nappies, change of clothes and bottles on the couch.

Katya was dozy, flushed, her eyes half closed. We'd got into the habit of leaving any serious talking until she and Peter were in bed. Today was Wednesday, so Peter wasn't a consideration. This waiting was a habit I'd encouraged. Ivan was the sort of person who'd discuss the fate of the planet, or our business, while bathing, feeding, cleaning up. But this evening I felt differently.

I changed from my work clothes into jeans and an old blue jumper. While I prepared a meal, I thought about coincidence, and how, if the contract with the ANU hadn't come up when it did, if Ivan hadn't taken it, he would be the one working for Moira Howley, not me. Ivan would have been the obvious choice because he knew about MUDs. I'd barely heard of them. All I knew was that they were some sort of role-playing internet game. The letters stood for Multi-User Dungeon, though whether dungeons were a necessary feature, I had no idea.

If Ivan had been the one to ring Moira Howley's doorbell earlier that day, what would he have made of her? And what would Moira have made of him? All the time I was cooking, and Ivan was feeding Katya, and I was feeding Peter's dog Fred, who knew it was Wednesday and moped, and Ivan and I talked in snatches, testing one another, I felt a mixture of pleasure and guilt and anxiety and gratitude.

Domestic life would always pull in too many directions at once, or else the bottom would fall out of it. What was Moira doing now? Washing up the dishes after an early meal? Sitting in a chair, hands clasped, a woman who looked heavier than she was, thinking about the bathroom mirror, and that, if she dared to stand in front of it to comb her hair, nobody would be looking back?

I glanced around my house with more of an accepting eye, the eye of a person who had more important things to think about than the fact that the housework wasn't being done. Originally bought for its renovating potential, it had become comfortable and shabby, offering few sharp edges or surprises. Most of the furniture Derek had bought, or brought with him. I'd become pregnant with Peter soon after we married, and until I took a job in a government department I'd had only scraps of part-time work, and consequently practically no money to call my own.

My living room was now a nest, the once glamorous sofa and armchairs covered with rugs so Peter could climb, and Fred could lie on them. To give Derek credit, he'd been generous about the house. Otherwise, there was no way I could have afforded to keep it.

I grated parmesan cheese, drained pasta, and wondered about the beginnings of obsessions, if Moira Howley could pinpoint such a beginning for Niall, if I ever would for Peter. Would I ever look back and say to myself, yes, that's it, it was then. Before I woke up one morning and the son I knew was gone.

I stopped outside the bathroom door to tell Ivan dinner was ready. He was bathing Katya, singing to her.

'*Varyag*,' I said. 'Isn't that a battleship? I remember you telling me that song was about a battleship.'

Ivan pursed his lips so that they disappeared between his moustache and beard. 'It's what my mother used to sing when she was bathing me.'

'Your mother sang you songs about battleships?'

'In the Russo–Japanese war. It sank with everyone on board. My mother was a proud woman in those days.'

'I heard it in your voice,' I said. 'The pride.'

Ivan threw me a reproachful glance, but underneath it I could see that he was pleased to be talking about his mother, which he hardly ever did.

I'd noticed Russian words and phrases finding their way more and more into his dialogues with his daughter. And Katya, as though she understood, deep inside some fledgling language part of her brain, that they were for her and no one else, lifted her arms and sang back 'Ka! Ka! Ka!' as loudly as she could. She never sang for me, though she would repeat the rise and fall of my voice when I was chatting to her.

Katya splashed and laughed, and Ivan laughed with her, lifting her out of the bath and wrapping her in a thick green towel. As usual, his front and beard were soaking wet.

He dressed her in the white one-piece terrycloth suit she wore night and day, and put her on a rug on the floor, while I served up bowls of pasta and matriciana sauce. Through the steam I recalled Moira Howley's eyes, how she would look anywhere but at her son's body mimicked on a screen.

I felt a sudden need to bring her forward, perhaps to make Ivan see something I was scarcely aware of myself.

'All the years until they're grown up and don't need you any more,' I said. 'And then nothing.'

'What does she want you to do?'

'Find out about her son's obsession. Help her to understand it. Put her in touch with the other players so she can talk to them about Niall, find out about them, what they did together. Why he got hooked. What happened.'

Ivan sipped his orange juice.

'What do you think?' I asked.

He took a moment to consider what I meant, then decided on the safer answer.

'Should be okay. Don't know what anyone'll tell you, but you should be able to make contact. You'll have to see if the game's still up though. What did you say it was called?'

I remembered the name printed along the bottom of the death scene, sitting in the envelope on my desk, along with Niall's photo.

'*Castle of Heroes.*'

Ivan made a face. 'I haven't done it before, but I think I know how. You'll need a Telnet Application, or better still, a MUD client browser. I think I can download one. You want to do it now?'

'Why not?'

Ivan had no trouble getting what he wanted, but then we ran into a wall. There was a message saying that the game was down.

'*Due to Ferdia's tragic and untimely death, Castle of Heroes has vanished for all time.*'

Surely it was Niall's death that mattered, not that of the character he'd played? There was something odd about the message. I couldn't help feeling that it was tongue in cheek.

'Kaput,' Ivan said, with a tinge of satisfaction.

'What now?'

'Well, you can't play it, if that's what you were hoping.'

I stared at the message, willing it to disappear, wishing I could roll the clock back thirty seconds and see another, welcoming one in its place.

'There's a web address.'

'Guys who run MUDs are pretty much totally up themselves,' said Ivan. 'This one's probably kept his homepage complete with pictures of his dog, cat and a description of what he had for breakfast.'

'Let's see.'

I reached out my hand for the mouse.

Ivan stood up, pushing back his chair. 'You can. I've had a hard day at the office.'

Castle of Heroes might no longer exist as a MUD, but its website did, plus several player homepages. I spent half an hour reading through them, staring at photographs and reading potted personal histories. Homepages are such variable things. Some people put them together in a completely straight-faced way, for others they're an opportunity to play a little with identity. For me, that night, they were a consolation prize. I sent off half a dozen emails to ex-players, all saying the same thing, that I was an old friend of Niall Howley's who'd only just found out he was dead. I wanted to talk to anyone who'd been in contact with him in the last weeks of his life.

By far the most elaborate of the homepages belonged to the God of the MUD, a man who called himself Sorley Fallon.

The highlight of his page was a photograph of a young man standing in front of a ruined castle. His dark hair was pulled back in a ponytail, his broad shoulders half turned to the camera. Though wearing ordinary clothes, jeans and an open-necked blue shirt, he looked like a younger Mel Gibson playing Brave Heart. Fallon, with his black hair and dark blue Irish eyes, was extraordinarily handsome, and this in itself made me suspicious.

Behind the photograph, and to the right, was a line drawing of another castle, not much more than a shape and sketch. In the left-hand corner, I read 'GOTO *Castle of Heroes*', the last three words in ornate script and blue to match their creator's eyes. I moved and clicked the mouse. The message on the screen said *Castle of Heroes* was no longer connected. I studied Fallon again. It was hard to see exactly where he was standing. Scrolling down, I came to information about a silver-smithing business, accompanied by more pictures, this time of a shop, Celtic bracelets, and a silver brooch so large and pointed you could use it as a weapon.

The shop was located in a village in County Antrim, Northern Ireland. The composition had an element of tourist posiness, but there something slightly off about it, just as there had been, I thought, with the message of regret about the MUD. It was as though their creator was standing to one side, not laughing exactly, but performing a verbal and pictorial sleight of hand that the initiated would know how to read.

He'd turned his homepage into an advertisement for his silver-smithing business, and this part of it seemed straightforward. The high-lighted words, the words you could click to move to another page, were green and decorated with a small shamrock at either end, an obvious touch on a site whose significance was far from obvious.

I stared again at the handsome face, the thoughtful, knowing blue eyes and mulled over how Sorley Fallon's expression, or indeed his presence, should be read. I had no previous experience of mudding, but living with Ivan, working with Ivan, had taught me that computers were great tools for making up lies about yourself. I was prepared for aliases within aliases, indeed I found the notion an intriguing one, and was grateful that the email addresses gave me some kind of lead.

My brief was to find out what I could about *Castle of Heroes*. Fallon was a logical place to start. But I didn't want to send him the same email I'd sent the ex-players. I needed access to any information Fallon might be sitting on without alerting him to the fact that I was after it. I decided to stop thinking about this for the moment, let it sit at the bottom of my mind.

Ivan had done the dishes, which I could read as a conciliatory gesture if I wished. I gave Katya her last feed for the night, put her to bed, then phoned Brook, a detective sergeant with the Federal Police who was also a friend.

I told him about the job, and asked if he could arrange for me to see the coronial brief on Niall Howley's suicide, plus the photographs.

Brook replied in his dry way that photos shouldn't be a problem, but the brief might be 'a bit more tricky'.

'Who was the officer in charge?'

'Bill McCallum I think. I'll see what I can do.'

Brook said he had to go. I wondered whether his girlfriend, Sophie, was with him, but didn't feel like asking.

I'd first met Brook when he was assigned to investigate a car crash that had broken my arm, and had been meant to do much more. He had leukaemia, and had been given my case as a kind of favour, because he'd wanted to keep working as long as he could. Since then, his cancer had gone into remission, and for the past six months he'd been enjoying a period of unhoped-for good health.

'You know what illness does,' he'd said once, looking at me appreciatively. I'd been seven months pregnant with Katya. He'd taken enormous pleasure in my pregnancy, almost as much as he did in Kat herself. 'It absolves you from responsibility. You're not responsible. It's just something that's happened. And it's a regime, treatment. You're in it, under it, you do what you're told.'

He'd laughed and rubbed his full head of hair. His laughter had been a wind at the end of a long inland summer day, a lifting under dry land, spending what no longer needed to be hoarded.

I'd laughed too, delighted with myself, with him, with life. We'd spent that afternoon as we'd spent many, not talking much, listening to music, drinking tea and eating sweet things.

I knew he couldn't understand why I wanted to take on cases, involve myself in the misfortunes of strangers.

Three

A crumpled arm half hidden by an angel's head, a leg twisted at a crazy angle – the body in the centre of the photograph looked like a doll, a clumsily made toy that had been tossed in a heap by some giant child tired of playing with it. Given that Niall had planned his suicide, had taken pains to get the computer graphic right, had spent time, presumably, deciding on the best position, it made sense that he'd also thought about creating this impression of abandonment.

Why? To make his parents and everyone who'd known him feel guilty? To haunt them? Had this been his intention? What about his fellow Heroes in the Castle?

In the police photographs taken to establish the position of Niall's body, the base of the Telstra Tower was a grey smudge in the background. If you didn't know what it was, it could have been any building, anywhere.

I fetched my hard copy of the castle scene and placed it on my desk beside the photographs. In key respects, the similarities were so strong they had to be intentional.

In both, the body was lying face down, yet favouring the right side. The position of the limbs was different. The twisted right leg of the computer image was, in the police photographs, hidden underneath the body. Yet the overall impression – black clothes, grey background, long bright hair – was the same. The young man who might just be sleeping.

Cold fingers danced along my spine. I was seeing what to the police must have been obvious. Niall's real death was a clever copy of his virtual one. He had died, in actuality, as he had already died in his imagination. The photographs captured the last twist of a play within a play. Niall Howley had scripted his suicide and the performance had gone off without a hitch.

I set aside the distance shots, and the next one hit me between the ribs.

In the photographs I'd looked at so far, Niall's face and the front of his body had been concealed. The earth at the base of the Telstra Tower was hard – baked, unyielding Australian earth – but its impact had been hidden. The first close-up shot showed the side of Niall's face and head squashed to an unrecognisable pulp, his hair dark with blood. Blood ran from what remained of his right eye and nose. There was no right ear. Bits of cheekbone poked through skin that the ground had torn away. His right hip and leg seemed disconnected, as though his clothes covered a body not just broken, but cut up into bits.

There were a number of differently angled close-up shots, the main purpose of them being to catalogue Niall's injuries. I wondered who had seen them apart from the police, the pathologist and coroner, whether Niall's parents had asked to. I felt a scarf of responsibility slip itself around my neck, a scarf that might remain loose and comfortable, or might tighten of its own accord. I'd felt so pleased with myself telling Ivan about my new case, sounding important to Brook on the phone. It hadn't taken much to pull the plug on that.

I sat back and looked out my office window. I'd been in such a hurry to see the photographs that I'd practically grabbed the envelope from Brook when he arrived with it. In spite of what he'd said to me, in spite of trusting him to pull whatever strings were necessary, I'd woken up afraid that he'd turn up empty handed, or ring and say, 'Sorry mate. No dice.'

Before I went to bed the night before, I'd packed away the files from my last job, a routine one for the Industry Department, and my desk was clear apart from a vase of flowers. I kept hard copies of my reports and notes in a double filing cabinet. The office was at the back of the house and offered an uninterrupted view of a trampoline and rotary clothesline. When I lifted my head from my work, I liked to look at the clothes gently drying in the sun and wind. I particularly liked to do this if someone else had hung them out.

While waiting for Brook, I'd moved all of Ivan's stuff onto one of the desks, and re-arranged the other to suit myself. Ivan tended to take over any space he occupied – it simply didn't occur to him that I might prefer to have my corner left exactly how I wanted it. Prunus blossom from our garden was in a bowl on the corner of my desk. Neither

Peter nor Ivan teased me any more about working with my nose against a bunch of flowers. Ever since Peter was born on a rainy September night almost ten years before, a few months after my mother died of cancer, I've liked to pick flowers and keep them near me.

I made copies of the photographs. I'd left all the inside doors open so I could hear Brook and Katya returning from their walk. A soft knock on the front door told me they were back.

Brook was looking sheepish and trying not to grin, an expression that meant everything had gone perfectly from his point of view. I peered around his shoulder at the tight bundle of baby, blanket, woollen cap, as neatly and perfectly wrapped into the stroller as an expensive chocolate.

'She stayed awake for most of it,' Brook said, as though I was criticising him for the fact that my daughter was asleep.

I handed him back the photographs, then said, 'Turn around.'

Brook raised an eyebrow, but did as I requested.

'It's new.'

Brook smiled over his shoulder. 'Forty bucks at Target. End of season.'

'It suits you. A jacket like that you can wear right through till December.'

'That's what I was thinking.'

'I didn't notice because –'

'Because you were too wrapped up in this.' Brook waved the envelope of photographs, then turned it around in his hands the way he'd once turned the Akubra hat he'd worn to cover his baldness.

'Did you say anything to Bill about my case?'

'Didn't know it was a case.'

'About Moira Howley.'

'Nope.'

'Oh,' I said. 'I might need to see him.'

'Shouldn't be a bother.'

'Thanks,' I said. 'It was nice of you to take Kat for a walk.'

'Favourite way of spending my day off.'

'How's Sophie?'

'Fine.'

'Are you seeing her today?'

'We're having dinner at the Taj Mahal.'

'Oh very posh,' I said, and laughed when Brook went red.

'Jealousy does not become you Sandra,' he said with mock pomposity, leaning forward to kiss me goodbye.

For so long Brook had been branded by his illness. Now he stretched and pulled, smiled and limbered, out from underneath the brand. His body was smooth, his greying hair neatly cut into his neck and around his ears. Yet I knew he dressed carefully and admired this trait in others because there was that in him which couldn't be smoothed out, which might ambush him still. This was what gave his eyes a shadow no matter what the time of day. Fear had put down roots as strong as cancer, and came to the surface more or less according to its own inclination. Brook dressed smoothly because crumpled was the best he could hope for underneath.

. . .

That night Ivan and I sat up in bed talking about Niall.

'I wonder why he did it.'

'Maybe he was inventing a past for himself,' Ivan said, fiddling with the doona, folding a corner, letting it loose, then re-folding it. 'And suddenly he was struck by the futility of it. Poor little fucker just could not see the point. The guy has to get a few points for originality. A bit of theatre, no? But his mother will suffer. You can't do anything about that.'

Ivan abandoned his fidgeting and fixed me with his black eyes, but just then I saw Moira Howley more clearly than I saw him, a woman who wore too many clothes, yet was diminished and truncated, sitting on a straight-backed chair, knees and hands together, bearing witness.

'Lie down,' I told Ivan. 'What is it about you that you've never learnt how to talk and be comfortable at the same time?'

'You're not going to complain about the cold.'

'Just lie down and give me back my half of the doona.'

Ivan did what I asked then rolled over with his back to me. I gave it an experimental pat.

'I thought you were tired.'

'I am.'

I put my arms around him, blew on the back of his neck and made the black feather curls, our daughter's curls, lift and tighten. I felt the tension underneath his skin. Our conversation had focused his frustrations with his own life and work. But I didn't think he'd made up his mind *not* to help me.

. . .

Katya woke in the thick dark before a spring dawn, and I got up to feed her.

The initial sensation of alarm, almost of repulsion, the sweetness as my tight breasts, overfull and strained, began to empty. The discomfort of being made to wait, though Katya waited and then took what was offered most days, most nights, without complaint, taking and receiving with an even hand pressed on a working breast. These pre-dawn feeds were when I felt it purest, cleanest, the sucking and the draining down and out. The act, basic and mechanical, a place to start from. She and I had started in the middle of the night, with a single cry as the doctor handed her to me, black hair crowned in blood.

When we came home from hospital, Ivan kept the fire going so I could sit by it at three in the morning and feed her. Now we'd reached a workaday routine. On Katya's creche days, I expressed milk early in the morning. Over the last few weeks I'd been finding I didn't really have enough to make it worthwhile. Katya took milk from bottles with the same wide-eyed calm she accepted it from me.

······

Four

The Telstra Tower pointed a long white finger at the plate blue sky. So blue, blue not of a distance, suggesting other times and places, other cities. Canberra laid out like a dream, smell of the bush, its fingerprints all over Black Mountain. The mountain squatting underneath the tower, and the tower so tall and white, so elongated, needle-thin, it looked like a child's rendition of what was architecturally impossible, a stick building where stick figures went to play.

I climbed towards it, my car protesting more at every bend. I'd grown up in Melbourne, and though I'd lived in Canberra for a long time, I still felt more at home in the damp and rolling fogs of the national capital's winter mornings than these bright, cloudless days. I wondered what the weather had been like the morning Niall's body had been found. I would soon be talking to the woman who'd found him. I had no doubt she remembered.

As I reached the top of the mountain and the base of the tower, a gust of wind swung my car hard to the left. My hands tensed on the wheel as I pulled back from an eight hundred metre drop. I gritted my teeth and made it to the car park, which was lined with acacias, the smell of their blossoms thick and heady. I locked my car and walked over to a fence that separated the car park and a walkway from the tower.

My view of the base was obscured by a corridor of trees and bushes. Looking around, I noticed that this corridor was narrow to the left, but widened considerably downhill to my right. I was early for my appointment, and intended using the time to get as close to the spot where Niall had landed as I could.

I studied the fence. It was surprisingly dilapidated, and low enough for even an athletic dunce like me to climb over without any trouble. Between a row of steps leading to the first floor entrance and the fence was a gap large enough for a smallish person to squeeze through.

I stepped over the fence and made for the spot where I estimated Niall would have fallen, using the photographs I'd copied to orient myself as best I could. The area I was in seemed to be the only one free of trees and bushes. Much of the ground was hard and bare, but spring was making itself felt in new grass and flowering wattle. Now that I was practically underneath it, looking up, the tower appeared like some impossible ocean liner standing on its end.

A number of viewing and broadcasting platforms were spaced out along it. The platform closest to the ground, hung with large white circular discs, each painted with the Telstra logo, jutted out at a height of what I guessed was about thirty metres. From where I was standing, this platform looked much wider than the three above it. How would anyone jumping from the higher platforms avoid hitting this wider one on his way down?

I climbed back over the fence and walked uphill along it. The currawongs were making a racket. I wondered how many native birds nested on the mountain. I'd once seen a currawong swoop down and take a young thornbill, not long out of the nest, balancing on my back fence.

Access to the tower was through two sets of doors, one at ground, another at first floor level. I'd have to check to see if there was a back entrance as well.

At the front of the main entrance I read the notices to visitors. Opening times were from ten in the morning to ten in the evening seven days a week, every day of the year except Christmas and Good Friday. There was a revolving restaurant and a canteen. Access to the viewing galleries was by lift and stairs.

A few minutes later, I was introducing myself to Olga Birtus, the kitchen hand who'd found Niall Howley. I held out my hand and Olga grasped it in her tiny one.

I felt brittle yet enduring bird bones through her skin. Her face was pale, made paler by powder and red lipstick, her dark hair wrinkled at the ends. She wore a man's heavy watch on her thin left wrist, and her eyes kept returning to it, as though the passage of minutes, if she marked them closely enough, would bring the interview sooner to an end.

I asked her what she'd been doing on the morning of 23 June.

'I see something through fence.' Olga jumped into the middle of her story, staring at me, then down at her watch.

'You were in the car park?'

'Am walking from car park. Very cold.'

I pictured Olga hurrying to get inside the tower.

'I see that it is body.'

She took a deep breath. 'I am fright, you understand. I go inside. My hands is shaking, so.' She held up her chicken wings and shivered. 'I wait. Beverley, she come ten minutes.'

'Beverley's your – ?'

'Supervise. My supervise.'

'What's her second name?'

'Pearce.'

Olga drew the double vowel sound out. Beverley had been late that morning, she explained, and waiting had been terrible. She knew she ought to go back downstairs and tell someone, but she hadn't been able to.

'What time did you arrive for work?'

'Is eight-twenty,' Olga replied immediately, obviously having answered this question often enough to roll it off her tongue. 'Beverley she come eight, I come twenty past. Beverley is late, but when she come I tell, and straight, Beverley, she telephone security. He come, and Beverley say, you come Olga, you show us.'

'What was the security guard's name?'

'Mikhail.'

'You took Mikhail and Beverley back and showed them through the fence?'

'I am thinking maybe drunk, you know, asleep. But too cold. That night freezing. Mikhail has phone. He ring to the police.'

'So none of you attempted to get through the fence and go to Niall?'

'Mikhail he go, after phoning to police.'

Olga shot another meaningful look at her outsize watch. I wished I'd tried to set her at her ease by first asking about her children, or telling her about mine.

'Was there anyone else in the car park when you arrived for work that morning?'

'Is fog,' said Olga, surprised that I seemed to have forgotten this. 'From five, six metres nobody can see.'

'But were you aware of anyone else? Any other cars?'

Olga shook her head.

'Where did you park your car?'

'Am parking close.'

'Close to the entrance?'

'Yes.'

'So if there had been other cars in the car park, further away from the entrance, you wouldn't have seen them?'

Olga frowned, as though I was trying to trick her. I bit the inside of my lower lip and decided to leave the question of cars.

'How did you get into the building?'

'Mikhail, he lets me in.'

'But you didn't tell Mikhail about the body?'

'No.'

'Why not?'

'I think Beverley is there. I tell Beverley. She know what to do.'

'But Beverley wasn't there, so you sat down and waited for her. Were you scared of Mikhail? Scared to tell him?'

Olga shrugged, withdrawing further from me.

'I won't keep you much longer,' I said. 'I was wondering, though, how was Niall Howley lying? What position?'

'He have head like this.' Olga rested her head on her right arm, fluffing out her brown hair over it, or attempting to. 'He lie so.' She raised her head. Her eyes glittered with what might have been anger. 'I am thinking,' she said, 'I am thinking, what a beautiful young man.'

. . .

Olga Birtus was one of the names on a photograph that showed her standing outside the fence in front of Niall's body. The other name I'd got from the photos was Mikhail Litowski, the back of whose head appeared in a shot taken from further along the car park. Birtus and Litowski. Did Olga's hesitancy to deal with Mikhail, her evident mistrust, stem from the fact that he was her countryman? I should have asked Olga where she came from. Among other things. I wasn't sure whether there was any significance in the fact that she'd waited before telling anyone about the body. Had there been something odd about it, something she'd needed to think about before she said anything? She'd told Beverley readily enough when Beverley turned up for work half an hour late.

I had fifteen minutes before my meeting with Litowski, a consequence of having rushed through my interview with Olga. I inquired after the canteen supervisor. As luck would have it, she'd left the Telstra Tower in August.

I took the lift to the top platform, deciding I'd use the rest of the time to scout around. I wished it was foggy. I wanted to see for myself what visibility was like on a foggy morning. It wasn't unheard of for Canberra to have fogs as late in the year as this, but it was unlikely.

The view was dizzying. I clutched the handrail for support, even though, since I was still inside the tower, I was separated from the 850 metre drop by thick walls and reinforced glass. The trees below me looked like matchsticks with spiky tops. The roads were grey ribbons, the cars bits of shiny Christmas tinsel, and the blue and purple mountains a border for an architect's or town planner's model.

The wind spun me around as I stepped through heavy doors to the outside viewing area. A steel fence with inward pointing spikes, a metre and a half high, ran along the edge. Before he jumped, Niall Howley must have negotiated those spikes. Surely there'd been signs of that – threads of cloth, even bits of skin or blood where he'd cut his hands?

It looked incredibly difficult. I wasn't even sure if it was possible. I'd have to ask the security guard about access to the lower platforms, but I guessed, in advance, what his answer would be. At ten o'clock at night, it would have been pitch dark outside the radius of the tower's lights. How big an area did the lights cover? And the next morning – slow winter wakening of birds, hunkering down of possums and other nocturnal creatures after a night spent foraging in sub-zero temperatures. There were kangaroos on Black Mountain. Every so often one ventured off it, crossing the highway that separated the hillside from the lake. Once I'd seen one hopping frantically along the grassy verge on the edge of busy Clunies Ross Street, a joey in her pouch.

I made myself complete a circuit of the viewing gallery, stopping short of actually hugging the wall, glad that no one else was mad enough to be out there with me in the roaring wind. Just before I got back to where I'd started, I came to a gate, with an arrow pointing to a further gallery. I'd thought I was as high as the public were allowed to go. A notice under the arrow said the upper gallery was closed. I tried the gate to make sure.

For a second, I considered hopping over it, but quickly dismissed the idea. There was a chance that one of the security people would catch me and I'd be in their bad books from the start.

I contented myself with standing on tiptoe and craning my neck. The upper gallery appeared to be a duplicate of the one I was on, but instead of a tall steel fence, sightseers were protected by one that looked to be only about half a metre high. I moved away from the gate and looked up again. There was the fence, running around the rim of the top gallery. Any adult could easily step over it. But if they did, and jumped, all they would do is land on the gallery I was standing on. The top gallery hugged the side of the tower much more closely than any of the others. Nobody could jump out wide enough to clear the platforms underneath it.

· · ·

Mikhail Litowski looked to be in his late forties. He wore his grey-brown hair so short it was an affectation. His eyes were black and round, two small black shafts drilled into his head. I'd pictured a man with Slavic features, high cheekbones, creamy skin. Litowski looked Indian, rather than eastern European. Standing next to him, I felt the contrast. I'd inherited the light brown hair and pale skin of my Scots and Irish ancestors.

Litowski looked at me as though I was a meal that had been carefully prepared, but still wasn't to his liking. His eyes tasted my insignificant height and overall appearance, the care I'd taken to dress for the interview.

Clearly my preparation did not measure up to the perfect knife creases in his trouser legs. He showed me a three dimensional model of the tower. I'd noticed the model on my way to the viewing galleries. You could scarcely miss it, since it stood in an open foyer, between the lifts and an information kiosk. Like many models of its kind, it had a wedding cake perfection, untouched by weather or by city dirt.

'Howley climbed over here.' Litowski pointed to a replica of the fence with the inward facing barbs.

'What about here?' I pointed to the lower platform, the one with the white discs. 'Couldn't he have jumped from there? It would've been much easier.'

'That is a secure area.' Litowski kept his eyes firmly fixed on the model, but I sensed the contempt in his black eyes for a person who didn't even know the basic facts. 'There's no way any member of the public can get in.'

'Who works there?'

'Technicians.'

'How many technicians?'

'Varies. Always minimum of two.'

'Twenty-four hours a day?'

'Well, no, not on that platform. There are always two technicians on duty, but they might be working somewhere else.'

'What about security?'

'The same. Always a minimum of two. Of course there are more during the hours when the tower is open to the public.'

'Who are you employed by?'

'The company's name is Swift.'

'The technicians are government employees?'

Litowski nodded. If you paid attention to his voice, you could pick up a faint accent. If you were just listening, not looking at him, if you didn't know his name, you might have said he was a second-generation Australian who spoke another language with his parents.

'How do the technicians get in?' I asked. 'I mean, say I was a technician coming to work, what would I do?'

'Well, you'd come in the security entrance. The guard on duty there would check your pass and sign you in.'

'Which pass is that?'

'Picture pass. It's got your photo, name and ID number. The guard enters it on his computer, then issues you with an access card.'

'An access card?'

'That's what gets you in. Say you're working on the broadcasting platform here.' Litowski indicated the one with the white discs. 'You have to go through this security door. That's what your access card's for. When you've finished your shift, you're signing off, you hand back the card. Access cards never leave the building. That's why I say that boy must have jumped from the public platform up here, because it's impossible for an unauthorised person to enter a restricted area.'

I nodded. I wanted Litowski to think I was taking careful note of everything he said. But I was used to security people – in particular I was used to computer security people – claiming their systems were foolproof. They were obliged to. If this man had any doubts he certainly wasn't going to admit them to me.

I asked politely, 'What happens if a card is lost?'

'An access card?'

'Yes. What if a card's lost, or even stolen, while a technician is at work? What happens then?'

'The technician would notify security and the card would be cancelled. No one could use it.'

'How is that done?'

'By computer.'

'So access to and from restricted areas is controlled by computer, and if you tried to use a cancelled card to get through a door, the computer wouldn't let you?'

'That's more or less the way it works.'

'And the technician who'd lost his card?'

'He'd be personally escorted in and out.'

'Just as a matter of curiosity, are there any female technicians employed at the tower?'

'No.'

'What happens at ten o'clock?'

'Ten o'clock at night? We clear the public galleries. All the outside viewing areas are checked, the café, restaurant, and basement. Then we lock the doors.' Litowski paused and added, 'I understand that Howley liked the tower, I mean that it was some sort of favourite spot.'

'Who told you that?'

'I can't recall exactly.'

'Where were you on June the twenty-second?'

Litowski answered with more hostility than the question warranted. 'That's none of your business.'

Any second now, I thought, he'll make some excuse and tell me my time is up. I hadn't prepared for my interview with him, or Olga Birtus, and that was a mistake. Instead of waiting for the coronial brief, studying it first, I'd rushed ahead. I'd used my association with Brook to get Litowski to agree to an interview, but he wouldn't respect my right to ask questions until I showed him I was serious and had done my homework. Maybe not even then.

'If he jumped from where you say he did, how did Niall manage to clear this lower platform?' I felt like a kid at a blackboard, pointing while the teacher stood to one side, ready to pounce on my mistake. 'He would've hit it, wouldn't he? Or landed on it.'

For the first time, I felt Litowski unbend a little. 'He could have cleared it by jumping out wide. Or else –'

'Yes?'

'Or else he hit the platform, as you say, and then kept falling.' Litowski sounded less certain. I could feel his guard slipping and willed it to slip further.

'If he did that,' I said slowly. 'If that's what happened, whoever was working there would have heard or seen him.'

Litowski began to speak, then apparently thought better of it.

'Where were the technicians at that time?'

'In the basement.'

'Both of them?'

Litowski's eye caught someone over my shoulder. 'Yvonne!' he called.

A young woman dressed as he was, except for a black skirt, was walking to the lifts. She stopped and looked back.

'I'll have to leave you now.'

'One last question. What was the weather like the night Niall died?'

'It was winter.'

'Raining?'

'Well yes, there was some rain that night.'

I thanked Litowski for his time and held out my hand. He looked at it with distaste before he shook it briefly, and marched away to join Yvonne.

. . .

I walked around the base of the tower, looking for the security door. A sign at the entrance to a small car park said *Authorised Vehicles Only*. That was okay, since I was on foot. There was a surprising amount of rubbish around the car park, including what appeared to be abandoned parts of a satellite dish. The security entrance was just a door set into the wall, opposite parking spaces reserved by registration numbers. A sign said *Absolutely No Unauthorised Entry*.

Next to the door, also set into the wall, was an intercom microphone. Presumably a technician arriving for work gave his name and the door was opened from the inside. My desire to speak to whoever was on the other side of the door was rapidly disappearing. Assuming he let me in, which was extremely doubtful, what were the chances he'd have seen Niall on 22 June?

I walked back to my car and unlocked it, but instead of starting the engine, I pulled a brochure out of my bag. I'd picked it up on my way out through the main doors.

The front of the brochure showed the tower with a storm behind it, forked lightning cutting the sky in half, as the tower itself did. There was a page of sociable photographs, people eating dinner in the restaurant, buying a coffee at the canteen, a stuffed koala at the souvenir shop. Technical details were given half a dozen short paragraphs. Telstra Tower provided essential communication facilities for Canberra. These included – I mouthed the words to myself – major trunk line radio telephony facilities, television and radio transmitters, mobile radio telephone and cellular phone base stations. A huge telecommunications centre in the middle of the national capital had to be among the top terrorist targets in the country.

I'd checked with the woman at the front counter. She'd told me Yvonne's surname was Radecki.

I phoned from my mobile and asked to speak to Yvonne Radecki. As soon as I introduced myself, I sensed her freeze.

'I'm sorry Ms Mahoney, I can't talk to you right now.'

'Later then? If you could suggest a time for me to ring back?'

'We're not allowed to talk to you. I'm sorry.'

'Would you mind telling me a bit about your work? Help me fill in some background?'

'I'd like to Ms Mahoney, but I'm afraid I can't.'

Five

We were a family. We'd grown up together. We knew each other's characters, their strengths and weaknesses. God's plan to execute Ferdia destroyed that. It turned us from a fighting unit into attacking one another.

I was very critical. I told Niall to appeal. I said to Fallon, 'What's got into you?' 'I make the rules,' Fallon said. He deleted my character and my password. When I heard Niall had killed himself I was devastated. I couldn't believe it. Some of us had been together for years.

Reading through the responses to the emails I'd sent out, it was clear that Niall Howley's death had shocked *Castle of Heroes* players. My impression was that they were deeply divided over the God's treatment of Niall, who'd played a character called Ferdia. I'd been doing some research into MUDs, and aspects of this one struck me as unusual. Of those I'd visited, most seemed to be run by a group of people who called themselves Gods, or Immortals. There were subsections of these, and their tasks were often set out on the MUD's website. It was common for different Immortals to build and maintain different sections of the game. In contrast to this, *Castle of Heroes* appeared to have been run by one man on his own.

Other information I gained from the half dozen ex-players who answered my email. Death in battle had been common, what kept players on their toes. You entered the game as an English foot soldier, and fought your way up from that. To become an Irish character was to be promoted to playing on the 'right' side. To become a Hero was to gain the power to plan battles and entry to the Castle, which was, if the English gained the upper hand in a fight, the only safe place to be. Soldiers who were killed in battle could be given new characters and start again.

A couple of months before Niall's death, I was told, something had happened to sour the relationship between Ferdia and his God.

According to a character called Sgartha, Ferdia had risen to a status no other Hero had ever reached before, to God's unquestioned second in command, with privileged access to the Castle. I asked Sgartha if this had made any of the other Heroes jealous, and he said it might have, except that God had turned on Ferdia, and begun accusing him of sabotage and treason.

It was really bad. Verbal abuse and threats. And the thing was, Ferd wouldn't defend himself. He just kept TELLING that he'd done nothing wrong. I guess that's a kind of defence, but it was so passive. I think at that point Ferd gave up. He started to disintegrate.

On other MUDs I'd visited, the TELL command meant that everybody saw what you were saying. There were other commands, like CHAT, for private conversations between players.

The dispute had gone from bad to worse, with God threatening to delete Niall's character, then God had changed his mind and decided on a public execution.

Deleting's no big deal. You gotta expect it, if you want to move up levels.

Sgartha was answering several of my questions in one.

You get knocked off as a Brit, if God's in a good mood that night, he'll bring you back as an Irish, low level of course. I mean, hell, Ferd'd been through that heaps of times. First, God closes sections of the Castle down. Nobody can go there, and I mean nobody. Some of the Heroes queried it. I mean like what's the use of privileges if you can't use them? God's reply – the Castle is under threat.

I'd established that the Heroes had the run of the castle, while the lower levels didn't.

Okay, like most of us thought, God's planning a new campaign. He'll open up the sections again when he's finished the changes he wants to make, and reveal the new campaign plan.

But then God gets really serious about this sabotage stuff and starts accusing Ferd of treason. At this point, some of us begin to wonder, you know, like what's really going on? Then God calls a special meeting and announces the execution. I didn't know what to think. It was obvious that God was way off on his own trip by then. There's no way he would listen. He remodelled a section of the courtyard for the execution, built a scaffold. The Heroes were supposed to stand around and watch.

At that point, Sgartha had quit the MUD. But his protest, it would seem, was too late for Niall Howley.

· · ·

I tried to will myself into Niall's shoes. I liked live theatre. During my adolescence and early twenties, going to plays and performing in them had been a kind of lifeline for me. I'd delighted in the chance to be somebody else. But this highly structured yet ad lib theatre of the internet left me cold.

To become so obsessed by a fantasy that you lost the ability to step outside it – that was on one side. On the other were Niall's break-up with his girlfriend, his relationship with his parents, and his work – I knew nothing yet about Niall's work situation, or his relationships with people at the hospital.

Moira Howley's instructions to me had been straightforward. Do the computer stuff. Find out about the MUD, uncover its secrets and explain them. But I felt that, if I was to understand what had happened to Niall and why, it was just as important for me to investigate his physical life in Canberra. Moira hadn't objected so far, but would she go on paying me to do that?

There was a risk, in any kind of theatre. It wasn't just you, alone with your imagination. You were dependent on other people for the make-believe to hold. There was a time – I was around sixteen – when I planned to make acting my career. When friends of my mother asked me what I was going to be, I replied defiantly, 'An actress', knowing how my mother disapproved. She considered my choice frivolous, and did not think I had the talent. Looking back now, I don't think so either. But who knows? I stuck with it long enough to begin to understand the simultaneous delight and danger of losing myself in a part, giving myself to it, not wanting to come back.

What had happened to Niall when that place of the imagination, his inner, yet shared sanctuary, had been destroyed? Perhaps the question I needed to ask first was what part he himself had played in the destruction.

Memories of my youthful aspirations gave me some kind of connection to Niall. I didn't want to think about this much, or question it, in case it fell apart. I needed some tendon or connective tissue to the person, otherwise Moira Howley's son was just an outline on a screen, or a pulpy mass at the bottom of a wall.

. . .

On Saturday morning, I printed out the email correspondence and put it in an envelope to take to Moira. My reason for choosing Saturday was that I wanted to meet Bernard Howley, Niall's father.

I knocked on the Howleys' front door and waited on the porch, Niall's computer balanced in my arms with the envelope on top of it. Ivan had examined the hard drive, but had found no files or documents except for the castle scene.

Moira let me in. She blinked as though her eyes hurt and it was an effort to focus on anything. I followed her into the living room, where I put Niall's computer on the floor. She stood waiting, clasping and unclasping her hands.

Bernard Howley walked in, startling me though I was expecting him.

He shook my hand with unsmiling gravity, looked me up and down, and asked me how long I'd been in the computer business.

Erring on the generous side, I told him three years.

I hadn't known what to expect, probably not a man who wore his grief as openly as Moira's, but not someone so closed and immediately hostile either.

Bernard's hair was silver grey, neatly cut and combed. He wore a shirt and tie under a beige hand-knitted vest. His trousers looked freshly ironed, and his shoes were polished.

He said stiffly that he would like a few words alone with me before I left, then, with a disdainful glance at Moira, turned to go. He closed the door behind him with a small, sharp clap.

I reminded myself that Moira had hired me, and I'd be working for her until she told me otherwise. I could stare Bernard down, or whatever else it took.

Moira sat abruptly on one of the vinyl-covered chairs.

I smiled, handing her the emails. 'Have a look at these.'

While she read, I looked at the crosshatched iron filings of hair curling at her temples, as though a magnet had collected them, brown cardigan with holes in both the cuffs, her expression that was cowering yet defiant.

After a few minutes, she said, 'They were his family. These people meant more to him than Bernard and I did. How could this have happened?' She hurried on without waiting for me to form an answer. 'How could I have been so wrong?'

'I'm not sure what you mean.'

Moira's lips became a thin, grey line. 'I let him down.'

'These people are sorrowing and angry. I think they've proved that by their willingness to talk to me. But there's nothing to suggest they were a replacement for you. Or for Niall's father.'

Unless her husband was deliberately eavesdropping, I didn't think he could hear us, but I was conscious of the need to keep my voice down.

Moira glanced at the last email. When she looked up again, her eyes grazed her scant furniture as though to fix each item in its place, then caught Niall's computer.

She stood up and walked over to it. 'Could you – do you think you could – call up this game? I mean, I know you couldn't do it here. We don't have the internet. That was Niall's. We didn't renew his subscription? Is that the right word?'

'The game's not running any more. It's been shut down.'

'What?'

'The man who invented the game and ran it – the one the players refer to as God – he's closed it down. It doesn't exist as a MUD any more, but there's still information about him, and some of the other players, on the internet. That's how I was able to contact them.'

'Did you contact this – does he have a name apart from God?'

'The name he gives himself is Sorley Fallon. That might be his real name, and it might not. He might not even be a he.'

'I don't understand,' Moira said. 'If these other players have the game, why can't they – ?'

'It's not something you buy over the counter. It's a live thing, or was. I mean people played it live.'

'What?' Moira asked again, impatiently.

'There were rules, and levels,' I went on, hoping that by staying calm and explaining I could win her trust. 'A player started at a low level and had to win points to move up. From what I can gather, most of the points were won by fighting, in battles between Irish and English soldiers. But where it differs from a board game is that a character, your son's character Ferdia for example, could talk, interact with other characters, plan battles by typing out what he wanted to do, and the other characters would respond, except they're not sitting in the room with him, they're in America or Ireland, or wherever.'

Moira was standing next to the computer as though connected to it by some thin, tough string. She still had the sheaf of printed emails in her hand. She glanced at it, then said, 'This is your correspondence with these people, but what I really want to know is what this character of my boy's was like. This Ferdia. What sort of a person was he?'

I began to speculate. She interrupted me to tell me she'd been born in Northern Ireland. Her parents had emigrated to Australia when she was six.

'I remember the war and the cold. And the day my mother bought me an orange.' She shuffled the sheets of paper without looking any further at them. 'I was just starting to read, the year we left. We didn't have many books, but my mother used to read them to me. In any case I knew the stories of the Irish heroes. Everybody does.'

I could hardly remember anything of my life before I was six. There were a couple of pictures that I'd worked on, worked over, until they attained a definite, yet shadowy life. They were like short rolls of film that ran a certain length and could never be enlarged or added to. One was of me walking up a laneway under overhanging trees, with my hand in someone else's. I'd ridden this memory hard, desperate to give form to the other person, convince myself that it was my father. In my self-appointed task of recollection, it hardly mattered that my mother insisted my father had left us when I was only a year old.

Moira asked, 'Where is it, do you think?'

'The Castle? I'm not sure. It might not be a real place at all.'

'Probably the north. Hard to imagine a southerner making all this up. Going to the trouble. Though I guess anything is possible.'

She waited for me to comment, and when it was clear I wasn't going to, she continued with a grimace, 'Probably a castle belonging to a rebel family. They all got screwed by the Brits, one way or the other. Some things never change. Even if one of these people did save a few passages of the game, what you're saying is – it'd be like reading the credits to a movie rather than seeing the movie?'

'Something like that, yes. But they liked your son.' I pointed to the emails, half embarrassed, to demonstrate that I'd been doing what she wanted, though I was no longer sure about this. 'They miss him, and some of them are grieving for him.'

'I'd say he was the clever one, Ferdia. He would've got to the top level, or whatever you call it, and stayed there.'

It was unsettling, the mixture of pride and remorse, yearning and defiance in Moira's voice. It seemed that, whereas I'd been looking for Niall Howley behind the character of Ferdia, trying to guess or deduce Niall's state of mind from comments *Castle of Heroes* players made about him, Moira wanted me to help her do the opposite. It was her son's other life that she was interested in.

The player tributes I'd brought her were some help, but they didn't come anywhere near satisfying her.

I opened my mouth to say I'd email the players back with different questions, when she said, 'That picture. The one he left. Do you think Ferdia really looked like that? Was that how he dressed?'

'I guess they'd have worn uniforms of some sort,' I said, nervous now about saying the wrong thing.

'Well, they wouldn't stand up in lines and march.'

I flinched. Moira noticed and reacted with a slow, derisive smile.

I decided that asking questions might be a better way to go. 'When do you think *Castle of Heroes* might have been set?'

'Maybe around the Armada. Elizabeth the first. If it's one of the great rebel Ulster families.'

My guess was that a time frame hadn't mattered much to Sorley Fallon. I suspected that his approach to history had been a ragbag one – pick a name here, a style of dress there. The main thing was the contest. The settings could vary according to his whim.

I didn't mind chatting to Moira about all this, though at every step I was bound to reveal my ignorance of Irish history. But I couldn't help being conscious of her husband's presence in the house, if not actually within earshot, then somewhere just outside it.

Moira understood, or else her own awareness of Bernard's critical and judging presence tipped the scales, because she roused herself and handed back the emails. I hesitated before taking them – I'd expected that she'd want to keep them.

I told her I'd send off some more. I hoped Sgartha and one or two others would answer my questions about Ferdia and his prowess in battle. Best, of course, would be to talk to Sorley Fallon.

. . .

I was surprised to find that Bernard Howley wasn't in the house and that it seemed as if Moira might have known this all along. She called through the back door to let him know that I was coming out, and for a second they could have been any older couple, habits known so well that a few half words were all they needed.

Bernard stood in the open air, framed by trees, bushes and a trellised fence. Two tall eucalypts in one corner, a clutch of three silver birches in another, gave the garden balance. In between were smaller apple and plum trees, flowering shrubs and creepers that gave off mingled, wind-shredded scents of acacia and fruit blossom.

Niall's father motioned me forward and indicated a green wooden seat in a spot out of the wind. He didn't sit down though, and, in the circumstances, I too felt like standing.

If I'd met him socially, I'd probably have thought of his face as pleasant. His features were small and regular, and his resemblance to Niall grew on me as we talked. I guessed his hair had been blond, and his blue, wide-spaced eyes suggested that the similarity between father and son would once have been striking. He was taller than Niall looked in his photo, with a heavier build.

He held himself very erect, one hand on the back of the garden seat continuing to extend the invitation I'd declined. Instead of looking at me as we spoke, he addressed some part of his own anatomy, his hands mostly, a forearm hidden under a shirt that smelt strongly, even out there, of dry-cleaning chemicals.

We began talking, of all things, about Niall's car.

'What happened to it?'

'The police returned it to us,' Bernard said, frowning at his finger-nails, 'along with my son's computer and his – personal effects.'

'Which were?'

'His wallet and his car keys.'

Bernard reminded me of Mikhail Litowski at the Telstra Tower, though they weren't alike to look at. It was the stiffly upright stance, the self control, though I sensed that in Litowski it would go much deeper.

'My son's wallet,' Bernard went on, 'was in the car. There was his driving licence, credit card, and about fifty dollars cash.'

'Nothing else?'

'Just his wallet and car keys. Oh, and his work pass. One of those clip-on passes.'

'Why would Niall be carrying his work pass? He'd finished work for the day.'

Bernard checked his spotless shirt cuffs and replied, 'I have no idea.'

'Where's the car now?'

'I sold it. Don't know about sold. Gave it away practically. The boy who got it couldn't believe his luck.'

'Do you have his address?'

'Somewhere,' Bernard said. 'If I haven't thrown it out. Look, where is all this leading? I really want to impress upon you, Ms ah – ?'

'Mahoney,' I said, thinking that he knew perfectly well.

'What help can you possibly be to my wife? You're not a trained counsellor. You'll only end up doing harm. Moira needs to be helped to put the tragedy behind her, not to dwell on it. If she's offering you money to perform some sort of an investigation, then I'm prepared to offer you a larger sum to stay away from her, from us.'

He finally looked at me, a long level stare. I was sure this had been planned as well, the timing of it, the carrot and the stick in one.

'Mr Howley,' I said, 'why do you think your son killed himself?'

I didn't think he was going to answer me, but eventually he did.

'Niall lost control, of this game – I don't know what else to call it, but game seems an obscene word – of his personal life,' Bernard paused and took a couple of deep breaths, 'God knows, I never thought Natalie added up to much, I thought Niall was worth ten of her in fact – '

'Moira told me that at the time Niall moved back here, after breaking up with Natalie, you advised her – she said your view was that neither of you should intrude. You should let him work it out for himself.'

I meant to be cruel, to pay Bernard back. He went pale and pressed his lips together, biting them. Then he said, 'We knew we had to let go. Whatever Moira says now she knew that as well as I did. It's hard, *was* hard, an only child, and one who'd always been so – '

'What happened that night?'

Bernard looked at me again, not a long, calculating, hostile look, but quick, appraising, wanting to know what his wife had said.

'I'm sure Moira's told you that Niall came home. Briefly. And that neither of us saw him.'

The wind picked up a notch and complained around a garden shed's aluminium corners. My wisteria would probably not flower for another four weeks yet, but Bernard's – I thought of it as his – was covered in buds about to burst. It had left its trellis way behind and climbed, a reckless child, above the fence and higher, threading its way around a crab apple tree and reaching long brown fingers out towards the silver birch.

It seemed out of character, to let the plant run wild, without a proper climbing frame, and nowhere near the house where it could use the eaves. It seemed out of character for Bernard, whose compost heaps against the back fence were shaped into perfect pyramids. Suddenly, I wanted to tell this man about my own garden across the lake, flowers on my desk bespeaking hope, good things to come as well as bad, this man with his attention to pruning and neat edges, so much of the outward appearance of careful treading, careful tending.

'It's all Moira's done these last few months,' he said. 'Blame herself. And me.'

'For what exactly?'

'For being hard. Insensitive. For not having recognised a cry for help.'

'What do you think?'

'I think that, with hindsight, it's possible to rewrite any person's history. And that's what my wife, very understandably, is trying to do. But unfortunately, it won't do her, or our son, any good.'

'What really happened that night?'

'I've told you. Niall came home and went to his room. He was there for a little under half an hour. I know the time because there's a wildlife documentary Moira likes to watch and it had just started when we heard the front door open, and it finished a few moments after Niall went out. Of course neither of us took it in. We were too tense.'

'What do you think Niall was doing in his room?'

'He destroyed all his papers, notes. He could have spent twenty minutes or so getting rid of them that night, although I'd have thought it would take longer to do such a thorough job. Since we didn't see him leave, we don't know what he took with him. He could have had a bag, a briefcase, anything.'

'Your son owned a briefcase?'

'Well no, he didn't actually, not that I'm aware.'

'There's also the computer picture.'

'There you are then,' Bernard said, as though this alone accounted for the time Niall had spent in his room, and his reason for returning to the house. He sounded annoyed, as though I was again asking unnecessary questions.

'Were you satisfied with the coronial inquiry?'

'It was a terrible ordeal. I don't want to be reminded of it.'

'Do you know the person Niall went out to meet?'

'Eamonn? Is that who you mean? Niall worked with him. Yes, you could say I knew him. As well as I knew any of my son's friends.'

'Did he come here, to this house?'

'Not very often. What I mean is, my son wasn't terribly outgoing, he didn't seem to need people all that much. Sometimes I used to wonder if he needed anybody. He didn't seem to miss the company of people his own age, or go looking for it. I guess you'd have to say Natalie was an exception to that. But take one example – Niall never wanted birthday parties. Even when he was quite young. When we asked him he said no thanks, he'd just as soon not bother.'

'But they were real friends for all that, he and Eamonn?'

'I believe so, yes.'

'Did you see Eamonn after Niall died?'

'Well, he came to the funeral.'

'Did you talk to him?'

'Not much. To tell you the truth, all of that's a blur.'

'So you know of nothing about the meeting with Eamonn, or anything that happened that evening or that day which might have triggered Niall's decision?'

'I've already told you what I think.'

'Are you angry with your son Mr Howley?'

'Angry? When your son kills himself, do you feel angry? You feel everything, yes, including anger. But it's nothing like the anger I feel towards you for coming here and asking such a stupid question. It's not a human scale of anger.'

He waited for me to apologise for being stupid, and when I didn't, he went on. 'You want to know what I think. I think my son was lost to me, not that night, but weeks, months before it, years. Now I can blame myself for that, or Niall, or circumstances. But blame – the word, the activity, has become meaningless to me. Just like the word anger, in the way you used it. You know, I can't remember a time when my son wanted to share his interests with me. There must have been a time, mustn't there, when he was four, five years old, when he couldn't help it? But I can't remember. I can't remember a time when he and I were open to the possibility, when he ran in to me and said, "Hey Dad, look at this!" Was that my fault? You see, this is where blame leads you. It's a road with no end.'

He paused, then went on, and now he sounded very tired. 'I do know that by March, April, when Niall and Natalie broke up, and Niall came back here, back home, it was too late. And he told us nothing. In the end he told us nothing.'

······
Six

I wrote to Sorley Fallon, expecting to be ignored. If I was serious about helping Moira, I couldn't put it off any longer.

I introduced myself then typed, *I need to find out why Niall Howley killed himself.*

I stared at this sentence, surprised at how personal it sounded. Up till then, I'd been thinking it was Moira's need, not mine.

Fallon emailed straight back. Over the next few days we had a sort of conversation.

I suggest you try talking to his family.

I'm already doing that. You'll understand that they're in a bad way, his mother especially.

I'm sorry.

A master of the short reply. Was he concerned, or just curious enough to continue?

I like your website.

Thanks.

What's business like there on the Antrim coast?

I get by.

Your jewellery's impressive.

I've some end-of-season specials if you're interested.

Can I take a raincheck on that? What happened to Ferdia? What went wrong?

It's a long story.

I'd established a link to Fallon, but a wrong move would snap it. *Not* making moves wouldn't get me anywhere either. I wedged my courage into my fingertips, and pictured Fallon licking his. How much of his jewellery business did he do by mail order? I imagined opening a well-sealed box on one of those brooches with a dagger pin.

While trying to work out my next question, I arranged to meet Niall's friend, Eamonn, at the hospital where they'd both worked, Niall as a radiotherapist, Eamonn as a nurse. I'd told Moira that I intended contacting Niall's former work colleagues and his ex-girlfriend, Natalie, who was away from Canberra on a field trip. She didn't argue with me, or insist that she'd only hired me to investigate the MUD. She did ask, though, for my latest news from Fallon.

Monaro Hospital had that special incandescence of new expensive places. We'd all seen the five-star accommodation ads on TV when it had opened to a fanfare three years ago. Tastefully decorated rooms with views of the Brindabellas. Especially tasteful flower arrangements, not those desperate floral loopings that surround the seriously ill. The ads for the new hospital had infuriated me. Since my mother died I'd developed, like many people I guess, a dread of hospitals as buildings.

I could have arranged to meet Eamonn in a bar in Civic, but I needed to see where Niall had worked. Being there wasn't as bad as I'd expected. The café was on the ground floor, not far from the main entrance, and this entrance, the shops surrounding it, the massed, shiny glass, the fountain, were exactly like the foyer of a large hotel. Only the number of people in dressing gowns and wheelchairs, the white coats of the staff, gave the place away.

One of the nurses who'd looked after me at the time of my car accident had been a man. He'd been taciturn, competent and kind, and I'd left my own stint in hospital well disposed towards male nurses in general.

Eamonn had the same gentle, though not self-effacing manner. The fine lines around his eyes and mouth suggested that he liked to smile, found quite a lot to smile about, didn't have to fake a cheerful expression for some poor patient who was feeling lousy. The prospect of half an hour spent talking about his friend's suicide apparently didn't make him feel he had to look like an undertaker either.

Both in its variety and quality, Eamonn told me, the food in the cafeteria was unusually good. He spent the first few minutes after we'd

introduced ourselves singing the cook's praises, then explained that
he and Niall had met at Dickson College here in Canberra.

'We did the same Year Twelve subjects. You know, physics, advanced
maths, the heavy stuff.' He smiled self-deprecatingly. 'We were both
interested in medicine. Well, I'd been interested in it since I used to
pinch my sister's nurse kit. Niall was coming round to it. His first
love, all through school, was computers.'

'And after school?'

'Radiotherapy,' Eamonn said mildly, carefully.

'I guess there's a fair bit of computing in that.'

'Sure.' Eamonn nodded. 'But it was the healing that was important
to him.'

'To you as well,' I said, sensing that he wanted this acknowledgment.

Eamonn smiled again, bending his head over his coffee and pastry.
I took a mouthful of my apple cake and pronounced it delicious, though
it wasn't.

'We decided we didn't want the full six years then residency. Well,
for me it was never really a serious consideration, but Niall toyed
with it. And his folks would've supported him financially. No worries
about that.' I heard a note of bitterness, but Eamonn's face wore the
same accepting, even amused expression. 'One weekend he read this
article on cancer and radiation therapy. I remember he brought it
to school on Monday to show me. That was it, his mind was made up
after that.'

'Where did he do his training?'

'Sydney. We both did. I came straight back. Niall stayed on for
another year.'

'Didn't you like Sydney?'

'It was okay.'

In spite of Eamonn's praise of the food, he was only nibbling at it.
'I guess I'm not exactly the adventurous type.'

'Do you like it here?'

'It's pretty amazing working in a place where absolutely everything is
new. Being the first. You walk into a ward and you think, this is going
to be what we make it.'

'And Niall?'

'Well he was the first too, of course. The radiographers all started together.'

'Do you live at the hospital?'

I realised I didn't know whether there was on-site accommodation for nurses.

'No, it's – I live alone.'

'Did you ever play *Castle of Heroes*?'

'I can't stand all that war game bullshit.'

Who had kept the friendship going? I pictured two shy seventeen-year-olds gravitating towards one another, discovering a common interest. But then? According to his father, Niall had been a reserved, self-contained young man. Was it reasonable to guess the friendship had been more important to Eamonn?

I wished Brook had been able to get me the police report. He'd probably come good with it, but I was too impatient to wait. I would have benefited now from knowing what Eamonn had said to the police.

'You saw Niall the night he died. How did he seem to you?'

'Excited, high, happier than I'd seen him in ages.'

'Happy?'

'He'd been depressed. I hadn't seen him outside work for a while. I thought he'd been avoiding me. I didn't like to push him.'

'But you were worried?'

'I don't know about worried. Niall was a moody guy – no it didn't worry me, though looking back of course it should have. When Niall was in one of his moods, the best thing was just to let him be. That's what I thought, anyway.'

'He'd always come round before?'

'Kinda. Yeah. I mean Niall was always quiet. I didn't mind that. I'm quiet myself. We kind of understood each other.'

'But that night was different?'

'Definitely. I hadn't seen him like that – like I said – in a long time.'

'And you asked him why?'

'Pardon?'

'You asked him why? What had happened?'

'He said he'd had some good news, but he wouldn't tell me what it was.'

'Did you have any idea?'

'I wondered if it was to do with his girlfriend. I knew they'd split up of course. I guessed that was maybe why he'd been down. I wondered if they'd decided to give it another try.'

'But?'

'I've got nothing against Nat. She's a nice girl, but Niall never seemed that heartbroken when they broke up. I mean, it wasn't the end of the world for him or anything.'

'Did Niall talk to you about *Castle of Heroes*?'

'I knew some dickhead had been giving him a hard time.'

'But you didn't take it seriously?'

'Didn't want to.'

'What did you talk about?'

'A bit about work. We didn't actually talk much. We had a couple of beers, and, you know, joked around. Niall laughed a lot. But he wasn't drunk, and he wasn't on anything either.'

'How do you know?'

'Because we'd got stoned together and this was different.'

'When you talked about work, was there anything in particular? Or anyone?'

'Niall's boss had been riding him a bit.'

'What about?'

'I don't know, to be honest. Have you met him, Dr Fenshaw?'

'I'm about to. What did Niall think of him?'

'Respected him. Admired him.'

'So he'd take any criticism seriously?'

'Oh for sure yes. He would.'

I heard something in, or under, Eamonn's tone. 'Admired – was there more to it than that?'

Eamonn blushed and didn't answer.

'Was there an argument between Niall and Dr Fenshaw?'

'Niall didn't go looking for trouble, but he was such an independent guy. Hated being told what to do. But he was terribly proud of his department.'

'Could the good news have been to do with work?'

'Well, possibly, I suppose, but – '

Eamonn stared at me, his calm gone, in its place a mouth that could not find a straight line.

I took refuge in practical details and asked, 'Did he have anything with him that night?'

'What do you mean?'

'Was he carrying anything? A bag? A folder, or envelope of papers?'

'No.'

'Did he say anything about where he was going after he left you?'

'No.'

'What was he wearing?'

Eamonn thought for a moment, then said, 'Jeans. Black jeans and a shirt.'

'Just jeans and a shirt?'

'Yeah, I think so.'

'Did he have a jacket with him?'

'Maybe he left it in the car.' Eamonn glanced at his watch. 'Sorry to cut this short, but I have to go.'

'What about your background?'

'Background?'

'Family. You've got an Irish name.'

'Oh that. My folks were born here. I'm about as Irish as –' Eamonn waved a hand, faltering, eyes on his watch again. 'How about Mahoney?'

I nodded. 'Did you and Niall talk about Ireland? Irish politics?'

'From time to time.'

'Which side was he on?'

'He wasn't political. I really have to go.'

I thanked him for meeting me and he agreed that if anything occurred to him that might help, he'd give me a call.

I watched his departing back with mixed feelings. I'd liked him straight away. At the same time a part of me was saying, be careful. Eamonn had been careful. Apart from Niall's state of mind on the night he died, he hadn't given anything away. He'd denied any detailed knowledge of the trouble Niall was in with *Castle of Heroes*. Why tell me categorically that Niall wasn't political? There was the game, for one thing.

I pushed my cake aside, wondering if my habit of leaving myself too much time between appointments was to create the illusion that I was busier than I was. I'd told Ivan I had a whole day of interviewing at the hospital. Why did I have to rub it in?

. . .

Over the phone, the head of the radiation and oncology department, Dr Alex Fenshaw, had made it clear that he was extremely busy, or rather his secretary had made the point on his behalf. In the end, we'd agreed on a short meeting, followed by a tour of the department with one of his staff, who would fill me in on the kind of work Niall Howley had done.

I found the department after making a few wrong turns along what seemed like a hundred dogleg corridors.

I told the receptionist who I was and that I'd come to see Dr Fenshaw. She checked her list. I wasn't on it, which caused a flurry for a few moments until I explained that I wasn't there for a consultation, but to see the doctor about a former staff member.

While I was waiting, I filled in the time reading pamphlets about palliative care. Dr Fenshaw finally appeared with a swish of white coat and long, dark-suited legs, ushering me through a doorway with a sweep of his arm. He was so tall that I felt physically diminished beside him, and I was sure the receptionist, who gave him a quick nervous smile as he hurried past her, had shrunk a good five centimetres.

He had that bearing-down look common to especially tall men. His mouth was wide and firm, curving upwards, lifted by his chin to make a point, to rest on that point for an instant before moving on. Yes, the hospital was wonderful. No expense was spared. His unit was especially wonderful. He was blessed by the dedication of remarkably talented young people.

'After decades of struggling inside the public system, going the rounds with my begging bowl outstretched.'

Fenshaw laughed at himself, stretched out his large smooth doctor's hands and flicked them over. He smiled winningly. 'After all these years I've landed on my feet.'

People could get better just by looking at this man. He knew it in the way his eyes flicked to a point just above my breasts. From someone else, this might have been offensive, or boring, or both. He apologised for being late, as an afterthought, and without being sorry in the least. His dark brown eyes smiled behind their glasses.

'Niall's mother's paying you, is that right?' His voice lingered on the words to give them weight.

'Do you know her?'

'She came to see me a couple of weeks after the funeral.'

'How did she seem?'

'Very upset naturally.'

'What did you say to her?'

Fenshaw moved his shoulders in a way that indicated the helplessness of a strong man used to helping. 'There wasn't much I could say. Sorry seemed a good deal less than adequate.'

'You felt responsible?'

'For what happened to Niall? I didn't know the extent of it until afterwards. I knew something was bothering him.'

I waited.

'It was a sin of omission, of oversight on my part, not to get to the bottom of that business with the internet. Niall was part of my team. I should have been paying more attention.'

'Did you argue with him?'

'I tried to find out why he was coming to work looking like he hadn't had a wink of sleep.'

'Did the other radiographers know what was going on?'

'Niall was a very private young man. That was part of his problem. What is it that his mother wants you to do?'

'Help her understand what happened.'

Fenshaw's pager blipped. 'Excuse me.' He half turned away from me. 'I'm needed I'm afraid.' His wide mouth turned down apologetically. 'One of Niall's former colleagues, Colin Rasmussen, will show you around. Please give me a call if I can be of any further help.'

'I'll do that,' I said, and thanked him for his time.

I stopped at the desk to ask for Colin Rasmussen. The receptionist told me to take a seat, he wouldn't be long.

I passed Fenshaw as I was walking to the row of seats nearest the door. His dark head and big protective shoulders were bent over a small girl. He smiled, bent even closer, said something to the child, who laughed, looking up at him. The woman standing with them, a tall woman, standing stiffly, carrying the child's features, chanced a smile herself, the stiffness cracking a little along her jawline, caught between gratitude and terror.

. . .

Colin Rasmussen held out his hand and introduced himself.

'I'm used to people staring,' he said. 'It's not that often you meet someone with different coloured eyes. Chimaerism, it's called. People with one brown and one blue eye. From different cell lines.'

'Different what?'

'A very early fusion of eggs, one expressing one set of genes and one another. I should have been a twin.'

'Oh,' I said. 'Does it affect your vision?'

'No.' Colin blushed as though he'd heard more in my question than I had intended.

I followed him out through the reception area and along a corridor. He held himself erect, not glancing back at me or making small talk. I stared at the back of his head, a good thirty centimetres above mine. He wore his fine blond hair tied back in a ponytail, as Niall had in the photograph Moira had lent me. But Colin was built very differently. Whereas Niall had been slight, but in proportion, Colin was tall and thin, with rounded shoulders and a concave chest. His ill-fitting white coat made him look a bit like an albino scarecrow. When he finally turned round and started talking to me, his brown and blue eyes startled me all over again.

But then he smiled, as though, having taken in as much of me as he could at first glance, then digested this impression with his back turned, he'd decided that I wasn't as much of a threat as I might have been.

He'd obviously given some thought as to what might constitute a satisfying tour of the department. One of the treatment rooms was vacant and he offered to show me that first.

He led me down a narrow corridor with a ninety degree turn half way along it, explaining that the design was an extra precaution against people wandering into a treatment room by mistake. Another precaution was a flashing red light above our heads. He opened a metal door and stood aside for me to go in ahead of him.

The great eye of a linear accelerator stared down at us from the centre of the room. The accelerator was attached by a long arm to the body of the machine designed for radiation treatment, and the whole was connected by cables to cameras and monitors flush with the ceiling. Colin picked up a small device that looked like a TV remote control and showed me how the eye and arm could be tilted in any direction. A narrow bench stood next to the accelerator, covered with a white sheet, and there was a steel shelf and cupboard in one corner. The cupboard was slightly open. Inside it hung a row of metal vests and on the shelf was a pile of hospital gowns.

'We have two Ventacs,' Colin said. 'All our equipment is state of the art.'

He flicked a switch and a double row of flashing numbers came up on the machine, repeated in the TV monitors. 'This one, the Ventac 2, is eighteen MeV and it's a dual energy machine which means it can produce both electrons and X-rays.'

'What does MeV stand for?'

'Million electron volts.'

Pressing another button on his remote, Colin raised the bench and tilted the accelerator so that the bench and huge eye were in line with one another. 'Relatively shallow tissue is treated with electrons. To reach deeper tissue, the electron beam is converted into X-ray photons.'

Part of the bench was solid steel, and part transparent. Colin pointed to what looked like a crosshatching of black wire under clear perspex. Again he pressed a button, and the bench was lifted higher. 'This is for the electrons to come up through here. A lot of our patients are treated that way.'

'Where are you while the patient's being treated?'

Colin indicated the wall opposite the TV monitors. 'The observation room's through there. The patient's being filmed from a number of angles. You can see it all clearly on the monitors.'

Neither of us spoke for a few moments. The reliable, unerring hum of the accelerator was the only sound, a sound so superior to human ones that it created its own form of indifference. Its eye took us in and reproduced our silence on the screens.

Colin returned the bench to its original position and replaced the sheet.

'How long did you and Niall Howley work together?'

'About two years.' Colin's face was turned away from me and I couldn't see his expression. I realised I should have asked my first question about Niall when we were facing one another. I sensed a change in him, a tensing of his shoulders, a self-protective narrowing of his chest.

'What was he like to work with?'

Colin was saved from having to answer when the door was opened by a dark-haired young woman in a white coat.

'Eve.' Colin smiled nervously.

Eve returned his smile in a way that showed she appreciated the effect she had on men.

'This is Sandra Mahoney. I'm giving her the grand tour.'

Eve's eyes barely grazed mine as she opened the steel door of a locker.

Still watching her apprehensively, Colin said, 'I'll show you the control room next.'

· · ·

Laughter came through the control room door as Colin opened it, and two young women turned to stare.

They were sitting at a bench in front of computers. Monitors above their heads showed the treatment room we'd just left. What had the joke been about? They weren't laughing now.

Colin introduced us, blushing again. Neither woman seemed willing to meet his different-coloured eyes.

I glanced up at a monitor. Eve was using the remote control to position the treatment bench.

Colin explained how the computer verified the treatment data against the settings she was choosing.

A man who looked to be in his late sixties entered the treatment room. Eve helped him take off his coat, and he walked unsteadily over to the bench.

I thought it would be better if we left the two women to get on with their job. Colin led me down another corridor and opened yet another door. 'I'll show you how we make the shells.'

He took a plastic face mask from a cupboard and smoothed his hand gently over curves of chin and cheek.

The mask, or shell, as Colin called it, was attached by staples to a wood and plastic stand. He undid these and pointed to a narrow headrest made of wood and yellow foam.

'This is where the patient's head goes.' His voice was warm and interested. Whatever had upset him was gone, or at least he felt able to set it aside.

'This cross here is the treatment area for –' He glanced down at a name written in black texta on the base of the mask. 'Anne.' Saying the name, he seemed to be recalling the person with affection. 'We make them here. Of course, each mask has to be made and fitted individually. These lines –' Colin pointed out the crosshatching on the side of the plastic neck, 'correspond exactly to tattoos on the patient. The tattoos are made with blue ink just under the skin. Lots of patients take their shells home with them.'

Colin glanced across to a cupboard, where masks like the one he'd shown me lay in a heap. They'd obviously belonged to patients who hadn't wanted to take them home, but Colin was remembering the ones whose attachment to a bit of wood and plastic might have equalled his.

'They have to fit absolutely perfectly.' He showed me how, once the head was in place behind the shell, the sides were stapled down. 'The patient mustn't move at all.'

'How long do they stay like that?'

'Five or ten minutes usually. Sometimes longer. Most of our patients, once we decide on a course of treatment, come every day. Ten days to two weeks would be average. The longest we've had since I've been working here is thirty-five days.'

'Thirty-five days straight?'

Colin nodded. 'Weekends are rostered. There's generally only one radiographer on at the weekends, but if we have to schedule more, then of course we do. In the case of that patient it was felt that to miss even one day would be dangerous.'

As Colin spoke, his greeny-blue and brown eyes sought mine, willing me to feel as he did. I thought of Eamonn and what he'd said about Niall's commitment to healing. Colin's skin was very fine. Colour ebbed and flowed beneath it. He was the type to blush easily and often, but it was his eyes that drew attention to themselves. It seemed as though, having that uniqueness, being born to, growing up to curiosity about it, he'd decided that there was no point in subterfuge, that he might strive *not* to be noted as an oddity, but this striving would always be thwarted.

He held the mask tenderly for a moment before replacing it.

The plastic face stared up at me. Odd how a mask with holes for eyes and mouth could stare, but it seemed alive in that moment, in spite of the black and red lines on its transparent neck. It wasn't a death mask, not an impression of a dead person's face fashioned for posterity or family record, but an imprint of a living human being, made for treatment, for healing.

'You know, a lot of our patients keep in touch, they come back to say hello. Their families. We get close to them. And they come from as far away as Orange, some of them. The patients live in at the hospital while they're having their treatment. We get to know them pretty well.'

'And the radiotherapists? Are you a close-knit group?'

Colin didn't answer immediately. He busied himself tidying the cupboard, bending down and rearranging the masks on the bottom shelf. With his back to me, he said, 'We do our job, that's what's most important. Let's see, what else is there? We make our own shields as well.'

He took what looked like a moulded wedge of lead from a shelf above the now neat face masks.

'These have to be done individually too of course. This one was made to go over a lung, to shield the healthy part of the lung from the electrons. We work with the technicians. We rotate all the jobs, so sometimes we're giving treatment, sometimes we're planning it. We use an X-ray simulator for that. I can show you in a minute. Sometimes we're doing technical stuff like this. This one here –' Colin picked up part of a lead face mask with one eye hole cut out. 'This was for a tumour at the corner of the left eye. Feel how heavy it is.'

I weighed the mask-shield in my hand and asked, 'Did Niall ever talk to you about what was bothering him?'

Colin stared down at the shield as though he regretted having let me hold it, tilting his whole body away from me. The effect was almost comical, like our dog Fred when he wanted to sneak a sandwich crust that Peter had left on the floor.

'I didn't really know Niall Howley.' Colin cleared his throat. 'Actually I didn't know him at all.'

'Did he have friends here, among the radiographers?'

'I don't know.'

'Did it ever strike you that Niall was hiding something?'

'No.' Colin went red, the painful blush of very fair-skinned people reaching right up through his scalp.

I handed back the lead mask and he replaced it carefully in its position on the shelf. He hesitated, then turned on his heel and left the room.

I followed, determined to go on asking questions about Niall, no matter how uncomfortable they made him. That question about having something to hide – wasn't the right answer yes, that his life was being taken over by a MUD? And why didn't Colin know who, in the hospital, had been a friend of Niall's? I was forming a disturbing impression, that not only were Colin's eyes different colours, but they looked in different directions as well, as though better to avoid having to meet mine.

He marched ahead and I hurried to keep up.

'Doesn't it strike you as rather contradictory? Niall cared about his work, and it obviously requires a great deal of concentration. Yet he sat up all night playing a computer game.'

Colin didn't answer. I persisted. 'What do you think?'

Colin turned to face me, frowning. 'I've already told you, I didn't know him personally.'

'Are you interested in MUDs yourself?'

'Of course not.' Colin turned away from me with an expression of disgust. 'I don't know anything about them.'

He went on to show me more glistening machines, one the X-ray simulator he'd referred to earlier. But I'd reached saturation point and barely took in anything about them.

He raised his head at the sound of footsteps hurrying past in the corridor. The door to the room containing the simulator was three-quarters shut, so he couldn't see who it was. I wondered if it was Dr Fenshaw, if Colin recognised his step, and had been listening for it, if that might explain the undercurrent of anxiety in his manner, an ear tuned through practice, an already nervous disposition, to his boss's footsteps.

I wondered whether, in common with a lot of other nervous people, Colin wasted energy worrying, that his instinct was immediately to worry, or whether there was something particular about Fenshaw that required attentive listening, and about Niall's death that required him to say no automatically.

The steps receded. Further off, voices rose and fell. The air-conditioning sighed. Colin was staring into space, hands in the pockets of his lab coat.

'What happens if something goes wrong with one of the accelerators?'

He started, shook his hands free. 'We'd get someone from the Biomedical Engineering Department. What I mean is, there are full-time technicians here in the hospital. If they can't fix it, Dr Fenshaw rings Sydney. We can have an engineer here within three hours of reporting a problem.'

'The manufacturers are in Sydney?'

'A rep. Wilton's an American company. In the very unlikely event of it turning out to be something the guy from Sydney couldn't handle, he'd ring the States. We can get parts from the States in under two days.'

Colin was controlling his voice with an effort, but determined to go ahead and make his point. 'The thing you have to understand about the treatment is – it's critical. I wasn't exaggerating when I told you about that patient who came in thirty-five days straight. We've worked over Christmas, Easter, so a patient won't have to miss a day. The Ventacs are incredibly sophisticated machines. Sure there are going to be minor technical problems from time to time. But it's important to remember that every minute they're operating here, they're saving lives.'

My stomach was knotting with the intensity of this. What had I said to bring it on? And what was it about Niall Howley that Colin didn't want to talk about? Was it that Niall had killed himself? Was this sufficient reason for Colin to want to dismiss him, and subtly, or not so subtly, put him down?

On my way from the radiotherapy department back to the side of the hospital where I'd parked my car, I recognised Eve, the young woman who'd come to set up the treatment room while Colin was putting the accelerator through its paces.

I hurried to catch up with her and, when I was half a dozen steps behind, called out her name.

She swung round and stared at me blankly.

'Eve?' I repeated. 'It's Sandra Mahoney. I met you a little while ago. With Colin Rasmussen.'

'Oh,' she said. 'Oh yes.'

I could see her caught between wanting to hurry on to whatever business she had waiting, and not wanting to be rude to me in case I was somebody official.

I walked up level with her. 'I won't keep you. I was just wondering, did you know Niall Howley?'

'He was the guy who died, right? No, I didn't know him.'

'Could you tell me who in the department he was friends with, who might have known him best?'

Eve looked startled, then guilty. 'Why do you want to know? Who are you anyway?'

'Niall's mother's hired me to see if I can find out more about what led to his death.'

'Oh,' Eve said. 'Colin –' She bit her lip. 'Sorry, I'm in rather a hurry.' She began to move away.

'Did Niall have any friends here?'

'They – we're all new, you see.'

'You mean nobody working in the department now was here when Niall was?'

'Except Colin. And of course Dr Fenshaw.'

'What happened to the others?'

Eve caught sight of someone out of the corner of her eye. 'Dominic!'

A tall, good-looking man was bearing down on us, lifting his hand in a quick salute.

'Nick! I'm sorry!' Eve's olive skin had gone a deep red-brown.

The man ignored me and smiled at Eve, giving the impression that he was annoyed, but prepared to let her make it up to him.

Eve turned to me. 'I have to go. I'm sorry.'

I thanked her and said goodbye, wishing handsome Dominic had been held up somewhere too.

. . .

Coloured arrows on the floor converged towards two men unaware of me, half hidden from me by the angle of a corridor. Colin's face was thin and flushed. His blond hair flopped forward, and his gestures were exaggerated, arms poking out of the too-short sleeves of his white coat. He was appealing to Dr Fenshaw, who was leaning towards him the way a man did when he was certain of his power of attraction.

It was only a moment before Fenshaw continued on along the corridor, Colin staring after him, red-faced and intent. I was sure that, whatever Colin was asking for, the answer had been no. He stood looking anxiously after his superior with his eyes from once discrete, lost twins. Then he too moved away, energetic suddenly, in a hurry, his white coat a spinnaker that the wind has filled.

I thought of following, then decided I didn't want either man to know I'd seen him. Though I'd left the accelerators behind a maze of corridors, I was aware, in my inner ear, of their constant, authoritative song, a long, one-toned exhalation.

. . .

I phoned Eamonn that evening and thanked him again for making time to see me. I asked if he'd been aware that there'd been a complete turnover of radiotherapists at the Monaro Hospital, apart from Colin Rasmussen. Eamonn said he'd heard about it.

'How many were there?'

'Six, I think. Six or seven.'

I asked him if he'd help me track them down. After a pause, he replied in his mild, pleasant way that he'd see what he could do.

I put the phone down conscious of the pressing in of memories. The huge, unquiet breath of the accelerators had followed me home, but it couldn't be something I associated with my mother's illness, because she'd had no radiation treatment.

There'd been wards with other women. I remembered how symmetrical and alike these women had looked, putting on a good face in pink and aqua bedjackets. Women of a certain age with a lifetime's practice at putting on a face.

The phrases, 'Just a few tests love.' 'Be out of here tomorrow.' And she was. But in a few months back again, to a ward identical in almost all respects. More tests. What had I been thinking of? Or was it that I had not been thinking, had refused to think? Had got back on the plane and home to Canberra and Derek?

The four or six bed ward. The women sitting against pillows primped for visitors. My mother's false cheerfulness repelling conversation. Not her cowardice, but mine.

. . .

'Hey you,' I said to Ivan late that night, pulling on his arm. 'Do you know what time it is?'

'In a minute Sandy. Don't wait up for me. Go to bed.'

'I did. Hours ago.'

Ivan had found a game similar to Niall's, and was playing it for all he was worth.

'Celtic magic,' I said crossly. 'Ruined castles. A bad guy lurking behind every rock.'

I recalled Ivan's cold side of the bed, my side cooling down, and was irritated because I knew it was a false opposition to set up – work and bed.

'It's given me an idea.'

'What kind of an idea?'

'Not a MUD,' Ivan intoned. 'MUDs are boring. I've got to work it out. Dangerous to talk about it too much. Words might steal it.'

I lay awake waiting for him, then I must have fallen asleep because he woke me with waves of bathroom air and a smell of toothpaste.

I lay against his chest and felt damp hair. 'What are you doing having a shower in the middle of the night?'

'The water splashed while I was cleaning my teeth.'

'You'll catch cold.'

'Australians have no idea of cold.' Ivan rolled over, getting comfortable. 'It's true Sandy. This doona is a heap of shit. I have to go to sleep now. Wake me up at seven.'

'You'll be stuffed.'

'I'll catch a nap at lunchtime.'

I liked the moonlight coming in between and under skimpy curtains, and had always resisted Derek's nagging that we should get proper, made-to-measure ones. But that night I would have liked the darkness to be total. Perversely awake – Ivan was snoring lightly in five minutes – I did not want to look at the bulk of him beside me, or rather would have preferred to see it only with my inner eye.

Black hair and eyes, and thick white skin, were transferable and travelled well. What would a childhood of Canberra summers do to Katya's? High cheekbones instructed eyes towards an almost slant. I wanted to say to Ivan, look, I may not know much about families, about yours practically nothing because you refuse to talk about it. But I do know this. There's never as much time as you think.

I stared at objects and felt my attempt to force a solid and recognisable shape from them to be a kind of joke against myself. A chill passed between my shoulderblades. I thought that maybe, on other nights, Ivan lay watching me asleep. Ivan didn't look for patterns in relationships, in people, but through the digital images he created, and that were his greatest pleasure, suspended now because of having to work eight hours a day at the ANU. It occurred to me that he needed me to be a certain type of person, a certain type of Australian person – down-to-earth and plodding. He'd remarked once that Brook and I were two of a kind.

Ivan's face was blank with fatigue in the early morning, that once favourite time for sex, in the days when it was still supposed to be a secret from Peter asleep in the next room, Derek in America. I pictured a man sitting in front of a computer screen, a young man with his life ahead of him, concentrating, deeply moved. Dead before his time, this young man now stood between me and Ivan, me and Brook, me and Moira Howley. Eamonn had described him as independent. Colin Rasmussen had had little time for him. As Ferdia, he'd been respected and admired, but had managed to make an enemy of God.

There was the question of knowledge for its own sake, whether such a thing was possible, and, if so, what its consequences might turn out to be. And the related idea that, for certain people – Niall among them? – idealism equipped them poorly for dealing with people for whom knowledge was a way to power.

······

Seven

I emailed Sorley Fallon.

Why did you decide to execute Ferdia?
  It was my MUD. I ran it. I could do what I liked.
  Why that form of punishment? What had Ferdia done?
  Ferdia turned traitor. Before that he was the best player, the greatest Hero the Castle ever had.
  Did you give Ferdia a chance to demonstrate his innocence?
  Dozens of them.
  Do you believe Niall was so devastated by your decision to execute Ferdia that he took his own life?
  That idea is absurd.
  Were you questioned by the police about Niall's death?
  No.

Civic police station was an ambiguous refuge with rain knifing straight down off the Brindabellas. September sometimes threw up days that were colder and wetter than mid-July, Canberra days that made people feel spring had made an appearance only to mock them.

I'd dressed with more care than usual for my interview with Detective-Sergeant McCallum, in a skirt, boots I'd cleaned the night before, a neat woollen jumper. Now my boots were decorated with frills of mud and the hem of my skirt had been in the wrong place at the wrong time when a car skidded to a halt at the Northbourne traffic lights. Because of the weather, all the Civic car parks were full, and even though I'd left myself plenty of time, I had to park way over on Marcus Clarke and ended up running and sloshing my way to the station.

Rows of wet people filled the waiting benches. Maybe it was the rain, the throwback to winter, maybe it was the fact that I'd sat up late the night before reading the police report that Brook had finally brought round, but I felt depressed.

Brook's helpfulness. The way he'd smiled and said, 'Here you go Sunshine.' Borrowing the report for me, so I could read it at my leisure, copy what I liked. His pride in his ability to do this, even with the delay. The dry courtesy of that generation of policemen. I'd asked him if he'd read it himself, if he'd known that all the radiotherapists who'd worked with Niall had left except for one, if he knew that Niall's best friend had described him as happy on the night he'd died. Brook said no to all three questions, the careful no of a man who'd done what I wanted, but reluctantly, who did not want to be pushed into telling me I should leave well enough alone.

I'd started reading and was immediately disappointed. There was plenty of technical information, lists of the bones Niall had broken in his fall. But as to motive, states of mind, leads pointing to other people and the parts they might have played – it was less than sketchy. I'd built it up in my mind as giving me a clear direction, something I should never have done.

Moira hadn't seen it, had not asked to see it. She hadn't looked at the photographs either. Her imagination supplied her with a horror that they could not match. Would they have added to it though? Would they have seemed unreal?

Moira spent each day alone in her house with memories for company. Did she count the hours till Bernard came home from work? Did she dread that moment when he walked through the door? I thought of the television set and two chairs facing it, a black joke surely, a rotten nasty joke. And of the mother sitting, hands fondling, biting at one another, in her son's empty room, watching a blank screen.

Dr Fenshaw's testimony had stuck in my mind. The beginning came back to me almost word for word.

I have known Niall Howley for a little over two years, since he began working in the radiotherapy unit. During that time, and in particular in the last six months, I was disappointed, indeed distressed, to find Howley's work deteriorating. His ability to concentrate and to perform even simple tasks could not be relied on. It became a habit for him to come to work tired, and indeed on more than one occasion, it looked as though he'd had no sleep at all. I tried to talk to him about what was bothering him but, I am afraid, got nowhere. On the day in question, Howley appeared much the same, that is, physically tired, withdrawn and uncooperative.

That day at the hospital, I'd watched with admiration as Fenshaw comforted a young patient, but was struck by his readiness to conclude that Niall had lost his professional competence to an interactive game.

· · ·

Bill McCallum's eyes were blue, deep-set, fringed with dark blond lashes. He smiled and half stood up, shaking hands across a desk piled with papers. I felt a kindliness approach, then fix itself on me, as though whatever I'd done wrong would be understood and eventually forgiven.

'I had a bit to do with Moira Howley around the time of the inquest.' McCallum settled himself back down behind his desk. 'How's she doing?'

'Not too well.'

I suddenly noticed that McCallum had no neck. His shoulder pads, with their Federal Police insignia, bunched his shoulders up to short grey hair, which, cut straight above his ears, added to the squashed effect. The band of his black trousers sat too high on a non-existent waist.

'Of the forty or so suicides we've had in the last year,' he was informing me, 'only two have been jumpers. Most people gas or hang themselves.'

Forty seemed a lot for a population of three hundred thousand.

My expression must have shown what I was thinking. McCallum said, 'Oh yes, it's more common than most people think. There are traditions. Not something ordinary folk think much about. Well of course suicides aren't reported in the press. Jumping's a tradition. Top of the Currong flats. Last year we had two brothers. Terrible that was, the second following the first.'

'Why didn't – ?' I began.

'Block it off? Knock it down? They'd find somewhere else.'

I wondered about the people living there, the non-suicides, and for a farcical, stupid moment pictured a young woman looking up through the window and saying to her toddler, 'There goes another one.'

Under his thick eyelashes, McCallum was returning my gaze shrewdly. I thought of Brook, how when ill, bald, chemoed to the eyeballs, Brook had had that cocky manner, that okay you might have got me but I'm still breathing you bastard look about him.

'Jumpers,' McCallum was saying. 'Jumpers are – well, in my experience jumpers are always badly disturbed. They choose to jump because it's so violent.'

He flashed me another quick, assessing look. 'That seems odd to you, doesn't it? You're thinking that all suicide is by definition a violent end to life. But only a very particular type of person chooses to jump. I've never come across an exception to that in all my years of police work. And never from the Telstra Tower. That's a first.'

His eyes, transforming his pale scrunched face, watched me, not impatiently, not accusingly, but offering knowledge based on experience and waiting to see what I did with it.

'And it's an awful thing. Just now I mentioned tradition. Well, traditions have to, you know, augment themselves, become more elaborate, and in the traditions of suicides and potential suicides, more crazy from our point of view. They have to go one more, do better than the last fellow.'

'You think that's what could have happened with Niall Howley?'

'Yes, I do.'

'But there's a puzzle, isn't there? How did Niall clear the lower platform?' I took my brochure of the tower out of my bag and put it on the desk between us, pointing to the broadcasting platform with the large white discs. 'The width here – the difference between this, where Niall's supposed to have jumped from, and this, is over a metre. How did he manage to jump out far enough to clear it?'

'I agree it seems unusual. Howley was very disturbed and very determined.'

But that doesn't make him Superman, I thought, biting my lip, determined to stay on the right side of McCallum since that was how I seemed to have started off.

'Did you consider the possibility that he jumped from the lower platform?' It was one of my frustrations with the report that there was no discussion of this.

'It certainly occurred to us, but there's no evidence to suggest Howley gained entry to any restricted area. You need a pass for that and Howley didn't have one.'

Perhaps I was right in assuming that, on this point at least, the police had made only superficial inquiries. Why go looking for unnecessary complications? Had this been their reasoning? I reminded myself that it hadn't just been this man, that he'd had detective-constables knocking on doors and asking questions. But it had been McCallum who'd read through all the answers, collated them, drawn his conclusions, and influenced the coroner, in turn, to draw his.

'Going back to this platform,' I said, indicating the higher public one. 'Were any bits of Niall's clothing found on the spikes? Or maybe blood, where he'd scratched himself climbing over?'

McCallum shook his head. 'You see, they don't think like you and me, these young guys. It all seems crazy, unbelievable to you, but that's because you're looking at it from the outside.'

'Have you had much to do with computer addicts before?'

In his experience, McCallum said, addiction was addiction. It manifested itself in different ways, but there was an underlying psychology which was depressingly the same. He told me the story of a young man who came to Canberra from Thailand to go to university.

'A mate found him dead in his room a week before his third year exams. Heroin overdose. Parents flew straight out here. I drove them to the morgue and left them with him. Of course we're not supposed to do that. If any of the blokes out there had dobbed me in – but they needed to be with their son to pray.'

'Where were you while they were with him?'

'Waited outside. Got a chair and sat down by the door.'

I pictured McCallum hunched on his chair, nervous, but not too nervous, of a reprimand. I rephrased my question. 'Have there been other suicides associated with over-use, or – addiction – to computers?'

'You mean computer games?'

I nodded, thinking that in Niall Howley's case I did, but I could think of other instances, cases that had been reported in the press, of boys who'd become so hooked they'd been unable to get up from their computers to eat, or sleep, or use the lavatory.

'Not here in Canberra.'

'Did you contact any of the other players, or the guy who ran the MUD?'

The answer had to be no, I thought, otherwise they would have been referred to in the report. There was also Fallon's no, but I still wanted to hear McCallum say it.

He frowned. 'Police resources are tight enough, without wasting them on no-hopers like that.'

'Was the coroner satisfied that playing the game led to Niall's death?'

'Yes.'

I heard a noise, turned round and there was Brook, appearing from behind a perspex partition, its wavery reflections and the angle of the light multiplying his new suit.

He winked at McCallum, and kissed me on the cheek.

'Hi,' I said. 'Are you on your way to court?'

'After lunch.'

I thanked McCallum and shook his hand again. 'You've been very helpful.'

'Not too gruesome?'

'If it is, that's hardly your fault.'

'This old man remembers.'

'Too well,' Brook said with a grimace.

McCallum leant back in his chair. 'Remember that time we were sent out to the Cotter? There'd been that double suicide and they couldn't find the head? We were on bikes and I raced you.'

'You always raced me.'

'One of the heads was in the back of the ute and they were beating the bushes for the other one,' McCallum explained for my benefit. 'This young couple tied ropes to a tree and then around their necks. Going down this slope to the river. Ropes ripped their heads off. Back of the ute was covered in blood. Sharp eyes here found the second head. It'd rolled more than fifty metres down the hill.'

Brook said, 'We were too young to be doing that.' He was dressed for an outing. His skin shone, and he seemed ready to lift out of clothes and buildings, grey skies and a downpour.

'I'd go to the pictures with him,' McCallum said, noting my appreciation. 'But he'd have to buy me popcorn and a coke.'

'It's a date,' Brook answered, grinning. He squeezed my arm. 'Phone me tonight. I should be home by eight.'

'You haven't forgotten?'

'Peter's birthday? How could I forget?'

. . .

On my way out of the building, I met Sophie going in. I was putting up my umbrella and she almost ran into me. Her umbrella still up, me struggling with mine. We stared at one another. Sophie was taller, but I was two steps higher, which should have given me a momentary advantage. Her dark hair looked darker, not bedraggled, in the rain. She wore a suit and shoes with heels so high that, had I tried to wear them, I would have fallen over. Brook wasn't a particularly tall man, short, in fact, for a policeman. Was Sophie trying to outreach him? She must have found a park close by, or else was far more adept than I was at negotiating puddles.

I silently congratulated her. She looked me up and down and I had a flash of Mikhail Litowski doing the same at the Telstra Tower – a sharp, confident, masticating look. She was Brook's age and a widow. She'd had her kids very young, so now, conveniently, they were off her hands. So much compatibility in what seemed a record time. But who was measuring? Anyone could see they'd hit it off. Had he told her how his wife had left him, taken their two children, not returned to visit even when he was in hospital?

We said hello, smiled, passed each other.

Meeting him at work. A lunch date. Now she was with him, he with her, a lightness that two, three flights of stairs did not account for. But wasn't Sophie too matt, too sharp, too limited? So careful with me. A mask that umbrellas and the rain, the awkward steps, excused. Brook laughing, glowing. I used to think his chemotherapy had made him transparent. The bad blood might come back, trick him and the doctors. But the other stuff, the stuff that made him Brook, that he walked about on, breathed with, felt with, had been made see-through by his illness and its cure.

I checked the time and sloshed back to my car. Three minutes left on the voucher.

. . .

After dinner and homework and Katya's bath, which Peter took charge of – Ivan was late, though he hadn't said anything about being late that morning – I sat down with a medical dictionary to re-read the post mortem the police forensic pathologist had performed on Niall Howley.

The first time I'd read it, my eyes had glazed over at lists of Latin names. Now I made myself slow down. The post mortem began with the doctor's name and address. A Federal Police logo occupied the top left hand corner of the page. The preamble said that this was to be a three cavity post mortem: chest, abdomen and head. It began with three more subheadings: heart, pericardium, aorta.

Again, I found the list mind-numbingly long. It began to seem as if the body parts, named one under the other on clean pages, had never belonged to a human being. Niall's brain had been sawn open, and the injuries it had sustained took up half a page all on their own. I contrasted the report with the castle scene he'd left on his computer. The young man perhaps uncomfortably asleep. How often had I gone in to check on Peter late at night and found him twisted in bed, feet on the pillow, sheet all nohow?

I flicked back over Bernard Howley's statement. It was even terser than I remembered from my first reading.

The deceased was identified by his father, Bernard Patrick Howley, at 11.15 am on 23 June.

Mr Howley stated that the deceased had left home on the evening of 22 June at 7.30 pm and had not returned. He had been wearing a black shirt and black jeans. A car found in the Telstra Tower visitor's car park was identified by Mr Howley as belonging to the deceased. In the car was a black umbrella, a grey woollen blanket and a wallet also belonging to the deceased. In the wallet was a Commonwealth Bank Mastercard, a Medicare card, *a Video Ezy and a library card, a photo pass identifying the deceased as an employee of the Monaro Hospital, and $48.35 in cash.*

The statement went on to outline some of the background – how long Niall had been living at home, his relationship with his girlfriend, Natalie Rowan, his interest in *Castle of Heroes*, how many hours he'd been spending online, his withdrawal from 'reality'. I assumed that this was Bernard's choice of words. Reading through his statement again reinforced the view I'd formed the first time, that there was nothing to tell me how he'd really felt about the manner of his son's death.

. . .

Dr Marian Huxley, the forensic pathologist who'd performed the autopsy on Niall, lived in a part of Canberra I'd always liked, and had always known would be beyond my means.

In our landlocked capital, suburbs nudged each other for the right to squat around an artificial lake. And it was part of the curse I shared with many Canberrans, the curse of having grown up within smelling distance of the sea, that the sight of this lake, coming upon it round the shoulder of a hill, brought a lump to my throat. It was an experience at once pleasant, even exciting when the light fell on the water in a certain way, and deeply disappointing.

I wound the window down, sniffed and there it was – dank weed, flaccid water, no salt, no wind to lift salt spray. But the lake was an expanse of something other than buildings, roads, something *other* – or at least the possibility was there. It was this that kept me hoping, and why I would have moved to Yarralumla like a shot had I been able to afford a house there, or even the deposit.

Dr Huxley lived in a part of the suburb where the house extension people hadn't yet moved in to create skylighted upper storeys, family rooms and double garages. Hers was a shabby, cement-rendered, mean windowed place in comparison with its glamorous neighbours.

The former police doctor opened the door to me herself. At once I understood that she lived alone. The house had the unmistakable feel of a person who'd long ago chosen solitude.

She was of a type I recognised from books and television, manners of a gallant Englishwoman, grooming slightly ragged round the edges now, the lean height, reach of empire in the eyes. I wondered how many of her kind could possibly have ended up working for the Australian Federal Police.

We circled each other conversationally for a few minutes. Dr Huxley spoke carefully, her English accent giving her words what might, or might not, be an ironic edge. Hers was an old English, as old as the spread of England's language to its colonies, yet Australian colloquialisms sat easily within it, as weeds sit easily within the lawn that holds them. I admired her beautiful floor rugs, her polished dark wood furniture, Turner reproductions on the walls, the view through the windows of the morning mist over the lake – even these a comment on the relationship between motherland and colony.

If the doctor was as perceptive as she looked, she probably saw straight through my flattery. She had coffee ready on a tray, with milk and sugar in silver dishes, so there wasn't that space afforded by her having to go and get it ready, a few minutes for me to nose around the room alone.

I asked her what she'd done when she got the phone call to examine Niall's body. She described the scene at the Telstra Tower on the morning of 23 June much as Olga Birtus had described it, thick fog bringing visibility down to five metres or so, hiding the tower so that the top of the mountain might have supported anything at all.

By the time she arrived, the police had taped off an area around the body, and a photographer was already at work. Dr Huxley had studied Niall's body for a few minutes before kneeling down and going through the formality of feeling for a pulse. She estimated that Niall had been dead for between eight and ten hours, taking into account the sub zero temperature of the previous night.

'In your post mortem,' I said, 'you give the cause of death as cerebral haemorrhage.'

'Probable cause of death.'

'Why probable?'

'The extent of that boy's injuries indicate that he died on impact. He hit the ground on the right side of the head, right shoulder and leg.'

I wondered how recently Dr Huxley had read her report. Did she recall it in detail? There'd been that slight body waiting for her on the cutting table, face up his injuries all too obvious.

'The most severe injuries were to the right side of his head and body,' Dr Huxley repeated in her careful voice. 'There was no indication that the young man died of heart attack before he hit the ground.'

'Would you have expected him to?'

'It happens. People who jump from the tops of buildings do suffer heart attacks before they reach ground level.'

'Did Niall die straight away?'

'Death could have been instantaneous, but not necessarily.'

These were the words the doctor had used in concluding her post mortem.

'You've seen this?' I handed over a colour printout of the castle scene.

Dr Huxley inclined her head and smiled. Her smile surprised me. There could have been a hint of complicity in it, but if so it was brief, gone before I could be sure.

'A forensic pathologist has no business with coincidence,' she said. 'Or with speculation. He or she examines the evidence and records it.'

'Was there a sharp stone, a rock, on the ground where Niall fell that could have caused the laceration on the back of the head that you refer to in your post mortem?'

'There were many lacerations.'

Dr Huxley smiled again. This time I thought it was to warn me. She had dry, pale olive skin, even white teeth that showed to advantage when she smiled.

'I mean the one on the back of Niall's head. If he landed on his right side as you say, then how did he hit the back of his head?'

'It could have been, as you say, a stone.'

'Did the police find a stone Niall might have hit his head on?'

'Ms Mahoney, you must understand that, in the context of the young man's injuries, the one you're referring to was slight, it – '

'It couldn't have killed him?'

'No.'

'Would it have been enough to knock him out?'

'I doubt it.'

'And the most likely explanation for how Niall got this bump on the back of his head is that he ricocheted, bounced from his right side to his back and then what? Back to the position he was found in?'

Dr Huxley hesitated, then nodded.

'Could Niall have hit his head on the way down?'

'What do you mean?'

'Well, I'm sure you're aware that the platform he was supposed to have jumped from. This one here' – I pulled out my now crumpled brochure of the tower. It was coming in quite handy – 'is a good deal narrower, in fact almost a metre narrower than the one beneath it. So in order to clear this lower one, Niall has to have made quite an amazing leap. I'm wondering if he could have got the bump on the back of his head, and indeed possibly other injuries as well, by hitting one of the jutting out bits of this lower platform on his way down.'

'Can I see that?'

I handed the brochure to Dr Huxley, who studied it in silence.

'It's not drawn to scale,' I said. 'But you can see my point.'

Dr Huxley looked up at me and said, 'I would have to think about that.'

'But is it at least possible?'

'Many things are possible. The boy's injuries all pointed to his dying on impact. They differed in severity of course. The one you're referring to is slight in comparison with those sustained by the right side of his head and body. But the bruising, bleeding and so on are all consistent with the impact.'

'Doesn't it strike you as odd that nobody saw, or heard Niall that night? I mean, you put the most likely time of death as between nine-thirty and ten-thirty. The public galleries close at ten. Up till then, there are still people around, guards checking. After ten the doors are locked, but there are people walking to their cars. Yet no one saw or heard a thing.'

Dr Huxley shook her head and opened her mouth to speak. I knew what she was going to say. Speculation was not her job. She was, or had been, a forensic pathologist. Her job had been to examine the body and report on her findings. All very well if the case was as straightforward as everyone seemed to believe.

'Could Niall have jumped from the lower platform? I don't mean, could he have got onto it to jump. I'm aware of the security restrictions. But could he have jumped from here, rather than up here, and sustained the same injuries?'

Dr Huxley frowned. It struck me that she was taking a long time to answer a pretty obvious question, one she would surely have considered.

'From a height of fifty metres everything collapses,' she said at last. 'If there is one bone left unbroken, that is something to remark on.'

I nodded, recalling the long list.

'From this height,' Dr Huxley indicated the lower platform, 'the injuries will also be very great.'

'So what you're saying is that above a certain height it doesn't really matter?'

The doctor looked annoyed. I knew she didn't like me putting words in her mouth, but her answers were so cautious that I couldn't help it. I bit my lip and waited.

'The boy would have been killed,' she said, 'if he'd jumped from either here, or here.'

I nodded, mentally urging her, go on. Was she merely reiterating that, from the heights we were considering, the differences in injuries were likely to be negligible? Or was she expressing a deeper doubt?

She said, 'Niall was a mentally unbalanced and a very determined young man.'

Familiar assumptions. I didn't think we were debating them either, but perhaps we were.

'Could someone have thrown Niall over?' I asked.

She gave me a long, considering look. I could see her good manners struggling with a desire to tell me to go away and stop bothering her, leave her in peace.

'When there is a struggle, when a person is overpowered, there is always some evidence of it. In this case there was nothing which suggested an attempt, however futile, to fight back.'

'Any bruises or scratches would be assumed to be the result of the fall, wouldn't they?'

'That is true. But as well as the lack of physical evidence, there was nothing pointing to murder. How could that young man have been overpowered in a public place? If he'd cried out, don't you think one of the guards or other staff would have heard?'

'I agree there are easier ways to murder someone. Unless the murderer's intention was to make it look like suicide. In which case he, or she, carried the whole thing off brilliantly.'

Dr Huxley said nothing and I knew I would get no more 'speculation' out of her.

I thanked her for her time, and added my usual request to contact me if anything occurred to her that might be of help. I was sure that she would never do this. When I'd phoned her, telling her I was working for Niall's mother, and stressing Moira's raw, abiding grief, I'd felt her reluctance to meet me, but an unwillingness to say, categorically, no. I was very conscious that one meeting was all Dr Huxley, and for that matter Dr Fenshaw, would allow.

My depression came back. Maybe I was wasting my time and everybody else's. If Niall had been attacked, he would have struggled, shouted. What did he have to lose? On the other hand, at nine forty-five on the night of 22 June there wouldn't have been anybody else on the outside platforms of the tower. Niall would have had the platform with the spiky fence all to himself. He wouldn't have needed access to a restricted area. All he needed to do was take advantage of the darkness and the time to ensure that he had no witnesses. All he needed to do, as the head security guard Litowski had said, was climb the fence and jump out wide enough to clear the lower platform.

Eight

Derek stood at my front door with a parcel in his hands.

'Oh,' I said. 'The party's not till Saturday.'

Anger flashed along his cheekbones. 'I should think I could see my son on his birthday and bring him a present.'

'Oh,' I said again. 'Of course. Come in.'

My house was small enough for a conversation at the front door to be heard at the back. We didn't even have a proper dining room, just a table and six chairs at one end of the lounge.

Four people were sitting at the table, Katya in her high chair pulled up close so she could feel a part of the proceedings, Peter, Ivan and Brook.

We'd just finished Peter's birthday dinner, his favourite burritos with spicy mince and heaps of tomato sauce. Easy to prepare and revolting to eat, but I'd gulped mine down in deference to Peter being master of the occasion.

Katya was posting bits of bread into the pocket of her plastic bib, while Ivan and Peter watched indulgently.

'Here's Dad,' I said.

Peter turned up a face decorated with kisses of tomato sauce, a smudge of lost burrito. His long, honey-brown hair fell into his eyes. He smiled up at his father.

Derek seemed about to kiss him, then thought better of it. He looked around the rest of us as though expecting an apology, then handed Peter a present wrapped in sailing boat paper. Inside was a box of technic Lego.

'Cool,' Peter said. 'Thanks Dad.'

I invited Derek to sit down. 'We're about to have the cake.'

He'd cut his hair since I'd seen him last, short for the change of season. His neck looked shaved and reddish, though that could have been his state of mind. He was dressed in clothes that suited him, casual without being sloppy, dark green cord pants, brown boots, a brown and cream patterned jumper over an open-necked shirt. It gave me a small shock every time I saw Derek, how well turned out he was, how not so long ago he'd been my husband.

'Thanks,' he said, accepting my invitation with his particular double-edged politeness, by a simple turn of his body showing his contempt for the slipping into middle-age approach he considered mine and Ivan's.

He frowned at Fred, who as a special treat had been allowed to sit by Peter's chair. Fred wagged his tail briefly, but kept his eyes fixed on the plates smeared with leftover burrito.

'Take him out,' I said to Peter.

'Mum!'

I grabbed Fred by the collar and marched him out the back door, biting my lip, thinking that two seconds in the door and Derek was already making me act in ways I didn't want to.

Brook looked at me with conspiratorial understanding over an armful of dirty plates. I scraped them into Fred's bowl while he began placing ten candles fussily around the cake.

Brook should have been graced with an apron, high under the armpits. I realised with a start that I'd never pictured him as a young man. Neither young nor healthy. It was as though he'd been born pushing a forty-something body that death was pushing from the other side. I'd never met a man whose domestic inclinations had been thwarted so thoroughly.

It was Peter who was coping. He'd undone his box of Lego, and was looking at the instructions with Ivan, at the same time talking to his father about school.

The singing and cutting of the cake passed quickly. Ivan boomed out the words in his strong baritone, with Derek's tenor a fraction of a second later. My own voice sounded like a breathy excuse offered up through cotton wool.

Peter bowed his head over his plate and smiled the birthday smile of a child being sung to. Katya whimpered, not understanding why the light had suddenly gone dim and flickering. Brook put out his hand and she grabbed it, then just as the singing finished she decided to join in, her one note loud and confident.

Peter took a huge breath and blew out the candles. We clapped and I reached for the light switch. Everybody blinked.

The evening had suddenly become uncharted territory. With a gesture that I knew was overdone, I grabbed a large breadknife and began dividing up the cake, flinging the candles to one side and plopping slices onto bread and butter plates.

Derek gave me the sort of glance he'd perfected for social occasions when I failed to measure up. I told myself that this was Peter's night. I'd said to Brook, when we were ordering the cake, that I wanted to keep it simple. After all, the party on Saturday, with seven school friends, and Derek and Valerie, was the main event.

We ate the cake, Peter still smiling, pronouncing his beautiful.

Derek asked about my new job.

'It's to do with a computer game that went wrong.'

I glanced at Peter, who was absorbed in feeding Katya crumbs of chocolate cake from the end of his finger.

Ivan was sitting at his end of the table like an extra piece of furniture in a science fiction movie. More or less predictable, but you never knew.

He roused himself and explained to Derek, 'Sandra's holding the mother's hand.'

'You know it's more than that.'

I tried not to sound hurt. I didn't think that comforting Moira Howley was a trivial or straightforward task, and I wasn't about to say that I'd come to the conclusion she didn't want my comfort anyway.

Katya banged her spoon on the rim of her highchair and bits of cake flew in all directions. Peter and Brook jumped up, Brook bending for the cake, Peter taking Katya's spoon and whispering in a big brotherly voice, 'You'll get in trouble.'

Derek looked on with an expression of disgust. I told myself that in a few minutes he'd drink his coffee and go. Maybe he wouldn't even stay for coffee. He'd go feeling he'd been wronged, adding to his store of grievances against me.

Brook said, 'I'll get the coffee.'

I heard him opening and shutting cupboard doors. He wouldn't be able to carry everything and he mightn't find a tray.

He turned around at the sound of my step, coffee jar in one hand, spoon in the other.

'Go on tell me,' I said. 'Say it. I'm a rotten mother.'

'Calm down Sandra. There's nothing to get so het up about.'

I caught my breath, but I was angry and Brook was a target within reach.

'Niall Howley jumped off the Telstra Tower.'

'And?'

'And maybe he didn't jump. Maybe he was pushed.'

'Who said that?'

'I did. It's what I've been thinking.'

'Bill McCallum knows his job.'

'I'm not suggesting that he doesn't.'

'What *are* you suggesting?'

'There's something about the computer picture, the way it was set up. And Litowski worries me, the security guy at the tower. He's lying. And McCallum – he's had to deal with so many suicides, especially young men, he's used to treating them in a certain way, and the bizarre aspects of this one, well, so many of them are bizarre, unbelievably bizarre, yet you have to believe them because they happen. You were there when he made that point.'

'I'm a bank Johnny. That's my job. What do you want me to do?'

'Talk to me,' I said. 'Let me talk to you. Think aloud.'

'You've got enough on your hands here.'

'Moira Howley? What about her hands? What if I feel some responsibility for them?'

'You've got a husband and a baby.' Brook was angry too now. 'And when you were between husbands? Wherever you were then, you didn't want me following.'

'But you were –'

'You think illness makes you want to be alone? Wherever did you get that idea?'

The phone rang in the hall. Ivan called Brook's name. He went to answer it and a few minutes later came back to tell me that Sophie wasn't feeling well.

'She knows it's Peter's birthday. She apologised for ringing.'

'You're going over there.'

'She said not to, but yes.'

'Of course. Tell Sophie from me I hope she'll soon be feeling better.'

In the ruins of the birthday dinner, I came up against something I'd been pedalling over without seeing. My family was fragile, held together by bits of sticky tape and string, but Brook needed it to be strong and stable. Whatever he'd needed before Katya was born, that was what he needed now.

While Ivan and Derek drank coffee and spoke civilly to one another, momentarily allied in condescension over my 'case', I lifted Katya out of her highchair and was rewarded by a sudden perfect smile, all smear and stickiness and pleasure. I hugged her to me, not caring about the shirt that had been clean.

It was strange the way allegiances shifted. The men I had to deal with might be well-meaning, but I was more aware, just then, of the contradictions each one held within himself. Derek and Ivan. Brook with new claims on his heart. Peter growing into double figures. Ideas of what was important were a shape my son was growing into. Or Peter merely obeying orders, hiding his discomfort because he'd learnt that no one paid attention to it.

Things I hardly ever looked at, like the table, became just then distinct and solid, with edges, corners that could bruise, scratched and stained in a way I had stopped noticing. I wasn't seeing them through Derek's eyes, the way I used to. I was seeing them through my own eyes, only more nakedly, and I didn't know whether to feel ashamed, or learn a new kind of indifference.

I carried Katya to the bathroom. It was too late for a proper bath. I sponged her hands and face, and she looked at me with her father's black, unwavering eyes.

'We won't let them get the better of us,' I whispered, remembering how simple life had looked when I was ten. My mother was nice or nasty. When she was nice, it was no more than my due. When she was nasty it was always her fault, never mine. A part of the simplicity may have been to do with numbers. I had no father, as opposed to Peter's – one? Two? One and a half? I had no Uncle Brook.

Maybe, for once in his life, Derek had acted on impulse, jumped in his car and driven over without picturing what it would be like when he got here. I sensed the battle behind his composure – resentment that Peter was spending his birthday with me, and that we'd also organised the party. But did Derek want to take over organising parties? In the past such work had been thoroughly beneath him. Was the realisation coming now that it was perhaps his own fault he was missing out? Somehow I didn't think so. I was much more aware of Derek's urge to take what he considered his, at the same time his scorn for the poor excuse for a family I'd gathered round me. Brook he saw as sentimental, old before his time, wheedling his way in where he didn't belong.

A few minutes later, I carried my daughter back for goodnight kisses.

Derek submitted silently to my implication that it was time for him to leave, only betraying, by a contraction of the skin around his eyes, his certainty that the decision ought to have been left to him.

I found Peter sitting on the back step with his arms around his dog, his face buried in Fred's rough brown fur. Fred had that special look of contentment that meant extra food, and I knew Peter had just given him a piece of cake.

I kissed my son and whispered, 'Happy birthday.'

I didn't even want to think about the washing up. I took Katya with me to the office to give her a last drink before I put her down. Soon perhaps this too would be dispensed with. But not yet.

Katya stared at me, her wide, almost slanted eyes blacker than the night outside. On this night, ten years ago exactly, her brother had been born.

With my daughter in my arms, I looked out at the just discernible shape of the clothes line. The back fence sat where it always did, half covered by jasmine that each year died of frost and then grew back. I'd planted it thinking it would hide the fence.

Did Katya see what I did? Was there any way that I could tell?

I sat down and undid my not-clean shirt. I squeezed my nipple, then with a moment's sharp anxiety poked under it. Was there enough for even this last supper?

Katya took my nipple in her mouth and sucked, eyes still wide, the night sky before us. Time would come – how soon? when she no longer wanted, needed. Or when my body said enough – how soon? Still there would be, on my side anyway, a need of the heart.

Behind Katya's ear I found a smudge of chocolate that I'd missed with the sponge. I smiled and touched it gently with my finger. Her springy hair was damp.

I looked around the room, feeling its stillness drain into me, then realised slowly, yet with alarm, that there was nothing of Ivan's visible in the office. I'd cleared all his possessions away, stacked them in cupboards out of sight. I thought again about men, their preoccupations and obsessions. From a child's grab bag of interests on to something else, drawing the young male out into – what?

And what about Niall Howley? I couldn't rid myself of the notion that Niall's so-called obsession with a MUD was – well, silly. Even after the blood and compost of the photographs, and the intimations of cruelty that seeped through what I'd learnt about *Castle of Heroes*. It was all so silly. A part of me continued to pull back and smile in embarrassment at each new turning of the story.

......

Nine

I rang Moira to let her know where things stood. In the course of the conversation I mentioned the clothes Niall had been wearing on the night he died.

There was a long silence, then Moira said, 'But Bernard couldn't have known what Niall was wearing. He didn't see Niall that day at all. Bernard had an eight o'clock meeting. He left for work before Niall was up. Niall ate a piece of toast that I made for him and had a quick cup of coffee. He was running late for work.'

Interlaced with confusion, there was pride in Moira's voice, that she'd helped prepare her son's last breakfast. 'And he didn't see Niall in the evening. He told me not to go in, and he didn't go in either.'

'You're sure of that?'

'Of course I'm sure.'

'What have you done with Niall's clothes?'

'They're still here. Hanging up in his cupboard. All his shoes and socks.'

We agreed on a time to meet and I put the phone down, thinking about what Bernard Howley had said to the police.

I picked it up again and dialled Bernard's work number. He answered on the second ring. I said I needed to talk to him in person. He protested, but I overrode him, and we arranged to meet at one o'clock.

I glanced at my watch. 12.15. Plenty of time for Bernard to phone Moira and find out what had gotten into me.

. . .

Hudsons of Dickson, with its tables outside under wide umbrellas, was the right place for summer lunchtime meetings. Today was too cold and windy to sit outside in comfort, and I realised my mistake in having said the name of the first café that came into my head. Inside, it was crowded with people lined up at the counter buying cheeses and servings of lasagna. The tables were too close together for discretion. I slid quickly into a vacant chair, practically pulling Bernard down opposite me.

'You lied to me. You did see your son the night he died.'

In the second before Bernard answered, I felt his relief. He wasn't a good liar. In his own stiff, unfriendly way, he was sincere, or at least wanted to be. A determined liar would have refused to see me, fobbed me off over the phone.

'Niall was excited,' he said, keeping his voice low. 'I knew something had happened. He was' – Bernard paused, then continued carefully, as though, now he'd decided to tell me, the words he chose had to be the right ones – 'more alive than I'd seen him in weeks. In spite of what I said to Moira about letting him work things out for himself, I'd become increasingly worried. So – yes, I did check up on him that night. Moira thought I was going to the bathroom. I didn't mean to spy on Niall or pester him. I just wanted to make sure he was okay. I knocked on his door and he said come in. I could see he was getting ready to go out again.'

'What about his room?'

'You're thinking of the papers he got rid of?'

'What was on his desk?'

'It was – I think it was clean – clear apart from his computer.'

'Are you sure?'

'I wasn't looking for anything. If I looked at his desk at all, it was just a glance. He looked at *me* without seeing me. I was used to that, but this night it was different. You have to understand that it was the closest we'd come to a conversation for a long time. I was as grateful as a small boy who thought all his birthday presents had been stolen, then found out they hadn't. I should have let it go at that.'

'There was another reason for going in to see your son. You weren't just making sure he was okay.'

'I might as well tell you. It might make you understand that it's better not to pry.' Bernard lowered his voice even further and I had to strain to catch it. 'My son's dead. Digging over the traces as you seem intent on doing will only cause harm. I found a letter once. In his room.'

'A letter?'

'About organising support. Money. For this Irish group. For a Republican group in Ireland.'

'Do you know its name?'

'The Austral–Irish Friendship Society,' Bernard said with contempt. 'Stupid name isn't it?'

'How do you know they're a Republican group?'

'I saw a reference to them in a newspaper article, in connection with supplying arms and explosives to the real IRA.'

'Do they have a branch in Canberra?'

'Sydney. I looked them up in the phone book. I had no intention at that point of confronting Niall with it, but – '

'Did you phone them?'

'They were founded to raise money for the hunger strikes of eighty-one. I couldn't get anyone to tell me whether any of the money was used to buy guns.' Bernard laughed to make sure I got the sarcasm. It was such a cutting sound that a couple at the next table looked up, surprised.

'Apart from the newspaper article, did you see or hear anything else to suggest what the money might be used for?'

'Look,' Bernard said, 'I know these people. My wife's family left Belfast to get away from them.'

'And your parents?'

'My mother was born here. Dad came out before the war.'

'What did the letter say exactly?'

'It referred to a concert. A benefit concert. It was very short. No more than four lines. The society was organising a Cranberries tour. There was to be a benefit concert in Sydney and another one in Melbourne.'

'Did the Cranberries come to Australia? Did the concerts go ahead?'

'Oh yes. I saw the advertisements in the *Sydney Morning Herald*. I pointed one out to Niall, to see what he'd say.'

'And?'

'He said he had too much on his plate right now to go to Sydney for a concert.'

'So you assumed he was hiding something?'

'Yes I did. Of course I did. I was concerned. I began to wish I hadn't seen the letter, but I had, and I couldn't forget about it. It preyed on my mind. Niall was so withdrawn, you see, so secretive.'

'The letter could have been genuine.'

'Yes, but if that's the case, why didn't Niall tell us about it? Why feign ignorance when I mentioned the advertisement? And if he was a member of this Friendship group, why didn't we know about it?'

'Did Niall show an interest in Irish politics in other ways?'

'Not to me he didn't.'

'With Moira?'

'They used to talk,' Bernard said bitterly.

'Where's the letter now?'

'I assume Niall destroyed it.'

'Did you say anything to Moira?'

'No. I kept hoping I was mistaken.'

'So you went into Niall's room that night to ask him about it?'

'I don't know if the intention was so clearly in my mind, but yes, I did bring it up. I wish to God I hadn't. Niall went cold again. He said I should know better than to accuse him of anything illegal and that he had to go. That was it. We parted on a note of mistrust, instead of how –'

'Do you still believe that – about Niall raising money to pay for guns?'

'I could have been jumping to conclusions. If I'd made it clear that night that no matter what he'd done –'

'Do the police know about this?'

Bernard shook his head. His voice was just above a whisper. 'Please believe me when I say dragging it all up can't do any good.'

. . .

I made some notes, sitting in my car, trying to recall exactly what Bernard had said, then drove to Turner to meet Natalie Rowan.

Niall's ex-girlfriend had been back in Canberra for a while, but reluctant to meet me, telling me over the phone that her relationship with Niall had ended over three months before his death, and that there was nothing she could do to help. When I persisted, she replied that she'd already told the police everything she knew.

After an initial hesitancy, Moira Howley had agreed to act as a go-between. Whatever she said must have worked because Natalie at last said she would talk to me.

She opened the door, and greeted me with the downcast eyes and blush of a shy person. She pushed her dark hair back from her forehead with the fingers of her left hand held stiffly all together, then looked past me to my car parked in the driveway.

I stepped inside quickly, and followed her down a short passageway. I don't know what I'd been expecting, student grot perhaps, stained smelly carpet that the owner was too mean to get rid of, hand-me-down furniture nobody looked after or cared about.

Under wide windows, a scrubbed wooden table held a glass vase of apple blossom. I'd stopped for a second to admire the tree on my way in. A combustion stove sat on brown hearth tiles at one end of the room. A wall had been taken out to extend the living area. Natalie motioned me to sit down on a plain two-person sofa, the cushions covered in heavy cotton. The floor was polished pine with rugs in a pattern of red, dark brown and cream. Nothing was expensive and certainly the room was no show piece of taste or acquisition, but the overall effect was one of light and ease.

A smell of sweet bread and freshly ground coffee came from the kitchen. Natalie asked if I would like a cup. She came back with coffee, milk and sugar on a tray, and a plate of warm cinnamon rolls.

I asked her what Niall Howley had been like.

'Before we broke up he started acting really weird.' Natalie flicked her brown hair off her face, then continued. 'I think the change had been coming for a while, but I didn't notice it, and then all at once I did.'

'What kind of change?'

'You couldn't have a normal conversation with him. He wouldn't tell me what was bothering him. He refused to explain. He wouldn't talk. It made me really mad.'

'Was there someone else?'

'I don't think so. I feel bad about it you know, because he's, well, he's dead. But he scared me. He was getting so weird. He'd be up all night, and then go to work. I'd say something to him and he wouldn't answer and I'd turn around and he'd have fallen asleep. Sex. Forget it. Going out to a movie. Forget it.'

'How much did you know about the MUD?'

'I knew he was playing some game on the internet. I didn't take much notice.'

It struck me that Natalie was spinning me a line, one that had possibly begun with heartfelt impressions, but had moved on from them.

'Didn't Niall talk about it?'

'Not much. Well, like at the beginning he did. But he knew I wasn't interested.'

'Did you know what it was?'

'Some war game wasn't it?'

'Did you know he'd fallen foul of the guy who ran it?'

'He just became, you know, really withdrawn. He spent all his time in his room. He didn't even want to eat together. I was relieved when he said he wanted to move out. I was upset at first, but then I was so relieved.'

I took a deep breath and told Natalie what Niall's father suspected him of having been involved in.

As Natalie listened, she gave me a look that I could imagine my daughter perfecting by the time she was three, a look that summed up her contempt for anybody over thirty-five.

'I'd be careful with Niall's dad if I were you,' she said. 'I'd check his story out with someone else.'

'Which part of the story should I check out?'

'I don't believe any of it, actually.'

'Did Niall ever talk to you about Irish politics?'

'Not much.'

'Did you talk about politics in general?'

'Well, we must have. I mean, people do.'

'Why would his father make up a story like that?'

Natalie shrugged. 'He wanted to pick a fight maybe. He sneaked into Niall's room and found some stuff and went ballistic. I'd say that was typical of him.'

'Did you know Niall belonged to a group called the Austral–Irish Friendship Society?'

'No.'

'Did he mention a Cranberries concert? Last summer, it was. In Sydney.'

'What about it?'

'Did you go to the concert, you and Niall?'

'Sydney you said? I couldn't get Niall to go to a movie in Civic, let alone drive to Sydney for a concert. Look, there's heaps of stuff I never knew about Niall. Obviously. Heaps. And there's heaps of stuff he never knew about me. He wasn't interested. And I got sick of trying.'

Natalie began to wind a lock of dark hair round and round one index finger. She looked up at me, suddenly intent.

'I'll tell you something about Niall's dad. He's a total control freak. Moira is too, only I don't think she's as bad as him. After Niall moved in here, one or the other of them was ringing up every five minutes to check he had clean socks. I'm not kidding. It was that bad.'

I couldn't imagine what it would be like to have two possessive, hovering parents. I wondered about Natalie's family. She didn't seem to fit with the picture I was building up of Niall. Was she a selfish young women, whose retrospective discomfort moved her more than the death of someone she'd been close to? Perhaps I was being too hard on her. She hadn't wanted to see me at all, but she'd made an effort to be hospitable. It didn't paint a flattering picture of their relationship that Niall had kept so much from her. But Natalie hadn't tried to dress this up for me.

Had Niall's parents been in large part responsible for his secretive behaviour? Again, I tried to think what it would be like to be an only child with two adults watching every move you made, the painstaking effort such a child, once grown, might make to keep part of his life private and unknown to them.

'What about Niall's work?'

'He didn't talk much about it. I mean, he talked about the patients, who was a hopeless case, who he thought might pull through. I guess to that extent he did talk about it. He worried about the patients, that's for sure.'

'Would you say his worry was obsessive?'

'What I'm trying to say is, Niall stopped behaving like a normal guy.

He was better when we met, like he was okay then. We did go to movies and stuff, and out with friends. But he began to close in on himself. I tried. I did try. A relationship's got to *be* something, not just two people sharing a kitchen and a bathroom.'

'And a bed?'

'Yeah.' Natalie laughed and stood up. She began to gather cups, saucers and plates onto a tray. 'Actually the sex part was never all that great.'

I followed her out to the kitchen, thinking that it helped to be moving, not just sit facing one another.

'Niall wasn't interested?' I probed, watching Natalie put the tray down on a spotless bench. 'Would you like me to wash those up for you?'

'Oh no.' She blushed and looked confused. 'They're nothing. I – I'm not usually so tidy. I cleaned up while I was waiting for you.'

'I was nervous too,' I said. 'I'm always nervous on my way to interview someone. Unfortunately, I think they can tell. It puts them off.'

Natalie smiled. 'You seem pretty confident to me.'

'How long were you and Niall together?'

'About two years.'

'Why do you think Niall became so interested in the MUD?'

'Why do some people get hooked on dope? It's in their personalities, I guess. You know, we met at a party? Isn't that how people always meet in Canberra?'

Ivan and I had met at work, which seemed to me to be just as common, but I didn't say so.

Natalie began to talk about what Niall had been like when they started going out, responding to my prompting that she try and get a fix on what had changed, what had made Niall change – she was certain that the change had come from him, from within. I let her speak without interrupting, hearing in her voice the note of people who've been over the same blunted points too many times.

'Who owns this house?' I asked her when she'd finished.

'My parents. They retired down the coast a couple of years back, but they decided to keep a house in town.'

'Do they stay here often?'

'Every now and then.'

'Did you and Niall live alone here, just the two of you? Or was there someone else sharing the house as well?'

'Just Niall and me. We had a bedroom and a study and a spare room where my parents stayed. We talked about getting someone else last year when my fieldwork started. Niall wasn't keen on the idea. I think he was looking forward to having the house to himself for a few months. But I – we – never got that far.'

Natalie bit her lip and blushed, as if realising too late that she should have put on a show of grieving for Niall. She began to wind a strand of hair round her finger again. She was an attractive young woman. She had a comfortable, spacious house at her disposal, offering Niall a freedom he couldn't possibly have while living with his parents. I wondered why Niall had moved back with them when he and Natalie broke up, why he hadn't taken a flat and lived on his own, or possibly with Eamonn. Could the reason have been money?

......

Ten

Ivan and I were on our way to visit the Telstra Tower at night.

I'd asked Brook if he could get me membership records for the Austral–Irish Friendship Society. He'd said, 'How do you suggest I do that Sandy? Community organisations don't take too kindly to coppers turning up and asking for lists of their members.'

I swung the wheel too sharply round one of Black Mountain's hairpin bends and gave myself a fright. I glanced in the rear vision mirror, catching Peter's small white face.

'The collective wisdom,' I said to Ivan, 'is that Niall has to have jumped from a public gallery because it's impossible to get into any of the restricted areas or the outside platforms next to them.'

'Who says?'

'The head security guy. He explained about their access cards. To get to any restricted area a technician has to go through three doors with one of these access cards. When you've finished your shift, you hand it in. They never leave the building.'

'Who keeps a record of what technicians are in the building when?'

'There's a guard on the ground floor who lets them in. He enters it all up on computer. I asked him about cards going missing, and he said that if anyone loses a card, the computer cancels it immediately.'

Ivan chuckled. 'Remember Clinton Haines?'

Haines's nickname was the Virus King. A few years ago one of his viruses, called Nofrills, had hit a thousand Telstra computers at once and wiped them clean.

'Do you think something like that on a smaller scale could have been the means for Niall to get hold of an access card, or to get himself into a secure bit of the tower?' I asked, glancing across at Ivan as the road levelled out.

Ivan grinned. 'Say he did – would that security dude have admitted it to you? No way. Far better to pretend that everything was running normally. No blips in security whatever.'

'He may not have known. Depends on how it was done. He might be as much in the dark as we are.'

Ivan didn't comment on my 'we'. Good, I thought. He's in a good mood. I hope nothing happens tonight to turn him off again.

He bent over to unstrap Katya from her car seat, while I breathed in the long night breath of the mountain. A mild night, air to open your skin to, herald if not yet promise of summer. The winter hadn't been particularly severe, damp and grey rather, recalcitrant fogs that hung around till lunchtime, rain rather than pipe-bursting cold.

Ivan ran towards the fence, kicking a pretend soccer ball to Peter. He dribbled the invisible ball towards a hole in the fence and shot for goal with a great flourish of his long right leg.

Peter cried, 'Not fair!' But then he laughed, a high childish laugh of excitement that Ivan was playing with him, the hole in the fence for a moment lit by a searching arc light from the crow's nest of the tower.

'Mum! Be on my team!'

I kicked the imaginary ball to him, and he shot for goal.

'Everything's so bright,' I said.

There was a display of antique telephones in the foyer of the tower. Ivan made a beeline for an early model Ericsson, explaining to Peter in a loud voice, 'Now this fella here was called the coffee grinder.'

We left him to enjoy the history of telephony.

On the way up in the lift – Peter was still young enough to get a kick out of pressing all the buttons – I recalled how, when Ivan and I had met, he'd been renting a leaky weatherboard bungalow in Turner, a gloomy house surrounded by grevillea so overgrown that it obscured all the windows, a house festering inside with unwashed socks and dishes, forgotten bacon in the fridge so old it had grown a magician's cloak. His pride had been a computer room that was part museum, half a wall covered with a black and white print of Alexander Graham Bell.

Katya's eyes widened with alarm as the lift shot up to the viewing galleries. Peter swayed from side to side and teased her. 'Woooh!' Katya opened her mouth to howl. The lift clunked to a stop. Peter ran forward through the doors without waiting for them to open fully, then he froze.

Though the floor was level under our feet, we seemed to be on an irreversible slope down and out towards a fifty metre drop.

The lake shone grey and silver. The water spout shot floodlit water high into the air. Commonwealth and Kings Avenue bridges were luminous bracelets, curved and sparkling, the kind children might demand at a show or kiosk, flash around fixed to their wrists, great hoops and whorls of light.

Katya held out her hands to the lights through the double glazing. A stone might fall from the bracelet, a single, irrecoverable jewel.

Peter pulled me by the elbow. 'I don't like it Mum.'

Ignoring his anxiety, I stood staring through the glass, mentally stretching out my own hands towards the shining drop. The tower was a spectacular upended Titan in its last freezing moments. And we weren't nearly at the top. I'd imagined Niall's fall as dark, private, anonymous. Much stranger, standing here, to recall how nobody had seen or heard it.

And before – Niall perhaps passing the point where I was now, looking out, or, eyes down, heading for the doors to the gallery. Once outside, no barrier beyond an iron fence, did he look down and note the awkward jutting of the lower platform, feel a lifting of the heart, perhaps, at this final challenge?

'Mum!' said Peter urgently.

We walked around to the small kiosk which sold souvenirs as well as drinks, chips and confectionery. A solitary man was sitting at a table, in front of him a polystyrene cup and a large, expensive camera. A tripod lay folded at his feet. He looked up at our approach and nodded.

I nodded back, understanding his impulse to make contact. The emptiness was unnerving, the walls cold, kiosk lights, lolly papers, stuffed koalas unnaturally bright.

I bought a packet of salt and vinegar chips and asked the woman behind the counter if the nights were always as quiet as this.

'Well, there's the weekends,' she replied.

I returned to the table where I'd left Peter holding his sister. The man with the camera had gone. Peter munched through his chips, sitting with his back to the glass. Working out his own method of coping with a grim situation, he took the car keys out of my bag and jiggled them in front of Katya, who laughed and tried to grab them.

'I'll take you back down to Dad now.'

We found Ivan, whose eyes were glazed over with the pleasure of a dozen unexpected antiques. 'Did you know that Melbourne had the telephone less than a year after Bell's initial breakthrough?'

'Amazing.'

'Don't be like that Sandy. A sense of national pride would do you no harm at all.'

'I promise to work on it,' I said. 'In the meantime, I need to take a look at the outside gallery. Be back in fifteen minutes.'

'Take your time,' said Ivan. 'We'll be fine right here.'

I don't know what I had expected – a wind like that morning when I interviewed Olga Birtus and Mikhail Litowski? There was nothing you could call a wind. I walked over to the fence and stared out between its iron bars. Had Niall done that before he climbed them, feeling at last that constriction of any kind was dreadful, not to be borne, the world too bright, replete with trivial illumination? And then, taking step after step, had he climbed up and over, into the night sky and beyond it, taking what he needed for the moment, letting go the rest?

This time, I took the stairs back to the ground floor. On the floor adjacent to the broadcasting platform, there was only a small area open to the public. More windows, though smaller at this level and set higher in the wall, a rope across the walkway with a *No Admittance* sign hanging from it, on the other side of the rope two steel doors whose signs proclaimed *Strictly No Admittance*. As I stood next to the stairwell watching the doors, a guard came out of one and stared straight at me, not with hostility, but surprised to see me there. Perhaps I was the only visitor to use the stairs for quite a while. The guard was a heavily built, middle-aged man. He went on staring, then seemed about to ask me what I was doing. I turned and continued my progress down the stairs.

. . .

A message from Brook waited for us on the answering machine.

'Found an interesting connection Sandra. Catch you tomorrow. I'm out for the rest of the evening.'

I phoned back immediately and got his machine. Where did out mean, if not with Sophie? Why hadn't he called my mobile, and why was his switched off? Brook persisted in his dislike of mobiles, using them only when he had to. In some ways, he was infuriatingly old-fashioned.

The phone display had made Ivan restless. He'd talked about it all the way home in the car. He was too keyed up to sleep, and so was I.

'We could check out that friendship society for ourselves.'

'I was hoping you'd say that.'

Their membership database was easy to break into. We found Niall Howley's name on a list, then began looking for any mention of the concert Bernard said had been the subject of the society's letter to Niall, better still a copy of the letter itself.

I scrolled through lists of dates, figures and names. My eyes were beginning to blur when I spotted Niall's again. He was credited with having sold a book of tickets to the Sydney concert, at a cost of nearly a thousand dollars.

He'd done well. Who had he sold them to? And, in spite of what he'd told his father, had he gone himself?

Success was a rush of energy we hadn't felt for ages. Ivan's black eyes shone. Who was it said that hacking was like sex? That night it felt like this was our particular discovery. I felt the long night breath of the mountain once again, in my throat, on Ivan's hair and beard. But then we left both the mountain and its tower behind, entering another, a surprising yet familiar space, where other mountains might appear or disappear, tricking eyes and minds, enticing human beings.

We stepped once again into that limbo land of snoopers, and I knew a part of me would want to return every night, now I'd been reminded of it, to send my furtive melody out along the wires, see who tripped on my filaments of song.

Ivan whispered, 'Sandy, it's okay. We're not late for a bus.'

'I always think – '

'They were asleep in thirty seconds. They're both knackered.'

'So are we.'

I took care of my own clothes, got my legs around him. Ivan was a big boat, second-hand and weatherworn, not yet a shipwreck in an unknown sea.

Sex was skin and blood and letting go, not bothering any more about how you looked because up so close it didn't matter. Hacking was up close too, so close there was no space for doubt or self reflection. Hacking was physical the way that skin was, skin under the palms of our hands, Ivan's and mine, the slippery, unexpected roughness. Perhaps the idea that the human will, or spirit, could leave the body, do its work and then return, had something to do with it. The body not diminished, but enhanced.

The surprise in Ivan's thick white skin was like the surprise of unexpected pain, yet his body had no sharpness to speak of. It was round and solid. A certain rivalry proper to pleasure stood between us. He shut his eyes and let me take the lead. I tangled my fingers in his chest hair, and he came like that. And then without me having to ask he opened his eyes again, face still concentrated, eyes wide and black as Katya's when I fed her.

. . .

In the unforgiving light of morning, Moira Howley sat and heard me out, folding and refolding her cold hands.

When I'd finished, she said in a small voice, 'Perhaps Bernard was mistaken.'

'You knew Niall was a member of the society didn't you?'

'I suppose I did.'

'And you knew he was helping them raise money?'

'Do you mean the concert tickets? As a matter of fact, Niall was worried. He was very busy, he wasn't sure if he had time, so – so I helped him.'

'How?'

'I sold them for him.'

'Why didn't you tell me that before?'

'I'm sorry, Sandra. I should have, I know. It's just that – I wish you could understand what it was like those weeks after Niall broke up with Natalie. Something was upsetting him, eating away at him, and he wouldn't say – and he and Bernard – well, they went from arguing to not speaking to one another, and back to arguing, and I was at my wits' end trying to figure out what to do about it. Then a letter came one day with the society's name on the envelope, and I asked Niall about it. I was careful to choose a time when his father wasn't home. And Niall said there were these tickets he was supposed to sell. I was so pleased to be able to help him.'

'If there turned out to be more to it than selling tickets, that wouldn't surprise you?'

'I want to believe the best of my son – does that seem so strange to you?'

'No, of course not.'

'I want to believe there was more to him than – well, if I say Niall was self-centred, I don't want you to take it the wrong way. I think he was as kind to me as he was capable of being. It's just that, when that letter came, I can't tell you how pleased I was.'

I hadn't found Moira's name in any of the lists, but I asked her anyway. 'Have you ever been a member?'

'I used to be. Bernard and I had a fight over it and I let my membership lapse.'

'Did you and Niall talk about the concert?'

'He was grateful when I sold the tickets, surprised that I managed to sell so many, I think. His hopeless old mother was good for something after all.'

'What was the money for?'

'We never talked about that.'

I took a deep breath and said, 'You need to make a decision. You need to tell me whether you want me to stop now, whether I've found out enough about the MUD.'

Moira hunched her shoulders obstinately. 'I can't say goodbye because I don't know who I'm supposed to be saying goodbye to.'

'Yes, you do. Forget about all this for a minute. Niall was your son. You knew him better than anybody. Say goodbye to the boy you knew.'

She shrugged again, and then, without giving me an answer, began walking to the door. Okay, I thought, I'm being dismissed.

I was halfway down the front steps when she called me back.

'Sandra? I have some money of my own.' She smiled, embarrassed. 'I mean, I couldn't have hired you if' – her voice changed and she began speaking precisely, choosing words with care – 'if I'd had to use my husband's money. Perhaps you ought to go and meet this man Fallon, talk to him.'

'You want *me* to go to Ireland?'

'What do you think?'

'Well for a start, I don't think he would see me. And even if he did, what would he tell me, face to face? If Niall was involved with a Republican group, and Fallon was perhaps involved in it with him, there's no way he'd admit that to me.'

Moira was nodding as if her mind had moved faster than mine, and she was waiting for me to catch up with her.

'He's answered my questions up to a point, but he hasn't offered anything.'

'I think it's worth a try,' said Moira firmly. 'Nothing Niall did, or didn't do, will make me love him less, or grieve less for him. At least I'm not afraid of that. And I'd rather know.'

She looked me up and down, nodding as if to say I might not be ideal, but I'd have to do.

'I'd go myself if I thought I could manage it.' Taking my silence, if not for assent, then the wish to do as she asked, she smiled. 'So you go Sandra. Beard this Fallon in his den.'

Her smile was soft, encouraging, with a deal of calculation in it.

I didn't feel like explaining my family situation to her. I said I'd think about it.

. . .

That evening, when Peter and Katya were asleep, I went into the office and sat down by myself to puzzle over her proposal that I go to Ireland.

Ivan was out with some of his work mates. I was glad. I wanted to concentrate on Moira. So much ground seemed to have shifted during our conversation that I had difficulty burrowing my way back to how I'd felt before it, to the sort of person I'd thought I was dealing with.

The difference wasn't in Moira's feelings for Niall, but I was sure now that she didn't want emotional support from me, much less someone to help her understand a MUD.

Why had she hired me? And what was her real reason for wanting to send me to Ireland? She couldn't believe anyone would tell me anything, and I might stumble on, or draw attention to, matters that were better left alone. Is this what Bernard had meant when he'd tried to dissuade me from asking any questions at all?

If Moira had been lying to me, what were Bernard's views underneath his stiff, censorious front? He'd painted Niall's membership of the friendship society in the worst possible light. Was that what he really thought?

None of this explained what use I could be. On the other hand, why was I expecting Moira to behave methodically, to consider each step before she took it? She mustn't know much. If she knew, for instance, that Niall and Sorley Fallon were members of a Republican group, and that Fallon had turned on her son for political reasons, she wouldn't want me fronting up to Fallon to confirm it. Fallon would laugh in my face, or worse.

I remembered Moira's quick, sarcastic comments about the Irish fighting the English in *Castle of Heroes*. She had assumed immediately that her son would be on the right side, and one of the best.

Perhaps she knew no more than that something had gone wrong – not what, and nothing about who else might have been involved. Perhaps she feared the worst, that Niall had betrayed the cause in some way unforgivable even to himself. What she wanted from me was to seek out some reassurance that this had not been so. She feared the worst, yet wanted to discover otherwise. She wanted me to come back and tell her that her son had not failed anyone, that he'd been a hero.

Again, I recalled the computer image, the body at the bottom of the cliff. Did the clothes, the position of the body, mean something to Moira that they didn't to me, or to the police? Moira Howley stood on the crumbling edge of a castle wall herself. What did she see when she stared down?

There was birth, illness, death, a continuity that, for me anyway, when my mother died, had been like little bits of vertebrae, once part of a healthy skeleton, scraps of crushed bone to scavenge and to cherish.

Was this what Moira wanted me for, to unearth a bit of shin bone from the compost? Perhaps she'd changed, or perhaps I'd been slow to pick up on the clues she'd given me. She was more resilient, and her desire to know ran deeper than I'd acknowledged, either to her or to myself.

. . .

'You've been burning the candle at both ends,' I said to Brook when I finally got him on the phone.

Brook laughed. Laughter took him under the arms with a lover's gentleness and lifted him clean off the ground.

'What about the friendship society?' I asked.

'It's a fundraising outfit.'

'And?'

'Howley's on an ASIO file. Couple of connections. That game gets a mention too.'

'There's an ASIO report on *Castle of Heroes?*'

There was a silence, then Brook said, 'Boss agrees it's worth asking a few questions. Bit delicate between me and Bill, but we'll sort it out. An officer in London's checking up on Fallon.'

Why wasn't that done before? I felt like asking, but instead I said, 'I could try asking him a few questions myself.'

'What?'

'When I go to Ireland.'

'You're joking.'

'Moira Howley wants me to.'

'I don't think that's a good idea at all.'

'Why not?'

'It's unnecessary. It might even be dangerous. What can you hope to learn, turning up like a bad penny from the antipodes?'

'I think I can manage Sorley Fallon. A Mel Gibson clone can't be all bad.'

I said goodbye and put the phone down thinking that the decision, after all, had been easy. All I had needed was the pressure of resistance. On the other hand, I'd pissed Brook off again.

We need to meet, I wrote to Fallon. *Name a date. I'll be there.*

I was thinking that if I could convince this Irishman of few words, then convincing Ivan that I had to go shouldn't be impossible.

What do you look like? Fallon's emails had not got any longer.

'The cheek,' I said to Ivan.

Ivan sucked the ends of his moustache. He was replacing a printer cartridge and getting ink all over himself. He'd forgotten the box of tissues. In a minute I'd have to go and fetch it from the kitchen.

'You could send him Julia Roberts or Pammy,' he suggested.

'That's a crap idea.'

Ivan had already told me Fallon would be eighty-one, completely bald, and that he'd knock me out with his potato breath.

'Well it was you who came up with *Brave Heart*,' he said. 'I didn't like to tell you at the time that Scotland and Ireland are separate countries.'

'If you weren't covered in ink I'd throw something valuable at you.'

Ivan looked around, miming astonishment that there could be such an item within reach.

· · ·

When I opened my mail a few days later, there were two attachments from Fallon. One was the Pamela Anderson I'd asked him to consider, pulled from one of the many thousand images of her that breathed around the net. The other was a photo of myself. I recognised it from *The Australian* a year or so ago, a case I'd been involved in that had got more than local publicity – me standing outside the Supreme Court looking as though I'd just been stung by a bee.

'Look at that,' I said to Ivan, who chuckled as though nothing about Fallon could surprise him.

The mixture of unyielding, authoritarian commander and playful, if laconic conjurer enticed me, as I suppose Fallon expected it would. At the same time, I felt as though a stranger had pulled a knife on me while I wasn't looking, and was holding it at a point just beneath my breasts. I swallowed hard, reminding myself that I'd begun this correspondence, *I* sought a face-to-face meeting with *him*.

······

Eleven

I sat in a Woking pub called the Three Fiddlers and willed myself to relax.

Woking was not London. 'Not actually in London,' was what Sgartha had written in his last email, when we'd arranged a time and place to meet.

It seemed part of London to me. During the train journey down I hadn't noticed any rural gaps. Not knowing what to expect, or how long it would take to get around by public transport, I'd booked into a hotel not far from Heathrow, and since the plane was six hours late and I'd arrived in the middle of the night, I'd been glad of this.

The hotel gave the impression of being crammed with flowered, overstuffed upholstery. My bedroom, up two flights of stairs, had a sloping, wide-beamed ceiling and two small leaded windows. I'd spent most of what remained of the night staring out through them, listening to the traffic, too keyed up to sleep, telling myself that I'd done it, I was there.

Sgartha had arranged to meet me for lunch at a pub close to where he worked, at a Formula One racing car factory. All of his suggestions I'd fallen in with gladly, afraid at every step that he would change his mind. Aside from my worry about this, I was riding the wave of promise and excitement that comes from having made an unlikely decision and acted on it.

I glanced up at the clock above the bar. Sgartha was already fifteen minutes late. Did I have the right place? Surely there couldn't be more than one Three Fiddlers in St John's Road, but maybe I should ask.

A soccer match on TV ended in a draw and the men who'd been watching it turned away with groans of disappointment.

A young woman walked up to me and said, 'Hello Sandra. My name is Bridget Connell.'

I sat there concrete-faced while she apologised for being late, then laughed, all good humour and Irish grace. She had a soft, clear laugh and short dark hair, thick and rough cut, so that it stuck up at the top of her head. She was expensively dressed in a silk shirt and designer trousers, with a well-cut woollen jacket. Beside her I felt frumpy, colonial.

We ordered at the bar, then sat facing one another. Bridget was drinking beer. I chose a cider. My hand shook as I clamped it round the glass.

'If you knew your Irish legends at all,' Bridget said, resting her chin in one hand, leaning forward, 'you'd have known Sgartha was a woman.'

I raised my glass. 'To the first of many lessons.'

Bridget grinned, while my list of questions skipped pointlessly around inside my head.

Our food arrived and she set to work on a plate of steak and chips.

I'd asked about the Castle scene, the body at the bottom of the cliff, during our exchange of emails. I'd brought a hard copy with me. I pulled it out and asked again, 'Did Niall send you this?'

Her eyes only grazed it, but the shake of her head was precise.

'Did he send it to any of the other players?' I'd asked this before as well, but I wanted to see her expression when she answered me.

'No. They would have said.'

'What about Fallon?'

'No.'

'What was it like being a Hero in the Castle?'

'It was an action MUD. We took that pretty seriously. It wasn't everybody's cup of tea. Players would join, stay for a few games as Brits, then get sick of it and leave. But those of us who didn't leave, who won our Hero's shields, well now, we each made a commitment.'

'What went wrong?'

'Fallon used to make us feel special, those of us who'd won our shields. Every now and again we'd review the levels a soldier had to pass in order to become a Hero. There was debate, you know, over how difficult to make them.'

Bridget paused and chewed a large mouthful with obvious enjoyment.

'What exactly did Fallon accuse Ferdia of doing?'

'Stealing the source code.'

'How did he react to that?'

'He denied it. Ferd was always very good on detail. Which bits of our army were where and what they should do next. It could get complicated. His reports were always accurate. You couldn't fault him. He was almost too perfect. Not that we – not that I minded. I thought he was wonderful.'

'Had Heroes been punished before? Banned, is that the right word?'

'Once,' Bridget said. 'But that was different.'

'How?'

'So far as I know – it was before my time – it was for a breach of security before a major battle.'

'Who breached security?'

'A character called Caffa. People talked about it because it had become a kind of symbol of what a Hero shouldn't do. Once a player is accepted in the Castle, given responsibility, he mustn't form allegiances outside it.'

'And this Caffa – how was he punished, if he *was* a he?'

Bridget smiled again, and pushed her plate aside. She'd polished off her meal in record time.

'He was banned. He had to leave the game.'

'Fallon went one step more with Ferdia? Banning didn't satisfy him?'

'There was a consensus to ban Caffa, I believe. A Castle conference. A decision was reached. With Ferdia it was Fallon's personal decision.'

'Why do you think Fallon made those accusations?'

'Either something had happened between them and that was his way of retaliating – '

'Or?'

'Or somebody *did* mess with the source code.'

'So the accusations could have been true?'

'It would've been totally out of character for Ferd to do that. Totally.' Bridget finished her beer and stared at my food. 'Aren't you hungry?'

I nibbled small holes in my sandwich while she ordered coffee and a slice of pie.

'You quit the MUD,' I said.

'That didn't help much, did it?' Bridget looked wan suddenly, and sad. Yet a smile seemed to be waiting in the wings of her mouth, ready to move up, lighten the pale clear skin around her eyes. I found myself liking her. I liked the way she'd tricked me into believing Sgartha was a man.

'How many other Heroes were played by women?' I asked, watching her dig her spoon into a thick wad of apples and whipped cream.

'Well, I wouldn't know now, would I?'

We laughed. Bridget said, 'It would be a bit strange if I was the only one.'

I was beginning to feel dizzy from lack of sleep. I took another ragged bite of sandwich and looked up to see her watching me, her head on one side, contemplating my confusion.

'And you never met Niall Howley, you never saw each other face to face?'

Bridget shook her head. 'I met Fallon once, in London.'

'When?'

'A few years ago.'

'Is Fallon' – I said his name carefully, holding it out between us, as Bridget had been doing – 'a member of any political party, or organisation?'

'Which organisation would that be?'

'Any one.'

If Bridget thought my question was out of place for an old friend of Niall's, then she gave no sign. 'Fallon doesn't like political parties. He told me that once. They all become corrupt.'

'What do you think?'

'That's why I came over here – to put a bit of water between myself and all of that.'

'But you and Niall corresponded, I mean as yourselves?'

Bridget nodded. 'Email and on the phone. And I sent him post-cards once or twice. He had a lovely voice.'

It gave me a small shock to realise that I'd never heard it. 'Was it common for players to become friends offline?'

'Sometimes.'

I waited, hoping Bridget would elaborate. Instead, she asked me if I'd like to see around the factory where she worked. Surprised and pleased, I thanked her and said yes. I paid for the food and she told me the drive would take about ten minutes.

'Was there any way Niall could have returned to the Castle after he'd been executed?' I asked as we walked out to the car park.

Bridget busied herself unlocking her car.

'I mean not return as Ferdia, but another character?'

She didn't answer until she'd exited the car park. I was impressed by the way she drove, leaning over the floor gear shift and changing gears fast.

'Ferd could have started at the bottom again with another password. Provided Fallon didn't figure out where he was coming from.'

'It's possible, isn't it, for someone to have impersonated Niall's character, Ferdia that is, without Fallon knowing?'

'That couldn't happen.'

'Why not?'

'Fallon kept close tabs on all of us.'

'Are you scared of him?'

Bridget didn't answer. She kept her eyes on the road, and I was aware of her discomfort. She turned into another car park, with fresh white lines and licence numbers painted on the asphalt.

'Did you think about the Castle when you weren't playing?' I asked.

'Yes, of course. Many times. I had dreams.'

'Nightmares?'

'A few. In my dreams, the roles were sometimes mixed up. I wasn't a Hero, or if I was, I was a different one. A couple of times I played –'

She paused and I prompted her quietly. 'Who?'

'God.'

Bridget took me through a large reception area, all tinted glass, soft beige leather and well-watered shrubbery. One wall was entirely taken up with shelves on which stood rows of gold and silver cups. My eye lighted on a couple from Australia.

She nodded to the receptionist, who looked back at her with a peculiar expression. I filled in a visitor's book and was given a small pass, while Bridget pulled a laminated pass out of the pocket of her jacket and pinned it on. I followed her up some steps, then through reinforced steel doors, while she explained that for security reasons we wouldn't be going into the part of the building where this year's model was being assembled. She smiled with what I was coming to recognise as pleasure in knowing things other people didn't.

'A man's world,' I commented, wondering if I should feel flattered at Bridget's assumption that I'd know what I was looking at.

'Yes,' she answered with another smile. 'And no.'

She didn't elaborate, and I was too full of questions I still wanted to ask about Niall to pursue the topic of her work.

While she showed me how they tested the car bodies for durability, and invited me to hop inside last year's Grand Prix model, she explained that she was an aeronautical engineer by training.

'I never thought I'd get this job, you know. You could have blown me over with a puff of wind.'

'Have you got family in Ireland?'

'My parents are in Derry. And one of my brothers, and my youngest sister. I go back fairly often. More often than I'd like to actually.'

'Why did you leave?'

Bridget frowned. I could see her thinking she'd already answered that.

'I got sick of it. And I was lucky. I went to university. I had a good job. But my brother, the one who lives at home, he had a nervous breakdown some years back, and he hasn't really had much in the way of work since. I'm trying to talk my youngest sister into coming over here. She can live with me while she finds a job in London. Her chances will be better here. And she'll feel better about herself. I did.'

'Niall was interested in Ireland,' I said, deciding it wouldn't hurt to improvise a bit. 'He didn't like the way his father wanted to deny their ancestry. Pretend it didn't matter.'

'Maybe it doesn't,' Bridget said, leading the way into yet another showroom through a well-sealed door. 'Maybe the best thing to do is to forget about it. In here – this is my baby.'

On the other side of the door was a large room, with what looked like a huge white half plane, half racing car sitting in the middle. It was much larger than a racing car, and a lot of the size was wings, designed, Bridget told me as we walked around it, to keep it on, not off, the ground.

The car was to have been the factory's attempt to break the land speed record, and the reason they'd hired Bridget in the first place. But bad luck had struck the project. After initial sponsorship, which had enabled her to design and build the model, the sponsors had withdrawn. It would cost several million pounds to build the actual car and trial it, and until they found that money, the project was on hold and Bridget was stuck with the Formula One.

She stroked the side of her great-winged, grounded bird. Both looked, for one peculiar moment, as though they were about to take off, Bridget with her upstanding hair and Irish luminescence. It seemed that they were land bound, if at all, by strings too light and thin for the human eye. And so it seemed too, just for the briefest time, that this extraordinary woman might indeed take flight with the thing she called her baby.

She seemed too unlikely, fey, irreverent to be its designer. Yet in her imaginative life she'd been, still was for all I knew, an island warrior, and everything from a British foot soldier to an Irish Hero.

She turned to me and asked, 'Why did you come all this way?'

'To find out what you thought of Niall and why he killed himself.'

Bridget patted the bird car as though to reassure herself. 'He was the kind of guy who never gave up. Stubborn as all get out really. Honest.'

'But he liked acting, playing roles.'

'Not half so much as me.'

'You mean for him it was a means to an end?'

'That's right. Oh he loved the Castle. And his buddies. He used to say he loved the feel of it. Knowing it was always there.'

'The challenge?'

'Yeah. That was like the role play, something he had to keep up, live up to, in order to keep being part of it, if you see what I mean.'

'I think I do. Did Niall ever talk to you about his family?'

'You mean his real one? In Australia? A bit. I got the impression he didn't get on with his dad. He felt sorry for his mother, but he found both of them overbearing. He did say that he hated being an only child.'

'You don't have that problem?'

'My folks are cool, and in any case I live a long way from them. You know,' she said, looking me up and down, then nodding as though she'd come to a decision, 'Niall wrote to me just before he died.'

'What about?

'The hospital where he worked. He was in some sort of trouble. He didn't spell it out. Something to do with the guy he worked for.'

'Dr Fenshaw?'

'Yeah. Niall obviously thought the world of this guy, but he'd done something that upset him.'

'What?'

'Niall never said. He never went into any of the details. I told him to go and talk to someone over there, someone he could trust. And to forget about all this shit with the Castle. He needed that like a hole in the head. Just quit, like I was doing.'

'Did he take your advice about talking to someone?'

'I don't know. If he did, it couldn't have done him much good, could it?'

'So Niall really admired Dr Fenshaw.'

'Yeah.'

'Like he admired Fallon?'

'I got the feeling even more so, but by the time Niall was telling me this stuff he was totally pissed off with Fallon.'

'Did Niall describe Fenshaw to you? Tell you why he thought so much of him?'

'You mean physically?'

'As a person.'

'He did say that he made you feel special, and that he was a perfectionist, that he drove himself as hard as he drove everyone who worked for him.'

'You really never met Niall face to face?'

'Never.'

'Do you feel you should have helped him more?'

'Of course,' Bridget said, with another wry face in which sadness fought with something tough and resilient. 'Don't you?'

. . . . . .

Twelve

I drove north from Belfast airport in a hire car, arriving at Fallon's village just on dusk. I was tired when I got there, but proud of the way I'd managed.

The village had two hotels and a few more bed and breakfast places. I'd booked to stay in the only B&B that was open in October. My guidebook mentioned Sorley Fallon's silverware and jewellery shop as one of a handful of businesses catering to summer tourists.

The light was fading as I pulled up. The countryside around was bare, practically treeless, the few trees already stripped of leaves. Small, stone-fenced fields neatly contained black-faced sheep, and stretched all the way to cliff edges, the ocean below them a grey shimmer in the evening light.

A woman wearing a tweed skirt and twinset showed me to a tiny upstairs room where I dumped my bags, then hurried out for a walk while there was still some light to see by.

People were about, two couples walking dogs, a woman pushing a stroller and holding a child of three or four tightly by the hand, others making their way towards the closest pub which, I was glad to see, served dinner from seven o'clock on.

I found the jewellery shop without any trouble. It was small and narrow-fronted, as was the shop advertising Aran wool jumpers next to it. Both were closed, but there was a light on at the back of Fallon's. I studied the finely-carved pieces in the window to see if I could spot any of the ones he'd photographed for his website. There were trays of bracelets, earrings, brooches, attractive but nothing out of the ordinary. I heard a noise and stepped back onto the street.

It was too dark to take the cliff path to the sea. I'd save that for tomorrow. I didn't have a plan for tackling Fallon, but I believed I had one card up my sleeve. Everything would depend on what happened when I played it, how Fallon responded, what move he chose next.

. . .

Fallon's homepage photograph didn't do him justice. He shook my hand, studying me with a smile of amusement, blue eyes of the Pacific seabed, not that other sea at the bottom of a cliff. If my flesh was a disappointment, then he was not about to say. His long black hair was tied back with a leather thong. He was tall, well-built, with the expectant confidence of someone who has turned strangers' eyes since he was a boy.

His shop was furnished with a couple of long, low display cases, two tables – one with a cash register and the other a computer, printer and modem – and a couple of chairs that looked as though no one ever sat on them. The windows facing the street were small, but an impression of light and space had been created by a large, sloping skylight towards the back. Under it was a workbench, covered with silversmithing tools and pieces of jewellery in various stages of completion.

Fallon was still smiling, waiting for me to explain myself.

'It's a quiet place you have here,' I said.

'The winters are quiet, that's true.'

His voice had an Irish way of holding together softness and its opposite.

'You prefer the winter?' I was afraid that my flat Australian vowels had already let me down.

'Very much so. And yourself?'

'It's cold, Canberra. Not like here though. Dry. The autumns are beautiful. Have you ever been to Australia?'

'I've not had that pleasure.'

He asked me if I'd like something to drink, and disappeared through a door set in the shop's back wall. There was another small building, a kind of annexe, behind the shop and a little to one side. It looked too small to live in, though large enough for a narrow kitchen. I guessed it was where I'd seen the light the night before.

His computer was running Windows NT, which took forever to

load. My host would be back before it did. I heard water running and prayed for some small kitchen calamity while I scanned icons for Fallon's internet service provider.

The second it came on the screen, I heard footsteps and flicked the power switch.

Fallon set down a tray with a coffee pot and two mugs that looked as though they'd been fired at a local pottery. He poured coffee, keeping his head lowered over the pot.

'Where did you work before you came here?'

'I studied computer science at Queens,' Fallon said slowly, as though he all day to fill in his biography. 'Then I worked in Belfast for a while. For IBM. Belfast drove me crazy. I'd started making jewellery when I was a student. I found I could sell quite a bit, you know, without really trying. I went to evening classes in silversmithing. One night a bomb went off so close it blew the electricity. We were sitting there, twenty of us, boys like me mostly, looking for an hour or two's escape, with our welding torches in our hands.'

'What happened?'

'Oh, the tech had its own generator, but by the time they got it going, the hour was up. Class dismissed.' He laughed. 'One Christmas I came up here and that was it. Love at first sight.'

I took a sip of coffee. It was good, hot and fully flavoured.

I looked at him over the top of my mug. 'Antrim's the most thoroughly Protestant county in the north. So I heard.'

'You heard correctly.'

'Why did you call your MUD *Castle of Heroes*?'

'It's from Yeats. Yeats liked castles. He bought one and lived in it during the civil war. Thoor Ballylee, it's called. And years before that, he'd found this castle in the middle of Lough Key. He had the idea of making it into a castle of heroes, the centre of a new cult.'

'You were following in the poet's footsteps?'

Fallon shook his head slightly, perhaps to clear away an unwelcome vision.

'Others might see it like that. I don't.'

He leant over to refill my mug. I've always liked being waited on by men. It calms me and makes me feel satisfied, as though I've just eaten a very good, but light and nutritious meal. It's a feeling of how life could be if the world were tilted just a little more.

Whether Fallon sensed this or not, he made a small ceremony out of pouring the coffee and watching me drink it appreciatively.

'Yeats is remarkable you know,' now there was something shy in his expression, as if he didn't know how his opinion would be met, 'for his interest in both nationalism and the occult. The two great passions, or forces in his life. And poetry, of course, though poetry wasn't so much a separate interest as an attempt to bring those other two together.'

'Yeats was a Protestant.'

'So was Wolfe Tone.'

'Did Yeats succeed, in your view?'

'Read the poems.'

'I studied them at university.'

Fallon inclined his head in deference to the superior knowledge conferred by universities. 'You know all about it then.' A strand of his hair came loose from the leather thong.

'What about the magic? Did you get that from him too?'

'He compiled books of fairytales, that's true. But the primary magic in my Castle is – I mean used to be – a staple of Irish folk tales.'

'Was Niall Howley a Republican?'

Fallon smiled and said, 'I suspect there's a type of Irish–Australian for whom we, the *Irish* Irish, are never good enough. You should visit Yeats's birthplace while you're here.'

'There's nothing I'd rather do.' I nodded to emphasise the point. 'But in the meantime – '

'Yeats was a game player, as all great poets are. And all great game players have a little of the poet in them.'

'Tell me why you decided to execute your favourite. And remember, I'm an Aussie blockhead, so you need to keep it simple.'

Fallon's stone blue eyes were cold. 'You should understand that Ferdia became erratic, irresponsible. I reprimanded him, then I threatened him with demotion. It made no difference. Then I caught him, or rather Niall, attempting to steal my source code. If he'd succeeded, he could have crashed the Castle any time he wanted.'

'How did you catch Niall?'

'My system recorded attempted break ins. He was logged on every time. It still amazes me that he thought he could get away with it.'

'Why would Niall want to crash your MUD?'

'I wish I knew.'

'Did you talk to the other Heroes about him?'

'Enough to convince them that the problem was serious.'

'So the execution was –?'

'I had to put a stop to it. He could have started his own MUD, but if he wanted to be part of mine, then he had to play according to my rules.'

At times it seemed that both of us were making a scrupulous distinction between Ferdia and Niall, at others that Fallon ran them together to suit himself.

'Who told you Niall was dead?'

'A friend of his from the hospital.'

Fallon roused himself, as though this was the point he really wanted to make. 'Do I grieve for him? Yes. I wouldn't be sitting here talking to you if I didn't. Do I blame myself? No, I do not.'

'Did Niall always log on from the same computer?'

'From memory, there was more than one.'

'Did you keep a record?'

I waited while he looked up the addresses, copied them, and handed them to me. One was Niall's. The other looked as though it could belong to Monaro Hospital.

'This could mean two players, couldn't it? Both claiming to be Ferdia.'

Fallon hesitated for a moment, then replied that, though he'd kept all his login records for a time, he'd recently got rid of them.

'What about the buildings, all the graphic stuff?'

'I got rid of that too.'

I reached into my bag, took out an envelope containing a copy of the castle scene and handed it across.

'It was left on Niall's computer when he died.'

Fallon glanced at it without apparent recognition.

'Niall sent it to you, didn't he? When?'

'It would have been the night he died.'

'June the twenty-second?'

'That's right.'

'Did he send it to any of the other players?'

'I have no idea.'

'Did you create it and send it to him?'

'Of course not.'

Fallon's voice was so mild, so soft. I listened for the edges, the cut under the sibilance and repeated, 'When?'

He thought for a few seconds, then said, 'It would have been after midnight. Your time.'

'Niall was dead by then.'

'Are you sure?'

'Absolutely. Someone sent you the picture after he'd pushed Niall off the tower.'

Out of Canberra, out of Australia, I felt free to say it. And having said it, it felt right.

'Do you know who it was?' asked Fallon.

'Do you?'

When Fallon didn't answer, I said, 'Niall was very different from Ferdia, wasn't he? From the character he played. You could say they were opposites.'

'What makes you think that?'

'I'm asking you.'

'Niall could be free in the Castle. He wasn't alone in that, but there were aspects of his life in Australia that seemed, from what he told me, to be very constricting.'

'He talked to you about some trouble he was in? He phoned you?'

Fallon said sarcastically, 'Before his *character* began behaving so destructively. Before our disagreement.'

'What *was* Niall like then? Why did he need this freedom that you say you gave him?'

'To express himself, aspects of himself that there was no place for in ordinary life, or that he couldn't find a place for. He'd been brought up very strictly. He was frightened of his father. There was a lot of anger there, but he'd learnt to hide it well.'

'Are you saying that you and the Heroes understood him better than his family or friends?'

'I'm saying that we came to, yes.'

'Understood what, exactly?'

'His determination. His devotion.'

'His devotion to Dr Alex Fenshaw?'

'Who?' Fallon's eyelids didn't flutter. His eyes became harder if anything, but I was sure he knew the name.

'Did Niall tell you he and Dr Fenshaw quarrelled?'

'I understood,' Fallon said, choosing his words with evident care, 'that they were a loyal and close-knit group.'

'Niall said that did he?'

'He implied it.'

'Did he expect too much of other people?'

'Possibly.'

'Did that make you angry?'

'Not until it became clear that I was losing him.'

Fallon picked up the tray and stood up. This time I followed him.

Autumn sun through a second skylight turned the back room into a cask of amber light. Fallon moved through it casually, yet with the strength of ownership. He set down his tray on a stainless steel sink and bent to open a small fridge. It struck me that he showed no concern about leaving his shop unattended.

'It's a lovely room,' I said. 'Rooms.' Not wanting to disparage the shop by my comparison. Behind this sloping globe of kitchen was there an even smaller, light-centred bedroom?

I waited till he stood up and I could see his face. 'Bridget Connell told me Niall wrote to her about trouble he was having at work.'

'If you've met Bridget, which it appears you have?' Fallon didn't bother to hide his distaste. 'Then I'm surprised you haven't worked out that she's a compulsive liar. Bridget tailors her story to her audience, whatever she feels will titillate them. Let me guess – she told you she used to work in aeronautics. She showed you around her factory. She likes doing that. She's the financial manager's daughter. He indulges her, to my mind, excessively. I expect she also spoke about her family, the poor brother stuck in Ireland recovering from a nervous breakdown, the sister she would like to help. Bridget is an only child.'

Each of Fallon's words tapped out into a silence that had not been broken by a single workaday noise such as the phone ringing, the fax machine whirring, not even an old-fashioned bell over the door announcing the presence of a customer.

'You don't have to believe me. Phone up. Find out for yourself. Bridget's father spoils her, but the receptionist has a mind of her own.'

The gracious host, firmly in control, Fallon led the way back to his shop and extended his hand towards the telephone. 'Please. It'll cost a wee fortune to call from your hotel.'

I gritted my teeth against his sarcasm, snatching at the phone. My hand shook as I listened to it ring, then asked for Bridget Connell.

There was a slight pause before a smooth English voice replied, 'I'm sorry, but we have no one of that name working here. We have a Mr Frank Connell. Would you like me to put you through to him?'

'No, thank you.'

Fallon leant back against the computer table and crossed his feet in front of him. He looked infuriatingly relaxed.

'Bridget was the longest-running player wasn't she?' I asked him. 'After Niall.'

Fallon nodded.

'She was loyal to both of you.'

'Up to a point.'

'You're trying to make a fool of me,' I said, 'because you think that way you'll get rid of me. You'll intimidate me and make me look stupid and then I'll leave. It won't work. Intimidation just makes me dig my heels in.'

Fallon laughed. 'Is that an Australian character trait?'

'I would have thought it was an Irish one.'

'May I make a suggestion? Whatever you think of me, think about this. The name *Castle of Heroes* is taken from Yeats, and some of the ideas, but physically my castle was modelled on a real one, on Dunluce. I'd like to show you Dunluce as it's meant to be seen. Will you let me do that?'

'When?'

'How about tomorrow morning?'

. . .

Though I'd been looking forward to it, I was scarcely aware of my sur-roundings as I walked to the end of the street and took the path that led down to the ocean. In the half light of the evening before, I'd thought the path went more or less straight down, and had been prepared for a scramble, but now I realised that it sloped gradually, following a contour of the basalt cliff. Getting down would take longer than I'd thought, and I was already feeling hungry.

The sea was iron grey, as was the sky above it, but there was little wind and it wasn't really cold. The path was narrow and I concentrated on not losing my footing. It took me about twenty minutes to reach a large sign, a red on white warning that bathing was unsafe, above the last slope to the beach. I wondered what the summer tourists did. There was sand, but it was coarse and muddy looking. Sea-scoured rocks covered most of the beach. Close up, the waves were huge, and so monochrome and regular that they seemed solid, not made of water at all, but some new form of plastic.

Ahead of me, a dog was taking itself for a walk, dashing at the shore-break, then madly backing off, barking at the waves. From a distance, the dog could almost have been Fred, but Fred wouldn't have shown that much energy or initiative unless there was a promise of food at the end of it.

As a child I'd learnt to pretend, to perform, no matter how I was feeling, and I took this for a commonplace that everybody learnt, and could put into practice when they chose. I would never be a good actor, but I understood the principles. How could I have been so wrong about Bridget Connell? And was I wrong about her? I wouldn't put it past Fallon to have bribed the receptionist to lie to me.

I knew now why Bridget's face had seemed about to break into a grin. It was complicity, the knowing smile of a fellow deceiver. She'd known I wasn't who I said I was, and she'd been waiting for me to catch up with her and share the joke.

Ivan had warned me that the trip would be a waste of time. He knew the sorts of people Bridget and Sorley Fallon were likely to be, people who delighted in game playing – well, that much I could have worked out for myself – but also people for whom secrets, aliases, were crucial, not an aspect of behaviour they could take or leave.

Fallon was a young man. I put his age at somewhere around twenty-eight, certainly no more than thirty-one or two. His way of life seemed unusual for a man of his age and looks. He'd known I was coming, and had prepared his story with its literary references and hard to swallow conclusions. I wondered if it would have been better to turn up unannounced. What would Fallon have done if I'd dropped out of the sky and surprised him?

Even as I was thinking this, I knew I couldn't have done it. I could never have got on the plane without a meeting already arranged. I thought of Moira, how she'd kissed me on the cheek, looking proud and hopeful as she'd said good luck.

The other reason I didn't think it would have worked for me to try to catch Sorley Fallon by surprise was that I suspected this was next to impossible. His self control ran so deep that it was scarcely touched by my appearance, even less by my ham-fisted questions. I wished I was a better interviewer. Maybe there was some course I could take when I got home.

Say Niall had been helping to raise money for a militant republican group, and Fallon was involved. Say Niall had said or done something that made Fallon angry, and Fallon had retaliated. Perhaps Niall had been expelled from the group, for which the execution of Ferdia had been meant as a symbolic warning. But even if all this was correct, where did it take me? Where could I go from here?

· · ·

I rang Bridget Connell's number from the B&B.

'Good one,' I said when she came on the line.

She laughed, a youthful, happy laugh, delighted to have fooled me. 'What did you think of him?'

'Charming,' I said. 'A perfect Irish gentleman. How do you get away with it?'

'At the factory? To tell you the truth –'

'Yes?'

'It bores me now.'

'The bird car's nice.'

'Isn't it though? You know, I didn't make any of that up.'

'It had a certain ring. Tell me about Niall and Dr Fenshaw.'

'Niall really didn't spell anything out, just that there was a problem at work and he was upset and worried.'

'What else was worrying him?'

A long silence, then Bridget said, 'He thought someone was stalking him on the MUD.'

'Who?'

'The stalker kept changing his character.'

'You recognised the same person behind different characters?'

'Niall said it was. Poor guy, he got so spooked. I watched his back for him. We worked a buddy system. It made him feel better for a while.'

'Did you think he was imagining it?'

'He had some idea who it was. Then everything blew up. Fallon went ballistic and announced that execution. I quit and told Niall he should too. I thought he was going to.'

'What about the stalker?'

'I saw him off a few times. He had different handles. Blacksnake was one.'

'That sounds Australian.'

'I did try and watch Ferd's back for him,' Bridget said. 'Everything was such a mess.'

. . .

Fallon said, 'You know, the name Dunluce is Irish for fort. There's been a fort here since the tenth century.'

Setting out, he assured me that the castle was by far the best viewed on foot from the coast path, rather than the road.

'You're in for a treat Sandra.' He swallowed the a's in my name. In the clear light of the morning, he seemed relaxed and open to any questions I might ask, chatting about the Antrim coast and the MacDonnell clan who'd owned Dunluce for centuries.

I felt myself slipping underneath a border, not a strong stark one, a cliff face, but milder, a creek bank maybe. On one side was the pleasure of this unusual young man's company. I did not like to think what was on the other. Apart from small birds, we were alone on the cliff path, but instead of letting this make me anxious, I decided to enjoy the sun on the grass, the cliffs and view of the sea.

'How did you feel about women players?' I asked, thinking once again of Bridget.

'Maeve, Queen of Connaght, was a woman, Cuchulain's greatest foe and a match for him in cunning if not bravery.'

'How did you feel about Bridget playing an island warrior?'

'Well now,' Fallon smiled. 'I thought she was just right for it.'

The ocean looked completely different. Instead of forbidding, solid-seeming walls of grey, it was blue and far enough below us to seem like something out of a travel documentary. It reminded me a little of the southern coast of Victoria, around Port Campbell. The wind was cold and I was glad I'd worn a jacket. The sky was blue as well, with a line of clouds close to the horizon.

Bridget might have rung Fallon after I'd spoken to her. They might have discussed how best to deal with me. I reminded myself how little I knew about these people, their allegiances and loyalties. They obviously thought lying to me would be easy. But maybe that wasn't such a bad thing. Maybe one of them would get too smart.

'You know Sandra, it's no shame to kill or be killed by a Hero,' Fallon said.

I didn't want to rehash the peculiar ethics of his MUD. We could spar back and forth for days about it without getting anywhere.

He continued in a hard voice, 'I built the Castle. I ran it. No one *had* to play.'

We walked in silence for a while. The path became narrower, stony. I let Fallon take the lead.

'I must say after meeting you I'm curious,' he said. 'You don't seem like the crusading type.'

'Crusading?'

'I'd pictured you as a do-gooder.'

'I feel sorry for Moira Howley, Niall's mother.'

'And that's all?'

'Actually, it's quite a lot.'

I stayed a few steps behind Fallon, not that, if he planned to push me over the edge, it would make a difference. The path, which had been wide enough for two people to walk side by side when we started out, narrowed gradually until it was barely wide enough for one. Mentally,

I measured the distance between myself and the cliff edge. One step off the path, another, then nothing but sweet air.

I glanced back the way we'd come, to the small, enclosed fields. I put out my hand to steady myself, feeling underneath it crumbling dirt, the ever-present basalt.

I said, 'Any number of players could have been dialling up from Canberra.'

Fallon didn't argue the point. He lifted his eyes to the horizon. 'Around the next curve and we'll see it. You're lucky it's a fine day. I've been up here in the rain and fog. All weathers.'

'Niall claimed he was being followed, stalked.'

Fallon was still looking out over the sea. It seemed that he answered reluctantly. 'It was an action MUD. One of the things it was *about* was being followed, chased, and killed.'

'Whoever was harassing Niall might have had a purpose outside the MUD.'

Fallon repeated, 'If he didn't like it he could have left.'

'Why did *you* like it?'

'Because it gave a purpose and a shape to life.'

We drew near enough to make out Dunluce's tower and gatehouse, the battered wall that was a continuation of the cliffs, protecting the buildings behind it from storms and savage winds. Under a clear sky, the castle looked benign, though it was easy to imagine its outline barely visible through fog, its grey stone struck by storm.

'Can we go inside?'

'Of course. It's open all year round.'

The entrance was right at the back and it took us a while to get there. We paid our admission to a bored-looking young woman who said hello to Fallon.

I would have been glad for him to stay and talk to her – indeed, I would have liked nothing better than to be left to wander around on my own – but after explaining to the woman, who looked amused to hear it, that he was showing the local attractions to his Australian visitor, he guided me with him through the turnstile.

The castle buildings covered so large an area that the outer wall might once have enclosed and protected a whole village. We crossed mounds of shockingly green grass, passed bits of walls with signs explaining what they'd once been attached to.

Fallon said, 'You can't get onto the outer wall. It isn't safe.'

'Well then' – I glanced at him to see how serious he was – 'I'll get as close to it as I can.'

I was feeling strangely detached from everything, from the ruins, the history. I was glad of the cold breeze around my ears keeping me alert, pleased to find that there were few other sightseers.

Fallon had told me as we were leaving the village that I should take my time, that he had all day if I did, as though what he wished me to see and understand could not be rushed.

A fence about twenty metres from the outer wall warned visitors to go no further. I climbed over it. With a grunt of annoyance, Fallon did the same.

Close up, the outer wall was obviously not in good nick at all. Parts of it were okay, enough to give a solid impression from a distance, but many stones had fallen, and it looked as though the next big storm might send great chunks of it crashing into the sea.

I walked to the edge and looked down. There wasn't a single bush, no vegetation other than grass and lichens. Closer to the ocean, there was only rock, a sheer drop.

Fallon stood a couple of metres behind me. I put out my hand and ran it along one of the stones that had become dislodged, nudging it to see how much it would take to send it careering downwards.

'Why did you want me to come here?' I asked.

Fallon walked right up to me and laid his hand on the same stone, not as I had done, out of curiosity, and to gauge its remaining strength. It seemed an act, a reminder, of possession.

'Who told you another player was stalking Ferdia?' he asked.

'Bridget Connell.'

'I thought we'd established Bridget is a liar.'

'That doesn't mean she can't decide to tell the truth. And Niall, the more I learn about him, the more he strikes me as a truthful person.'

'He was loyal.'

'To you?'

'I wanted to believe he was.'

'If Niall told Bridget he was being stalked, surely he would have told you too.'

'You forget, he and I weren't on the best of terms.'

'But you were in a good position to catch the stalker. Being God.'

'I was that.'

'What did you find?'

'Nothing out of the ordinary. On a busy night, there could be twenty hits from new players. Some would only last five minutes.'

'But they all had to sign up and be given a password and a character?'

'Of course.'

'And they wouldn't all be logging on from the Monaro Hospital.'

Fallon was silent.

'Trust me,' I said. 'I'm trusting you.'

His eyes took on a glittering hardness, and he looked up past me again, to the open sea. Perhaps he was remembering Niall, or Ferdia, or some fusion of the two that shone in his mind more brightly than any living person. His eyes darkened even further, and his face closed in on itself, becoming ugly. He looked suddenly much older, fixed. I saw how he would be when youth left him. I'd ceased to matter, my niggling questions and reasons for asking them. It was as though the wind and the elemental fastness of castle and cliff had stripped a layer from him, revealing what was underneath.

Then he shook his shoulders as though preparing himself for some final effort. 'I didn't kill Niall, if that's what you came here to find out.'

'Who did?'

'I don't know.'

'Was it the same person who sent you that picture?'

'I honestly don't know.'

'Help me work it out.'

The towers and dark stone walls were as deserted as if there were never any sightseers, as if the gulls had the fortress to themselves.

'Don't you find,' I said, 'this whole business of castles and battles a bit old hat? After all, Tony Blair's just shaken hands with Gerry Adams, and most of Northern Ireland, so I understand, is trying to look forwards, not backwards.'

Fallon said coldly, 'It remains to be seen whether Blair, like so many British prime ministers before him, will prove to be a Judas.'

'So what about Niall?'

'Is politics just a game to you in Australia then?'

I bit back a retort.

'You know I think it must be,' Fallon said. 'All very well to condescend to us, then fly back home to sleep snug in your bed.'

'But there is a possibility of compromise?'

Fallon winced. 'Niall did what he felt he had to do, Sandra. I think you should take that back to his mother, or whoever sent you here. And then I think that, out of respect for our mutual friend, you should let the matter rest.'

......

Thirteen

I returned the car to the office of the rental company, and was booked on a flight to Sydney via London early the next morning. My one night in Belfast. I decided I would walk, not plan where I was going, just walk. There were a lot of people in the streets, young couples with babies and toddlers in the universal, tag-along position, women of my age and older, carrying their shopping home.

Puddles of rainwater reflected streetlights, and the whole centre of the city seemed floodlit, black and silver. I had a weird impulse to stay, find out something about the place. I could ring Ivan and say I'd been unavoidably delayed, or else say nothing. Go AWOL. Abscond.

The street I was in gave onto a large square. I stood staring across it at the city hall. I remembered seeing the square on television, after the 1995 ceasefire, when Bill Clinton had lit the lights on a huge Christmas tree. The cameras had focused on reflected light, just as my eyes were doing now, the shadowed square with foreign dignitaries muffled up in coats. Music, and a tree bursts forth.

Tonight, the square was empty. It was too early for Christmas decorations. I didn't feel like stepping out across it, but decided rather to skirt around the edges. In my pocket I had the address of the Bobby Sands wall mural, and a vague idea of finding it. I thought of Sorley Fallon, trained in the lightning time frame of computers, choosing to spend his energy crafting legendary battles which the Irish always won.

I loved walking at night. It was funny the way something as simple and apparently innocent as streetlights reflected in a puddle could flip through memories and give them a connection.

I recalled the night I'd sneaked through Canberra's back streets to visit my old boss, suspended on charges of computer theft and fraud, my broken arm in a black sling, afraid that I was being followed. Nights when I was young, scouring Europe on my own. I'd never got as far west as Ireland. I'd stood and stared for hours at Italian and French buildings, top-heavy with the kind of history bewildering to a third generation Australian, content at the time to let impressions mean as much or as little as they would, rain and light and shadows.

A fool's journey. I'd been warned. Ivan and Brook had both warned me. I thought of Moira Howley and what little I had to take back to her, then of Yeats's poem, *The Second Coming*. When I got home, I'd ferret out my *Selected Poems* and refresh my memory.

It was the nature of ambushes not to be predicted or foreseen. Just as it seemed to be in the nature of some people – I thought again of Fallon – not to be bowled over by an ambush, but to set about turning it to their advantage. What did such people learn about themselves and others as a consequence?

Being young and single, studying poetry at university. Looking back, I realised that those years had been the time of greatest peace between me and my mother, years of truce, when I was no longer at home, under her winged shadow, before I joined the workforce and began, once again, to disappoint her. My mother had expected me to hold fast to her values and to act on them, and at the same time to be everything she wasn't.

A shape with lion body and the head of a man,
A gaze blank and pitiless as the sun

Niall Howley in flight, an Icarus no one would make a poem of, however much his mother might yearn for a poem, or a song of praise. In flight on a winter's night in Canberra, unwitnessed until a tiny Polish kitchen hand on her way to work was startled by a shape in the fog, a burst of yellow hair.

Fallon in mind again. The beast in the poem seemed connected to him. The reckoning took an immediate and cruel form.

· · ·

I'd scarcely taken two steps inside my hotel room when the phone rang.

'I found something,' Ivan said. 'In Niall's room. Tucked into the cover of one of his textbooks, would you believe?'

'How –?' I began, but Ivan cut me off. 'Something the little bugger didn't want anyone to know about.'

'What?'

'Numbers.'

The line went fuzzy for a second. It had been as clear as though Ivan was standing next to me.

'What numbers?' I shouted.

'No need to raise the roof, Sandy. Your ears might be gummed up, but mine are perfectly okay. Don't worry. Have it cracked by the time your feet hit the tarmac.'

There was a metallic crash in the background.

'What's that?'

'Just Kat getting into the saucepans. I fronted up to Ma Howley. Asked her if I could have a look around her son's room. That woman's a witch, but she let me. I tell you Sandy. Our local constabulary. Their standards have been slipping.'

I thought of Bill McCallum and his turtle neck, his memories of heads rolling, a ute awash with blood. I thought about who else might have scanned Niall's shelf of textbooks and decided they could stay.

Ivan dictated the numbers to me. 'Sort of a diagram underneath. Stables, bakery, hall –'

'A diagram of the Castle?'

'Could be. It's not called anything. Looks like a kid's drawing. Peter could do better with his eyes shut.'

'Niall's handwriting. I forgot to ask Moira if it was his writing on the back of the photograph. I think it's probably hers. See if she's kept something with his writing on it.'

'Done. I don't think she minds me *that* much.'

'Where was it again?'

'On a scrap of paper folded inside the cover of a physiology textbook. Nice touch that. Give me a few days. Pity there's not more. Anyway,' Ivan said happily, 'I found it.'

'Did Moira mind? About you going through his books?'

'Didn't seem to. I wore my best jumper and I've cut my hair.'

'Well done. Have you told her?'

'Nup. I'll leave that up to you.'

'How's Kat? And Peter?'

'Tip top. Hey, guess what? She's got another tooth.'

'And Peter?'

'Rang up to say g'day. Sounds fine.'

'Did you talk to Derek?'

'Nah. Don't worry Sand. He's fine.'

. . .

Would Sorley Fallon know what the numbers meant? Why a diagram of the Castle? Did it mean anything? It could be years old, a meaningless doodle. Why hadn't I searched Niall's room?

I rang Fallon, who wasn't answering, then Bridget. I read her the list of numbers. She claimed never to have heard it before.

'Did Niall say anything to you about a hidden file?'

'I'm afraid he didn't.'

'Did he tell you he was putting together information that he had to hide?'

'What information would that be now?'

'To do with the MUD maybe, the accusations against him, the way that he was being persecuted?'

'If he was hiding information, what did he intend to do about it?'

I wanted to be the one asking the questions. 'Why didn't you tell me before about the stalker? You could have emailed me.'

'I'm not used to trusting people.' There was a pause. Had Fallon rung and told her I'd asked for *his* trust? Had they laughed about it? 'Email's not secure, and – and when I offer someone information, I like to know how they intend to use it.'

'Who was the stalker?'

'That I don't know, truly.'

'Was it Fallon himself?'

'I did think of that. But why would he?'

'One of the other Heroes?'

'I'd swear on Sgartha's reputation that it wasn't.'

'Can you do something for me? Can you contact them and ask them about these numbers? There's a diagram of the Castle underneath them, a kind of floor plan,' I went on, hoping this was accurate. 'Did you ever download a floor plan of the Castle?'

'Fallon would have it.'

'He says he got rid of all that. Can you ask about the stalker too?' Before Bridget could object, I said, 'Fallon knows that Niall was murdered.'

Silence on Bridget's end.

'Did he warn you against talking to me?'

'Actually, I think he was quite impressed.'

Fourteen

Peter's face was huge and white, a full moon at the airport.

'Mum!' he cried. 'Mum!' As though he thought I'd disappeared for good.

Katya was a tight lozenge of baby-in-a-blanket, solemn and wide-eyed.

I can't sleep on planes, at most had had three hours since London. Ivan looked as though he'd been managing on less.

As soon as the kids were in bed, he got down to business.

'Who's Fallon got his email account with?'

'Pegasus,' I said, recalling a young Irishman making coffee in a tiny, light-filled kitchen.

Ivan smiled, a different Ivan, focused and determined. 'We might even be able to get away without a password.'

The sleuth in him, that the necessity of making a living had forced underground, had come to life while I was on the other side of the world. What had he unearthed? A line of numbers with an awful lot of noughts.

200180001602080415000

It wasn't much more than thirty hours since we'd spoken on the phone, but already Ivan had exhausted all the well-known encryption devices Niall might have used. He'd been at Weston Creek, talking to the police encryption people.

His description of the diagram was accurate – a pencil sketch such as any child might have wiled away time creating. No attempt at scale or perspective, and the rooms' rectangular boxes joined to each other without apparent purpose, but each with a handwritten name and a number after it in brackets. It was Niall's handwriting, and recently done, but that was all the police had been able to establish.

I felt as though I'd passed beyond physical exhaustion and out the other side, but it simply didn't occur to Ivan that all I might want to do was fall into bed.

It took us a few minutes to track down the Pegasus site. While we were looking, Ivan explained that some providers ran a list of clients online at any particular time. If we were lucky, Pegasus would be one of these.

The site featured all sorts of information, useless to us, about how long the service had been running, the benefits of signing up, how their costs were incredibly competitive. At the bottom was a list of present users. It grew as we were reading it.

'Fallon isn't there.'

'That's because he's probably asleep, or seducing some poor peasant girl.'

'I think he's gay.'

'Whatever. When the fucker *is* online, here's what we'll have to do. This might, or might not work – if he's using Telnet – which he may do if he's still into MUDs.'

'I don't think – ' I began, but Ivan cut me off.

'Some versions of Telnet use an old FTP server, which is lovely from our point of view because it's got a hole big enough to drive a truck through.'

I waited, knowing better than to interrupt again, but I was thinking: one, Fallon had given up MUDs; two, he wouldn't use a dodgy server. He was too smart, and too particular.

'It'll be fiddly Sand, but once we catch him with the server open, we should be able to download any files we want.'

'Isn't there a simpler way?'

'Well you can try and guess his password.'

I felt suddenly alone and frightened. Fear caught up with me, a slice between the shoulder blades.

I put my arms around Ivan from behind. He'd trimmed his hair and beard himself, a bathroom mirror job with the nail scissors. Springy black hair upstanding at his temples, short behind his ears, gave his face a leaner, older look. I was never so reminded of his foreignness as when he was concentrated on a task.

His eyes left the screen reluctantly, and he turned to face me like a startled Buddha, a man transported too quickly from one time frame to another.

. . .

Next morning was cloudy, threatening rain.

Moira Howley said, 'That Fallon does sound like rather a cold, manipulative kind of man.' Her voice was tentative, not yet disappointed.

'Well manipulative certainly. You know you were wrong to tell me you couldn't manage a trip to Ireland. I think you would've managed splendidly.'

'Me?'

'Let's go out into the garden,' I suggested.

Two compost heaps were neat pyramids without, it seemed, a single piece of refuse out of place. The wisteria was in full bloom now. Wind blew the smell of it up against the house.

Moira breathed in deeply. 'Bernard says my clothes smell. He takes his to the drycleaners. I *do* wash them. He sees me.'

I slipped my arm through hers.

Leave the house behind our shoulders, I wanted to tell her, walk out of it, as you're doing now, only more emphatically. Leave the shell, or else let life creep back. If you let it, it will begin to, bit by bit. Leave behind those two chairs in the living room.

'What else did Fallon say?'

'That Niall was a good person. Loyal.'

'Did he mean it?'

'Yes.'

'I thought he might – accidentally on purpose, you know – ' Moira hesitated, lifting her chin to the damp air. Her cardigan fell open on a crumpled T-shirt. She laughed at herself and her expectations. 'At least you established one thing. The young man exists. He's flesh and blood. If only Niall had had the sense to talk to someone.'

She stared across the garden without seeing it. Now she'll dismiss me, I thought. She'll thank me for having done my best, and write me a final cheque.

I said, 'You waited up for him, didn't you, the night he died.'

'No. Well, yes and no. I normally go to bed between ten-thirty and eleven, and that night I was very tired. I couldn't have known, I didn't know, that something dreadful was about to happen, but I was more tense than usual, and that made me tired. And then there was Bernard. But I stayed up anyway, till after eleven. I suppose it was about eleven-fifteen, eleven-twenty, when I went to bed.'

'What about Bernard?'

'Do you mean, did Bernard wait up for Niall? No. He went to bed at the same time I did. Sometimes Bernard stayed up late, well usually he stayed up later than me, but he'd had an early meeting that morning.'

'Did you go straight to sleep?'

'Yes. I woke up later, though. Funnily enough, I thought I heard Niall coming in.'

'You what?'

Moira stared at her hands. 'It's cold, isn't it? I wish the sun would come out, just for half an hour. I woke up. I thought it was because I'd heard a noise in the passage. I lay awake for a few minutes, but I didn't hear anything more. I thought to myself, well, he's home at any rate, and I went back to sleep.'

'Why didn't you tell me before?'

'It's not important. I must have been mistaken.'

'What time was it?'

'I'm not sure, I didn't look at the clock. I don't like to know the time when I wake up at night. It makes it harder to get back to sleep. Anyway, it couldn't have been Niall because the police – they say he died before midnight. He probably died around ten o'clock.'

'Was Bernard asleep?'

'I think so.'

It didn't seem to have occurred to Moira that the noise might have been made by someone else.

I opened my bag and took out the diagram.

'In one of Niall's books, you say?' Moira's voice was petulant, confused. 'What does it mean?'

'Have you seen it before?'

Moira shook her head. 'Why didn't the police find this?'

'I don't think they looked hard enough. Did Niall ever say anything to you about information that he had to hide?'

'What about?'

'His work perhaps? Did he tell you about some trouble he was in at work?'

Moira shook her head. Her personality, what I thought of as the force of it, the energy, was slipping away. She was interested in Sorley Fallon and my trip to Ireland, but not this. Or else it was too much suddenly, this new piece of information. But was it really new? If Niall had hidden something, who better to entrust with knowledge of his hiding place than his mother? She'd misled me before, not by outright lies, but by omission.

'Did Niall mention any of these numbers? Singly, in pairs, a group?'

Moira smoothed the sheet of paper flat with both hands, then held it at arm's length. She said, 'Niall's birthday, that's January, and Bernard's is in April.'

She made to give it back to me.

'Keep it. Something might come back to you.'

. . .

I met Brook in Civic for a bite to eat. Time was, before Kat was born, before Sophie, we had lunch together once a week.

I took his arm and we walked in step. Four people greeted him on the way to Bailey's Corner Café.

'Do all these people know that you're a cop?'

'Canberra's a conceited country town Sandra. And you forget how long I've worked here.'

He looked well and happy. 'You've brought the rain back with you.'

'It was sunny in Ireland,' I told him. 'The sun shone on Dunluce Castle.'

'You're back safe, that's the main thing.'

'Thanks for minding Kat.'

'I only did it once.'

We sat down and ordered BLTs. We talked about the diagram.

'There's not enough to work with. So the guys at Weston say. There's no prints on it but Howley's.'

'How old?'

'Probably only a few months.'

'You still think he killed himself, don't you?'

Brook didn't answer immediately. When he did, it sounded as though he was letting me down gently. 'The kid was fixated on that game.'

I took a bite of my roll. 'How did your officer in London get on with Sorley Fallon?'

'He's making inquiries.'

I waited.

'That's all I can tell you Sandra.'

'One of the computers used to play *Castle of Heroes* belongs to the hospital,' I said. 'Can you find out who had access to it at the times Niall was supposed to have been logged on?'

'You think it was someone else?'

'It might've been Niall in his tea break. It might've been someone we've never even heard of. It's just that Niall doesn't strike me as the type who'd use a hospital computer to dial up a MUD.'

'Who would?'

'Somebody who wanted to get him into trouble. Someone, another player, or players, was stalking Niall online. He told Bridget Connell and Sorley Fallon about it. There's more. That castle picture was sent to Fallon the night Niall died. After midnight.'

Brook stared at me, his attention finally caught.

'There could have been a delay in transmission.'

'Moira Howley says she thought she heard someone in the house late that night. She thought it was Niall coming home.'

'Did she get up to look?'

'No.'

I'd almost finished my roll and Brook had hardly started his. 'What's the matter? Aren't you hungry?'

'There's something about the smell.'

'Bacon?'

'Mayonnaise.'

'You have to eat.'

'Sophie thinks I should go on a health diet to clean out my system.'

'Your system looks fine to me.'

Brook smiled. Responsibility was not to be sloughed off, but balanced.

Forgiveness was sweet, but did I want to be forgiven? How could I lay claim to Brook's attention? There were a dozen claims on it. Some said Follow me, Love me, Take Pleasure In Me. Some said Duty.

I said, 'Here's what I think. Part of the fascination for Sorley Fallon was exerting his control over what *couldn't* be controlled. There could have been one player accessing the MUD through that hospital computer, or there could have been more than one. It could have been Niall Howley playing Ferdia each time, or it could have been someone who wanted Fallon and the Heroes to *believe* that it was Niall. I think we should be looking for someone who'd been playing cat and mouse with Niall for months. They spooked and frightened him. They wore him down, and then they killed him.'

Brook refused to comment on my theory. He pushed his plate away and said he should be getting back.

I went off to do some shopping, thinking it was odd the way I projected bits of myself into relationships – floated, rather than projected? I thought of the tide coming in, and an underwater plant, dried and parched from that long wait through the ebb, stirring and lifting in response, a green branch here and there. That could be Ivan now his mind was working again, swapping notes with the encryption people, his imagination lifted from the everyday. It could be the picture I was building up of Niall Howley, feeling my way through the confusing testimony of those who'd claimed to be his friends. It could be Brook with his smile that said, just so far and no further.

Fifteen

Before going out to the hospital again, I read over the section of the police report containing Eamonn's statement. Detective-Sergeant McCallum hadn't queried his account at all. Eamonn had told McCallum that Niall had been happy. Had McCallum accepted this? You couldn't tell from the report. It wasn't long since I'd met Eamonn, but a lot had happened, and my view of events had changed.

As I drove over the lake, the thought of the diagram sitting in my handbag was like a rip when you're out swimming in the surf. Not strong enough to be dangerous. Not yet. But with the element of danger that belongs to the sea, to waves and undertows and cross-currents.

At the inquiry desk, I was told that Eamonn was on ward eleven. Luckily, I ran into him in the corridor outside it, so I didn't have to interrupt him with a patient. He was obviously in a hurry, but I wasn't going to let that get in my way.

I watched Eamonn study the numbers and the sketch beneath them, remembering his calm good humour the first time we met, the plateau of acceptance he seemed to have reached concerning Niall's death, if not the reasons for it.

He looked up, his face impassive. 'Where did you say you found this?'

'In one of Niall's textbooks. Did he ever mention it to you?'

'No.'

'Did he say anything about information that was secret, that he had to hide?'

'No. Look, I'm on my way to get something. It can't wait.'

'Did Niall give you anything to keep for him?'

'You asked me that before.'

'Did he send you the castle picture?'

'No.'

'Are you sure?'

140...

'It's not something I'd be likely to forget.'

'What about the other radiotherapists, the ones Niall worked with?'

'I know I said I'd help you with addresses. I will help. If I can.'

'Why did they all leave at once?'

'I don't know.'

'Why didn't you tell me that there'd been almost a complete turnover of staff?'

'It didn't seem important.'

'Was Niall asked to leave?'

'I don't know.'

'But you knew Niall was having difficulties with his boss. What did he tell you?'

'He said whatever problems there were, the department would deal with them.' Eamonn paused, then added, 'He was loyal to Dr Fenshaw.'

Again, the undertone in Eamonn's voice I remembered from before, as though loyalty masked a connection that was deeper and more interesting.

'Were they lovers?'

'No.'

'Were you?'

'What?'

'You and Niall.'

'No.'

'Fenshaw?'

'It's none of your business.'

'Fenshaw has a lover here on the hospital staff doesn't he?'

'Look,' Eamonn said, beginning to walk away. 'What difference does it make?'

'Fenshaw and Colin Rasmussen have a thing. Or did.'

'I don't have anything to do with either of them personally. I told you that.'

'Was Niall jealous?'

'Of Colin Rasmussen? That's absurd.'

'That last night – did Niall mention a specific date to you?'

'No.'

'You said he was happy and excited. That's what you told the police. Did they ask you why?'

Eamonn stared at me, his grey eyes angry. I was glad I'd made him angry. 'It was the day after, for God's sake. I know you mean well, and you're doing this for Niall's mother. But it was the next day – I might've said anything.'

'You said Niall was happy.'

'I've been going over and around that since the last time you were here.' Eamonn lowered his head and scratched at his hairline, as if he could scratch away both his thoughts and our conversation. 'I should have picked up on it, shouldn't I? I should have seen he wasn't happy. Some sort of crazy – '

'Or relieved that he'd finally made up his mind?'

'That's just it – if you'd known Niall – he was the last – '

'You don't believe Niall killed himself?'

'I have to believe it, don't I? It happened.'

'But you don't believe it. Why didn't you tell the police about your doubts?'

'I don't know. I just thought – whatever had happened – maybe it was better.'

'Is it possible that Niall met someone later that night who turned what he thought was good news into the worst?'

Eamonn shook his head and said he didn't know. 'I don't think you should come here any more.'

'Why not?'

'I just don't, that's all.'

'Are you embarrassed to be seen talking to me?'

'Not embarrassed – '

'Scared?'

'I have to go.'

'I'm sorry for upsetting you,' I said.

. . .

Dr Fenshaw was bearing down on me from a yellow arrow in the middle of a long corridor. He leant forward, smiling confidently. His white coat made other men's look grey.

'I didn't think I'd be seeing you again. I thought by now you'd have done your duty Mrs Mahoney.'

I smiled back. 'Then you mustn't have thought my duty would take me very far.'

We were a few steps from some benches by a fernery. A man in a wheelchair was sitting motionless, staring at the plants.

'Clearly I was wrong,' said Fenshaw with another smile. 'But, forgive me, what more can you accomplish?'

'Why do you think Niall Howley killed himself?'

'Niall became mentally and emotionally unbalanced.'

'Is that why you wanted him to leave?'

'Who told you I wanted him to leave?'

'Did you try and fire him?'

'Of course not.'

'What about the others?'

'What others?'

'Did all the radiographers who left have mental and emotional problems, or was it only Niall?'

'Who have you been talking to?'

'Some people who met Niall through the MUD.'

I watched Fenshaw perform an act of re-arranging. It was a tribute to his skill that this re-arranging went on behind a surface that remained open towards me, still disposed to like me, even prepared to be hurt if I failed to meet his frankness with my own.

'You're right, of course,' he said. 'Niall wasn't the only one with problems. The team did get off to a rather shaky start. They're pulling together much better now.'

'What about Colin Rasmussen?'

'What about him?'

'Why did he stay when the others left?'

'Colin's an extremely bright young man, and he's matured a lot in the last year or so. He's learnt his limits – his and other people's. There was a danger, for a while, that he'd burn himself out. But I think he's past that now.'

'Who burnt themselves out?'

'Apart from Niall? I'm not sure it's really fair to go naming

names. Has Colin been talking to you about his former colleagues?'
'He answered my questions about Niall.'
'If a member of my staff has been indiscreet, then I need to know.'
'No one's been indiscreet. Your staff seem extremely loyal.'
Fenshaw leant forward again. It struck me that, earlier references to begging bowls notwithstanding, he was unused to having to ask twice. He pulled up the sleeve of his white coat a fraction, and looked at his watch. If he wanted to maintain the fiction that he was the one doing the dismissing, then that was fine by me.

Once I was away from him, his words began to crumble at the edges, topple sideways, as though gravity itself was altered by his presence. I wondered who he would interrogate besides Colin. I hoped it would not be Eve, and wished I'd said something to lead his suspicions away from her. Did a young bright woman such as Eve attract him, as she attracted younger men? Was he inclined both ways?

. . .

Home again, having fetched Katya from the creche, and heard Peter's school news while I made him a snack, I got out the police report, and flicked back through the statements and interviews. Not to have contacted Sorely Fallon, or any of the MUD's ex-players, struck me as a much more serious oversight now that I'd met him and Bridget.

The pathologist's lengthy detailing of injuries. McCallum's statement – a neutral description of the scene, Niall's body, how it had been found. An open mind as to how it might have got there. But by the time McCallum recorded his interviews with Eamonn and Dr Fenshaw, there had been a shift. The assumption of suicide had taken root.

A number of questions and answers followed Fenshaw's statement, the first few to establish the size and nature of the unit, and some general facts such as how long it had been operating.

Then Fenshaw was asked:

'Did the deceased report for work on 22 June?'
'Yes.'
'Did you speak with the deceased during the course of the day?'
'Yes, I did.'

'How did the deceased appear to you?'

'He appeared withdrawn and upset.'

'Did you ask him why?'

'It was my understanding that Howley had become very involved with, addicted to in fact, a computer game, and I assumed that this was the reason.'

'But he remained on duty at the hospital that day?'

'That's right. I believed that Howley was capable of performing his duties. He carried out a full day of treatments and left, as you're no doubt aware if you've seen the log book, at six-forty. I'd tried to talk to Howley about his problems but he wasn't an easy young man to talk to. He resented, I think, questions about his private life.'

The phone rang by my elbow. Brook said, 'I spoke to Moira Howley. She's very nervy isn't she?'

'Give her a chance. What do you expect?'

'Didn't deny hearing a noise that night. Didn't deny any of the stuff about the friendship society either, though she insisted Niall never told her what happened to the money once it got to Ireland. Only thing she asked me was did I have to tell her husband that I'd been to see her.'

'How did you get on with the hospital?'

'Spoke to the CEO and put in a request for the computer logs for the month before Howley's death.'

'You could have a shot at Niall's friend Eamonn,' I suggested. 'He knew about all the radiographers leaving except for Colin Rasmussen. And he knew that Niall was hiding something. Ask him about the night Niall died. Ask him why Niall was so happy.'

. . .

The modem light began to flash at me. In the same instant Katya started crying. I called out to Peter to see what was the matter.

Just give me thirty seconds, I said under my breath, cursing Sorley Fallon for his timing.

The crying stopped. I clicked print and crossed my fingers.

Katya was under the sofa and Peter was busily bricking her in. All I could see between the bottom of the sofa and Peter's line of blocks were two eyes and a brush of hair.

Peter stood up. Perhaps he'd got as far as picturing his sister unable
to escape. The set of his shoulders said he'd done what I wanted him to.
He'd shut her up.

I pulled Kat out and carried her into the office. The pages were
rolling out blank. The screen had reverted to the Pegasus homepage.

. . .

Ivan said it was a pity Fallon had cottoned on and shut the hole so soon.
He was careful not to elaborate on his disappointment. The bags under
his eyes were as thick and crepey as the ones underneath mine. I could
feel an argument getting ready to break cover and run.

A knock on the door which we nearly didn't hear turned out to
be Brook.

He looked uncertain of his welcome. 'I was just on my way home.'

'We tried a trick on Fallon,' I said, leading the way down to the
office, explaining what we'd hoped to do.

'Too quick on his feet for us,' Ivan said morosely.

Brook wasn't in the mood for handholding. 'If I was a bit bigger,
I'd put you both over my knee and spank you.'

Ivan and I caught each other's eyes.

Brook said, 'Go ahead and laugh,' and Ivan, 'Time for a cup of tea.'

Brook followed him to the kitchen. I listened to their voices circling
one another, seeing in my mind's eye a journey, a progression, though
at the same time thinking we were three lost children following a trail
of breadcrumbs.

Over coffee and frozen muffins, which were edible so long as you
heated them in the oven rather than the microwave, Brook said,
'I couldn't get the logs for the hospital computers.'

'Why not?'

'I rang the CEO and he seemed fine with it, but half an hour later he
called back to say he'd had a bit of a chat with their solicitor and
decided it might be sensitive and confidential information. I've applied
for a warrant.'

He delivered this in a flatter tone than usual. He took a bite of
muffin and his expression changed to one of physical discomfort.

'Spit it out,' said Ivan. 'Here, I'll get you a serviette.'

Brook drank some coffee and wiped his lips. He could be infuriating sometimes, the way he parcelled out his attention between small matters and large.

'When will you get the warrant?'

'Tomorrow. I'll be able to unplug the computer and take it, but if the solicitor's up to the mark, he'll have a court order within a couple of hours and I'll have to take it back.'

He pursed his lips. It might have been the aftertaste of frozen blueberries.

I remembered that he must have had a reason for calling in. 'What's up?'

'Nothing.'

'Sophie?'

'No.'

'McCallum?'

Brook crushed the serviette in his left hand and put it on a plate. I stared at the mess of crumbs and then his hand, which kept the tension of a balled fist even after he'd straightened out his fingers.

'Another kid died today. There's no question this time that he took his own life. I told Bill he needed a change, and he told me I was past my use-by date and wasting everybody's time. Maybe I should get sick again. Make the bastard feel bad.'

I didn't know what to say. Should I remind Brook that McCallum was a mate and he'd come round? Is that what I believed?

Instead I asked, 'How did you get on with Bernard Howley?'

'He thinks Fallon was in Australia some time in the new year.'

'Jesus, why didn't he say so before?'

'Claims he was protecting his wife.'

'Did he tell you about the concert tickets?'

'He says he didn't know Moira was selling them. He says there was one evening, shortly after Niall broke up with his girlfriend, when he was acting very strangely. Some family occasion which had been planned for weeks and Niall announced at the last minute that he couldn't go. He wouldn't give a reason. Bernard wonders now if he was meeting Fallon.'

'Did Moira know?'

'They weren't talking to each other much. He doesn't think Niall told her.'

'He's guessing.'

Brook nodded. 'Ready enough to jump to conclusions, but that doesn't mean he's wrong. I've got someone going through airline records.' He sighed. 'I best be going. But be warned you two. No more back door visits.'

Sixteen

I heard the postman's motorbike and went outside to bring in the mail.

There was a letter from Bridget Connell, on notepaper with a floral border, a Woking postmark on the envelope. I held it to my nose. Faintest whiff of Bridget in silk shirt and catwalk trousers, Bridget caressing a huge flightless bird.

'*I don't trust email any more,*' she began, in a loose, back-sloping hand. '*The world is full of malicious eyes and ears.*'

'No kidding,' was Ivan's comment when I read the letter out to him that evening.

In response to Bridget's probing, one of the Heroes had said yes, he did recall an incident where Ferdia was being followed. It had been during a foraging expedition outside the Castle. The player doing the harassing had been Blacksnake. His threat had impressed the Hero, who claimed to have recalled it word for word.

Things fall apart; the centre cannot hold. Playing crusader turning out harder than you thought? Do-gooders end up with blood on their hands. Get out of Canberra. Take your doomed quest elsewhere.

The incident had stuck in the Hero's mind not because of the taunting – taunts were common – but because Blacksnake seemed out to get Niall, not Ferdia. He knew where Niall lived, and had the means to carry out his threat in person.

They'd gone back to the Castle, where Blacksnake had not been able to follow. The Hero had asked Ferdia if he was okay and Ferdia had said he was. He was safe from Blacksnake in the Castle, and outside it, Blacksnake didn't have the shield and layers of protection Heroes painstakingly acquired.

The Hero hadn't said anything about the incident. The MUD was getting pretty chaotic by then, and it wasn't long before he, like Bridget, decided to quit.

'By the way,' Bridget added as a postscript, 'thought it might interest you to know that Sorley Fallon was charged a few years back with hacking into British government computers. He got himself a hotshot lawyer and the charges were dropped.'

For a second, I suspected Brook of holding out on me. But if he'd known about the hacking charge, he wouldn't have missed the opportunity of pointing out the kind of shady character I'd got myself mixed up with.

I imagined Blacksnake watching over my shoulder while I roamed the streets of Belfast, trying to recall lines from *The Second Coming*. Were Heroes in the habit of quoting Yeats to one another?

. . .

That night I checked my incoming mail. There was a message from Fallon.

I take a dim view of folk messing about in my computer.

I hit reply and typed, *I agree. Absolutely. The dim view is mutual.*

Ivan was standing behind me, reading over my shoulder.

'He'll sick the Irish mafia onto us. He's mad. They're all completely mad.'

I recalled Fallon's tidiness, washing up the coffee mugs in the kitchen behind his shop. Colours of autumn, and the absence of even the suggestion of a customer. Ferdia's symbolic execution a tidy man's solution to a problem. I thought about the edges soft Irish voices could acquire, edges that could hide under sibilance as a knife can be hidden in a sofa cushion.

'No he's not,' I said. 'Just used to playing things at more than one remove. It's a hard habit to break. What we need to do is make him see that this time it's worth breaking.'

'I'm not quite with you.'

'Let's send him the diagram and see how he reacts.'

'He won't.'

'What have we got to lose?'

. . .

In the morning Moira said, 'I could have confided in the police myself if that was what I wanted.'

I stood on her front porch, knowing it was too late for an apology. She did not invite me in, or ask me what I was carrying in the manilla envelope I held under my arm.

'Bernard – the police have got Bernard to say that he thinks Fallon was here, in Canberra.'

'You don't think that could be true?'

'I'm sure it isn't. Niall would have told me.'

Moira's face was doughy, and the lines under her eyes cut deep into her cheeks, but there was a strength in her that had not been there before.

I'd brought a copy of the log from the hospital computer that had been used to access *Castle of Heroes*.

'Could you do one last thing for me?' I said. 'I need your help to begin a process of elimination.'

The business with the logs had turned out pretty much the way Brook had predicted. When he'd arrived at the hospital with a warrant, neither the CEO nor the solicitor had been able to prevent him taking the computer. But before the afternoon was over, a Supreme Court order had arrived instructing him to take it back. Brook and the constable assisting him had duly obliged, but not before they'd down-loaded the logs for the two months before Niall Howley died.

Moira stood to attention facing me, willing me to leave.

'Niall *did* tell you what was troubling him didn't he?'

'Trouble. He used that word.'

'Did he say what kind?'

'No. I begged him. I begged to be allowed to help, take some of the burden, whatever it was. Was it political? I asked. He said not your ordinary kind. I reminded him about the tickets, how I'd sold them. I waited for him to tell me more, but I could see that in his mind he'd moved away. He said he should leave me and Dad in peace. He apologised, said he knew he'd been a disappointment as a son. I begged him to stay, said he could come and go as he pleased, I wouldn't bother him. He didn't say any more about moving. I counted it a small victory at the time.'

I took a deep breath and said, 'I think Niall met someone at the Telstra Tower that night, but it wasn't Fallon, or anyone from Ireland. Whoever it was had been playing *Castle of Heroes* though, and causing trouble between Niall and Fallon. Fallon gave me the address of a computer at Monaro Hospital that was used to access the MUD. I've got a printout of the logs for April, May and June. I want you to look at the dates and times and tell me if you remember a time when Niall wasn't at work, when he couldn't have been using the hospital computer.'

Moira wrapped her hands around her elbows and stared at me.

'He didn't kill himself?'

'No.'

'And his death isn't connected to that game?'

'Perhaps, but not the way we thought.'

She faced this with an eerie calm.

I handed her the printout. She sat down where she was and began to read it.

After a few minutes, she said, 'Saturday April twenty-sixth. That was Bernard's birthday dinner.'

'Niall was there?'

'Oh yes. His fiftieth. We went out for dinner. To Santa Lucia's.'

'You were together at the restaurant,' I pointed to the time recorded on the log, 'at nineteen past nine?'

'Our booking was for seven-thirty. Bernard drove home. Not that any of us had much to drink.'

'So Niall could not possibly have been at the hospital?'

'I just told you. It was Bernard's birthday. Niall gave him a book on gardens of the world. We'd been planning it for weeks.'

Moira went back inside the house. She'd said nothing about a final payment, or, alternatively, about paying me to continue. I hoped that, when she'd had time to think about it, she'd be as keen to discover the identity of her son's murderer as I was. I watched the door close behind her and felt a pricking at my temples, as though I wore a coronet of chestnuts' spiny shells, as though *Castle of Heroes'* elusive double player had taken a further step out of the shadows.

· · ·

I phoned Brook, who said he'd been talking to the hospital sysop, who'd reported someone dialling up the MUD from one of the radio-therapy department's computers.

'What happened?'

'Not a lot, it seems. The CEO passed the information on to Fenshaw. Fenshaw said he'd deal with it.'

'When was this?'

'Some time in April.'

'And when it went on? When it didn't stop?'

'The CEO said he spoke to Fenshaw several times.'

'That's all he did?'

'Apparently. He's worried now.'

'A deer in flight?'

Brook said dryly, 'More like a hyena.'

I laughed, then said, 'Our man in Ireland.'

'Yes?'

'Do you know anything about a hacking charge? One that didn't hold up?'

'No,' Brook said immediately.

If it was true, and the London officer who was supposed to be checking Fallon out hadn't passed it on to him, then the officer would pay. Brook wasn't in the mood to forgive sloppiness or oversight.

· · ·

When I checked my email, there was a message from Blacksnake.

It's a small world Mrs Mahoney. I suggest you keep your head down.

At a sound behind me, I swung round, half expecting to see a stranger with a gun, or knife.

My hands were shaking, and I had to wait a few moments before I could shut the computer down.

I shouted at Fred when he appeared in the doorway, thinking it was probably him I'd heard. I made sure the front and back doors were locked, then went around the house locking all the windows.

. . .

When he read it, Ivan was inclined to dismiss Blacksnake's warning. Ivan took the view, based on previous experience of stalkers, that if Blacksnake wanted to remain invisible, he would.

'He hasn't changed his identity. He's still Blacksnake,' I said.

'If he suspects you're getting close to him, he will.'

His address was America online, which meant he could be coming from anywhere.

'Niall told Bridget he thought the stalker was somebody he knew.'

'Don't reply,' said Ivan. 'Just resist the temptation.'

Ivan didn't believe that Blacksnake would show up on our doorstep, or climb through the bedroom window with an axe between his teeth. The point of being a net stalker, as he tired of explaining to me, was that you spooked your victim from a distance. I wasn't convinced.

······

Seventeen

In the middle of an October afternoon, Sydney was hot, summery, sticky. Cronulla beach was crowded. A lot of the crowd looked like they hadn't had to live through a winter anywhere. Brown, fit people jogged along the esplanade. In their shiny wetsuits, the surfers over the point hung nose to tail like live sardines.

Katya was so completely covered in melted icy pole and sand that you could have used her to scrape the paint off a wall. She banged her hands in the shallow puddle Peter kept filling up for her. Since I'd joined them, he'd fetched three full buckets from the sea. As fresh sea water splashed into the hole, Katya yelled and laughed. More sandy water splashed up and found its sticking place.

'Mum! This boy came and wanted our bucket and Kat barked at him. Just like Fred!'

'Oh dear,' I said. 'I hope she didn't scare him.'

'Nah. He just wanted a loan of it. He brought it back. Mum? Can we have fish and chips for tea?'

'I don't see why not.'

I glanced across at Ivan, who'd arranged the umbrella so that Katya and her puddle had most of the shade. He'd curled himself around the edge of it, a cloth hat perched on top of his rough hair.

Eamonn had sent me several addresses. I'd picked Tanya Wishart's because she'd been the first to leave the radiotherapy unit. In fact, she'd left well before any of the others, before Niall Howley died. I'd just returned from seeing her.

Ivan looked at me and raised an inquiring eyebrow.

'Thumbs down, I'm afraid.'

'Mum, I'm thirsty and we've dranken all the fruit boxes.'

'Drunk,' I said. 'We've drunk.'

Ivan was taking care to keep his expression neutral.

'Let's clean up Kat and put her in the stroller. I'll carry it over to the path. And see there?' I pointed to a kiosk. 'Could you take her over there and buy some drinks? She'll like that.'

Peter grinned. 'Pinch Mum.'

I watched the proud set of his shoulders for a few moments, then rolled over so I was lying next to Ivan.

'Do you want to have a swim?'

'Maybe. So the lady didn't talk.'

'You should get wet at least.'

'The tide's coming in.'

'So?'

'So the waves are getting bigger.'

'Wimp. There's always the pool.'

'What do you think, that the waves stop at the wall and say, I mustn't go there, there's a big fat Russian who only likes going in up to his knees?'

'You should learn to surf. I'll make you.'

'And you're making excuses.'

I sighed. 'She was cagey as hell. She said the job here was a better one, and moving back to Sydney meant she'd be close to her parents who could help with the kids.'

'Why'd she go to Canberra in the first place?'

'Dunno. She's divorced. That's maybe got something to do with it. When I asked her why six of them had left at once, she said she didn't know.'

'I've told you before Sandra. You've got to bluff. It's no good if this lady, or whoever, gets the idea that you know bugger all. People only tell you what they think you already know.'

I shaded my eyes and counted heads till I found Peter's. He was still in the queue outside the kiosk. Across the sandy paths, I felt his thin shoulders bent towards his sister, his cheerful taking on of duty.

. . .

Over fish and chips in Cronulla Street the weather held, our luck held as a family. Peter spread his capable good humour so that it flowed over and around us, mingling with the warmth and grit and tiredness of the evening.

Whatever Moira thought of the turns my investigation was taking, she'd been generous enough, and brave enough, to tell me she was willing to pay me to continue. I thanked her silently now for having given Peter and Katya a day at the beach.

We'd chosen an outside table, in a tourist street now practically deserted. Katya was nodding off in Ivan's arms. It had been a day of firsts for Kat. First swim in the sea, first icy pole, first chip, which she'd chewed contemplatively, then spat into Peter's outflung hand.

Ivan was taking ages to finish his last chip. At times like these I was made uncomfortably aware just how alike he and his daughter were.

He started forward, began to scrabble in his pockets, and pulled out a crumpled, greasy copy of the diagram. I was about to tell him I was too tired when he barked at me, 'When did that girl leave the hospital?'

'February sixteenth. Why?'

'There it is!' Ivan jabbed with a chippy finger at the middle of the page.

'There is what?'

'Don't you see Sand? Sixteenth of February! It's not a bloody code at all!'

Ivan slapped the bit of paper down on a spill of tomato sauce and lemon juice, snatched it up again and began wiping at it madly with his handkerchief. 'Knew the bastard wouldn't beat me!'

'Are you saying that Niall wrote down the date Tanya Wishart left the hospital then hid it in his physiology book along with a sketch of the Castle? Why on earth would he do that?'

'That's for you to find out babe! If it was me, I'd bloody well get back over there right now!'

. . .

Peter and Katya were asleep practically as soon as we got back to the hotel, Peter in front of a tape of *Cool Runnings*, which we'd promised him he could sit up and watch.

I poured Ivan and myself a nightcap out of the fridge.

'BLS or gin?' I asked, holding up two cans.

Ivan was standing in front of the windows, staring down at the lights and the long flame of the oil refinery. When there was a break in the traffic, you could hear the sea.

'Those cans cost an arm and a leg. And they taste like shit.'

'I don't care. We're celebrating.'

I poured two glasses and handed Ivan his. 'I've been thinking. Tomorrow morning early, I'll go back to Tanya. Catch her off her guard.'

Ivan made a face, but whether it was the gin or what I'd just said, I couldn't be sure. 'Have to be out of here by ten. I dunno.' He half turned to me and winked. 'S'pose I could stand another hour or two of beach bunnies.'

There was the traffic outside, the small click and ping of flip tops opening, the tinny smell of spirits from a can. Ivan had turned the sound right down on *Cool Runnings*, but left the picture on, something that normally annoyed me.

He lifted Peter into bed. To the sight of four Jamaican men flying down a snow chute in what looked like a huge old bomb casing, I took off his T-shirt and rubbed my hand through springy chest hair.

Ivan said, 'You're drunk.'

'If only. There's no gin in those things at all.'

'You taste of gin,' he said.

I pushed him back onto the queen-sized bed, thinking that it was a shame to mess up such white, perfectly laundered sheets. It must be lack of imagination, but I could never feel the people who'd been in a hotel bed before me.

Ivan licked my nipples. I laughed and pushed his head down. 'I had a shower.'

'Dur,' said Ivan. But he did what I wanted. I knew by then he would.

I scrunched my bum into the impossible sheets, and Ivan's fingers slid in and found their place. And then his tongue.

I lay quietly, my mind straining for some hint of sea beneath the traffic, Ivan quiet beside me, his skin thick, pale, marked by a childhood spent out of the sun. A bodily quietness and waiting.

. . .

At seven-thirty the next morning, Tanya Wishart glared at me and said, 'What are you doing here? I haven't got time to talk to you. I have to get to work, and Cheryl's sick.'

Tanya's eyes were huge and puffy, with great grey patches underneath, but I could see the woman she had been, fine-skinned, dark-haired, with a long stride.

A wail came from inside the flat, followed by a burst of coughing.

'What about your parents?'

Tanya made a dismissive movement.

'Can you take Cheryl with you?'

She stared at me and I felt the settling of exhaustion in behind her eyes.

'You mean the hospital creche?' Her voice slowed, losing the anger it had no energy for. 'They won't have her if she's sick.'

'Maybe I can help.'

'You? How can you help? I really need to take her to the doctor. Look, I've got to go. I told you everything yesterday. I've got nothing more to say.'

Tanya turned to go back inside and began to shut the door. I put out my hand to stop her.

She turned to me accusingly. 'Last week Cheryl's brother was sick. I took time off then. Now she's got what he had. And we're short-staffed. That's why I'm working Sunday. I've got a full day of treatments.'

A small child's cry joined the baby's. I was left standing in the doorway.

I walked along a narrow hallway to a living room. I could hear Tanya talking softly in what I assumed was a bedroom on the other side. I found a phonebook and started looking up babysitting agencies.

Tanya came in carrying a red-faced baby who'd cried herself into exhaustion, with a boy of about four clinging onto her leg as though he was afraid she'd disappear.

I smiled at the boy and said hello. He was too miserable to return my greeting, or show any interest in who I was and why I'd suddenly appeared.

'It'll work out,' I said to Tanya. 'Just take things step by step. You have a meal break, don't you?'

'Mum?'

'Sweetie, you should get dressed for Justin's.'

'But I need your help!'

'No you don't.' Tanya bent down awkwardly, moving Cheryl to her left hip and caressing her son's splotchy face with the back of her hand. 'You can manage. Your clothes are on the chair. Have a wash first, and then we'll get some breakfast.'

Gently, she disentangled the boy's fingers from her dressing gown. He scowled at her, but turned around obediently enough. I thought of Peter, glancing at my watch. It was not quite seven-forty.

Tanya stood up with a sigh.

'When you get to work,' I said, 'arrange for Cheryl to see a doctor and take her in your lunch break.'

'But what'll I do with her till then?'

'Your son's going to a friend's, is that right? What about asking if Cheryl can go too?'

'I can't do that. It's good of them to have Billy, and it's inconvenient, really, on a Sunday. It's not as though Justin's mother's a friend of mine or anything. They just play together at preschool.'

Tanya nodded towards the phone book. 'I've tried three of those already. All they've got is recorded messages. It's too early. And it's Sunday.'

'I'll look after Cheryl.'

'You?'

'I know I'm a stranger, but if you got a babysitter out of the phone book, he or she would be a stranger too.'

'I don't think –'

'I've got two kids of my own. I know we haven't met in the most trusting of circumstances, but I'll take good care of Cheryl. I give you my word. I'll come with you. I'll walk up and down with her. I won't be far away.'

· · ·

Within half an hour of walking Cheryl, I was extremely sick of the corridor outside the district hospital's radiotherapy department. Cheryl whimpered unceasingly, tossing her head from side to side. I sat on a bench and kept the stroller moving, first with my hand and then my foot. A man hobbled along the corridor on crutches, slowing as he came level with me. I frowned in case he was thinking of stopping for a chat. Tanya had left a bottle of juice and I gave Cheryl some of that, then, though I'd said I'd stay inside, I spent the next hour and a half circling the car park. A few minutes before it was time to meet, I was back outside the department's double sliding doors. Tanya was waiting. She began running as soon as she saw us.

I followed them to outpatients, gritting my teeth, aware that all Tanya wanted was to escape into her appointment with the doctor.

We sat next to each other on orange plastic chairs and I handed her the greasy, torn piece of paper with the numbers on it. I explained that I thought four of them, 1602, might represent the date she left Monaro Hospital.

Tanya stared at the figures over the top of Cheryl's head.

'Who gave you my name and address?'

'A friend of Niall Howley's. Not someone from radiotherapy.'

After what seemed a long time, she said, 'If I tell you what I think, will you promise to leave me alone? Never come back?'

I nodded.

'Those four numbers are the date I left. And the ones immediately before them, these ones here –' Tanya pointed to the sequence 20018000, 'They're a date too, and a radiation dose.'

'A radiation dose?'

'Yes. Eight thousand rads is the treatment dose a radiotherapy patient received on that date. That is, January twentieth.'

'What happened to the patient?'

'Barry. His name was Barry. It was an overdose. He died,' Tanya said quickly, as though, now she'd begun, she wanted to get it over with as fast as possible.

'What dose should Barry have received?'

'Two hundred rads. Doses of over five hundred can be fatal.'

'What happened?'

Instead of looking at me, Tanya played with the edge of Cheryl's blanket, rolling it in her fingers the way you'd roll a cigarette, then letting it fall loose again.

'I loved working for Dr Fenshaw. He made everyone who worked for him feel special. We were part of, I don't know, it was like a grand adventure.'

'What went wrong?'

'The other radiotherapists were younger than me. None of them had kids. They didn't really understand, though some, like Niall, were sympathetic. Then, when I got pregnant with Cheryl – it wasn't a planned pregnancy.'

She fell silent. I felt cocooned with her in the waiting room, and prayed that the receptionist wouldn't call her daughter's name.

She started again at another point in her story. 'Sometimes I go to bed at night and I can't remember a single thing about the day. Or the day before. Whole weeks are just a kind of fog. I talked to Gavin – my ex-husband. Dr Fenshaw said he'd find a replacement for a year, to have the baby if that was what I wanted, take my time. He was great. Then Gavin dropped a bombshell on me. He told me he'd met someone else and wanted out of the marriage. He didn't want Cheryl. He didn't even want to have much to do with Billy.'

Tanya paused again. I could see that her story wasn't a line set out for her to follow, but made of material, some sort of embroidered carpet perhaps, and she knelt in the middle, and every time she turned her head another section caught her eye.

'You were the person who administered the overdose, weren't you?'

She nodded.

'And Barry?'

'He was burnt. All along his left side, and his hip.'

'Were you alone when it happened?'

Tanya didn't answer straight away. 'At a certain point, my mind kind of – well – blacks out. I was working with Colin. I was in the control room. Normally we swap jobs, but since I was pregnant I couldn't give treatments. I was in a state, with Gavin, and trying to work out whether to have the baby, what to do. Colin was setting up the table while I typed in the treatment data. There's a set of checking procedures you have to go through and I did that. Then I pressed the P key to start the treatment, and instead of the message Treatment In Progress, I got one that said Error 53.'

'What's an Error 53?'

'I've no idea. I'd never seen it before. What the computer does is check the data you type in with the settings in the treatment room, to make sure they correspond. If you've made an error keying in, or the person setting up has made an error, the computer will tell you. It won't allow treatment until the error's been found. So I thought it was most likely that.'

'What was the error?'

'That's just it. There wasn't one. I started from the beginning and re-entered all the data. Then I hit the P key again. There was a yell from the treatment room and on the monitor I saw Barry jump, try to jump up from the table. Colin and I rushed in and he was burnt all along his side and shouting in pain.'

'You and Colin rushed in – Colin was with you in the control room?'

'At that point, yes.'

'What was Colin doing while you checked the data?'

'I don't remember if he was there the whole time. It took a while to re-enter the data, and Barry was waiting in the treatment room. The phone rang and Colin answered it. He says he left the control room for a few minutes and when he came back he – Barry – had been burnt. I don't remember Colin going out. I wasn't concentrating on what Colin was doing.'

'So you re-keyed your data and then hit the P key?'

Cheryl moved on her mother's knee and began whimpering again. Tanya looked up hopefully as a patient came through double sliding doors at the far end of the room. The receptionist called out a man's name.

'Not before I called Dr Fenshaw,' Tanya said. 'But Dr Fenshaw says I never called him. It must have been while Colin was out. Colin said I must have typed in the wrong dose twice. But I don't see how I could have. I mean, of course I can see how I might've made a typing error, but when I checked it all, my figure was the same as on the Ventac's settings in the treatment room, and the same as on the treatment sheet that we were working from. The right dose was there. I didn't go back and alter it afterwards. I'm not a criminal.'

'So what *did* happen?'

'I've racked my brains over it. I just don't know. I think it must be something in the Ventac itself, not in our checking system. But the technicians said that wasn't possible. Dr Fenshaw got an engineer down from Sydney. This guy took the Ventac apart but couldn't find anything. He said it was impossible for that machine to overdose. All I know is, what couldn't happen, did.'

Before I could ask Tanya any more questions, we were interrupted by a nurse walking over and telling us that Dr Chan would see Cheryl now.

Tanya stood up and thanked me for looking after her daughter. I said I'd wait. She frowned and shook her head, then followed the nurse through the sliding doors into a consulting room.

I thought back over what she'd said. She hadn't mentioned the phone call to Dr Fenshaw straight away. What she'd said was that she'd re-keyed the data, hit the P key, and the patient had been burnt. She'd also said that she couldn't remember whether or not Colin had left the control room. What was Colin's responsibility in all of this? Should he have checked the re-entered data line by line? What had he been doing outside the control room? Who had phoned him, if indeed anybody had? And *had* Tanya phoned Dr Fenshaw, or did she only wish she had?

I thought of Eve, who'd said nothing to me about the overdose, though she must have known. And Eamonn. Word of an accident like that would have been around the hospital in no time. I could understand Eve and Colin not wanting to talk about it, but Eamonn? Why had Eamonn given me Tanya's Sydney address unless he wanted Tanya to tell me?

She came back looking much happier. 'It's okay. Cheryl can stay here for the afternoon. She'll probably just sleep. I could've brought her in this morning. I panicked.'

'What did Dr Fenshaw say when you rang him to tell him about the Error 53 message?'

Tanya bent down to pick up Cheryl's bag, which she'd left under one of the chairs, answering reluctantly.

'He said I was upset, overwrought. He told me to take time off. He came to see me. He was furious with Gavin.'

'What did you think?'

'The Ventac 2 is unreliable, but no one's been able to find anything wrong with it. I'd never had an Error 53 before, but every now and again it would throw up a message that made no sense. The messages weren't in any of the manuals we had, and the hospital engineers couldn't reproduce them. So we overrode them. We weren't allowed to take that step on our own, but in practice what happened was that we'd check with Dr Fenshaw and he'd give the okay to go ahead with treatment.'

Tanya hoisted the bag over one arm. 'I have to go now and get Cheryl settled down.' She began to walk towards the sliding doors. This time I followed her.

'Did Fenshaw come and check the treatment data himself?'

'In the beginning.'

'How did he feel about it?'

'He was dismayed, shocked by Barry's death. What do you think?'

'I mean how did he feel about the technical fault in the machine?'

'They're still using it. What are they going to do? Take it to the tip? It's been checked and double-checked and rechecked. No one can find anything wrong with it.'

'Does Colin physically check the data every time?'

'If he's rostered on. I mean, in pairs you check for each other.'

'What did Niall Howley think about the overdose?'

'Look, I –' Tanya paused just in front of the doors and sighed. She said that Niall had come to see her at home. She hadn't been able to bear the thought of going back to the hospital. Her voice cracked, but then she gave a small smile and said that Niall had been great.

'Was there an inquiry?'

'An internal one. Of course. The suppliers sent a rep over from the States. And there were our engineers. It was kept quiet. And the hospital board let me know they wouldn't make a big deal of my negligence.'

'If you kept quiet as well.'

Tanya nodded

'What about Error 53?'

'They couldn't reproduce it, like I said. Niall tried. He spent hours over it.'

'He was that involved?'

'He was determined to find the fault. Well, it wasn't as though the engineers weren't. Everybody tried to. Niall would find stuff on the net about Ventacs in the US and Canada and ring me up to tell me about it. But all I wanted by then was to get away. I felt as though I was going mad. Niall couldn't understand that. Well, he didn't have kids. He wasn't even married.'

'What about the American and Canadian Ventacs?'

'The Two relies a lot more on software safety checks than the older models. There aren't the hardware locks. They were considered superfluous by the manufacturers and they added to the cost, so they were dropped.'

'Was that raised at the inquiry?'

'I haven't seen the report. I didn't want to.'

I realised I hadn't asked Tanya how she felt about Niall's suicide.

'It's pathetic,' she said, moving forward. The doors opened. She was one step away from disappearing. 'I didn't believe it when I heard, and I don't believe it now.'

She swung round to impress her last point on me. 'I meant what I said about leaving me alone.'

I thanked her and she accepted my thanks with another sudden smile.

I thought of Niall surfing the net for information about Ventacs late at night. Had Natalie, or his parents, actually *asked* him what he was doing? Would he have told them? Or would he have replied with some off-putting reference to the MUD? Was this the point where Ferdia the Hero had gone to Niall's head? Ferdia who'd risen to a level no other Hero had risen to before. Was it possible that, after excelling in the fantasy world of *Castle of Heroes*, Niall believed he could tackle and solve the problem of the Ventac single-handed? Had he come to believe it was his personal quest?

Eighteen

I left Brook messages, unable to reach him on any of his phones, then rang Eamonn and asked him what he knew about the accident. Eamonn replied in his mild way that he was aware a patient had been burnt while receiving radiation treatment, but he didn't know any of the details.

I asked him why he hadn't told me before, to which he replied with infuriating mildness that I hadn't asked him.

Now was the moment to accuse him of lying to me, and for one or the other of us to hang up. Instead, I reminded myself what he'd said the last time we met, when he'd asked me to stay away from the hospital.

'Tanya Wishart told me Niall spent hours searching websites to try and establish a performance pattern for the Ventac 2.'

'I'd appreciate it if you didn't tell anyone who gave you Tanya's address.'

'I won't. Niall wouldn't have left his information lying round for anyone to find.'

'I don't know what he did with it. I told you that.'

'The Ventac 2 is still in use. Colin Rasmussen showed it to me.'

'Look, I'm sorry. I've done all I can to help, I really have. Please don't phone me. Please don't contact me again.'

. . .

Ivan went off to the ANU early the next morning. I strapped Katya in the car seat and drove to Brook's flat, praying he'd be home and on his own.

The puzzle of Niall Howley's death was like a Rubik's cube. I'd been holding it one way and trying to get the colours to match. Now I'd turned it upside down and was looking at it from the bottom up, it was different altogether. I was seeing the cube from a different angle, but I'd added a colour. I still couldn't get the blocks to match.

Brook kissed us both and led the way into his small, neat living room. He said he was sorry he hadn't rung back, but he'd been working late the night before.

His flat was what you'd expect of a man in his forties living on his own. The scrubbed wooden table always had a bowl of fruit sitting in the middle, and Brook belonged to the class that left sauce bottle, salt and pepper shakers arranged like a table decoration too.

'Have you two had breakfast?'

'Yes, we're fine.'

'You'll bear with me while I make a cup of tea.'

'I know what Niall was doing in the weeks before he died,' I said, and told Brook about meeting Tanya, and the overdose.

Brook made tea and toast and listened without interrupting. I'd forgotten how good he was at puncturing the drama of a situation, especially a situation of my making. I sat Katya on the floor and gave her my car keys, pursed my lips and waited.

Finally Brook asked, 'What makes you think this girl was telling you the truth?'

'Why would she make up such elaborate lies?'

'If it's true, why didn't she go to the police with her version of events?'

'She needs to go on working, and the hospital board made sure she understood the benefits of leaving quietly.'

'And?'

'And she was bewildered, scared that it *had* been her fault.'

Katya reached over and tapped Brook's foot experimentally with the keys. He leant down and picked her up, which was unnecessary since she was quite happy on the floor. He held her briefly against his chest before looking at me over the top of her head.

'Fenshaw rang Bill McCallum to complain about me. Wanted to know what was going on, why I was out at the hospital wanting to go through their computers, what I was up to when the coronial verdict had been clear and uncontested.'

'What did McCallum say?'

'That the boss had spoken to the coroner and they'd agreed some new information had come to light which needed investigation.'

'And?'

'And I wasn't there to eavesdrop on the conversation, but I have the feeling that Bill let Fenshaw draw the conclusion that he agreed with him about it all being a waste of time.'

I pictured McCallum's bunchy, ill-fitting uniform, his recollections of old times, his blue eyes saying trust me.

I repeated what I'd told Brook in the café. 'It wasn't Niall who wiped his hard drive that night and loaded the castle picture for his parents and your colleagues to find.'

The phone rang in the hallway and Brook went to answer it.

I thought how strange it was, the way certain places made possible the saying or withholding of a thing. The veranda of my house. Brook with those photographs in a buff-coloured envelope. Kat asleep in her stroller. Brook's shy smile, offering pictures of a death he didn't want to know about. The coronial report, its broken bones too numerous to hold in the mind at once. The quiet neatness here, the way walls could hold in balance and determine what went on between them.

Go through it with me, I would say when he came back. He'd smile and say, 'Okay Sandy.' And we would go through everything, step by step, so that pieces connected, so that it began making sense. Places would come forward between us, the Telstra Tower, Dunluce Castle on a windy day.

'That was Sophie.' Brook came back smiling like a boy. 'I've been flat out all weekend.'

'And?'

'She's been very understanding.'

I waited.

'We're having lunch.'

I swallowed the lump in my throat. 'Why not front up to Fenshaw unannounced, see how he reacts?'

Brook was still smiling from the sound of Sophie's voice. 'I have to get the facts right first.'

'At least you can request a copy of the accident report.'

He was all charm suddenly, willingness to help. 'Oh yes, I can do that all right.'

· · ·

I spent the rest of the morning washing sand out of clothes and buying groceries. Katya's black eyes scanned shelves of cereal packets at the supermarket. I remembered Peter's love affair with dog food tins, in the days before we found Fred, a starving puppy licking up lines of worms around puddles at the school playground.

I stopped in the middle of the aisle to watch my baby smile at a stranger, upright and calm in her ringside seat, hands with a beautiful even spacing on the trolley bar, a gymnast's sense of balance. The frailty and courage of the choices children made, their insight for what mattered. A sense of foreboding in that bright place, surrounded by confectionary on special. Feeding Katya – this was gone now. It appeared that only I regretted it. Katya, as far as I could see, had put the experience behind her.

. . .

Brook rang in the afternoon. 'Well the fat is in the fire now,' he said cheerfully. 'I asked Fenshaw about the Wishart woman. He wanted to know where I'd got her name. I asked him why she left, and he said that, with a baby on the way and a marriage breakdown, the work became too much for her. I asked him whether he fired the others too and he told me hard luck stories about his underprivileged youth.'

'The accident report?'

'It's classified confidential, but I should have the authorisation by tomorrow.'

. . .

I held the floral paper to my nose and inhaled a smell that was innocently, subtly suggestive of a wealthy English garden. I drank it in as though it was a balm of some kind, a soothing draught that had all but evaporated.

Bridget's handwriting was open, loose. The beginnings and ends of letters crossed a border of roses and forget-me-nots. Her message was businesslike and introduction swift. Another of the Heroes had got back to her with a story about Ferdia and his shadow. This Hero who, like the previous one, Bridget did not name, had been struck by Ferdia's timidity, how, with his reputation for audacity, Ferdia hesitated before making the simplest move, to make sure all his hard-earnt shields and protections were in place. He passed up moves that newer players took advantage of, and seemed content to slip back, let others make the running, take the glory when the risk paid off. He was not the Ferdia this Hero had expected from his reputation, not a character to emulate, admire.

The incident he recounted to Bridget involved a plan to strengthen forward defences. Everything was organised but, as they were about to leave, Ferdia changed his mind and said he'd stay in the Castle. He didn't even stay long on the game that night. A few minutes after his back down, he logged off. The group had left the Castle at the appointed time. In the band of hostile soldiers who immediately approached them, the Hero recalled one who was clearly waiting for Ferdia. He took his aggression out on the other Heroes when he discovered Ferdia had remained behind.

. . .

I phoned Bridget. It seemed the natural thing to do.

'I like the paper.'

'Thanks.' She sounded wide awake. 'I've got a heap of it.'

'A birthday present?'

'Years of,' Bridget said.

'You must have disappointed someone.'

'My mother. She hasn't given up yet.'

I bit my tongue because it was on the tip of it to say, wait till you've got children of your own.

'Sandra? I meant to put this in the letter. It was when we were talking about quitting, Niall and me. I'd emailed him to say I'd decided to. It was just getting too creepy. Niall emailed me back to say he was thinking about quitting too. The only thing holding him back was that if he quit then it would look like he was guilty. That's what Fallon and everyone would think. I remember him saying that he was waiting for a decision and that if it went his way he wouldn't give a stuff about who was lying in wait for him outside the Castle.'

. . .

Tuesday was a creche day. It was threatening rain again.

I rummaged in the hall cupboard for my umbrella, recalling, as I pulled it out, that Peter and Fred had had a tug of war with it and broken half the spines. I shoved it and a coat into the back seat of the car and drove over to the hospital.

The first big gobs of rain hit the car window. I shivered, though it wasn't cold. It was going to be one of those October cloudbursts I usually relish, spring blossoms scudding along footpaths, the lift under the diaphragm that the combination of warmth and heavy rain can bring, that makes you feel your clothes are suddenly too tight.

The main car park was full. I drove up and down a few times, hoping to see somebody leaving, but the squat cars under steady rain looked permanently fixed. I left and drove around to the car park at the back, finally finding a space in a corner furthest from the main building. I struggled into my coat and put up the umbrella, which was even more mangled than I remembered. Resigning myself to getting soaked, I began the long trek to shelter.

Heavy rain muted the hospital's luxurious façade. Close up, I began to feel the by now familiar mixture of dread and excitement. From blurred shapes, the buildings became clear, all-of-a-piece, still new and shiny with self-importance, not having yet worked out what might endure.

I'd received a letter in that morning's mail from Zhou Yang Zhu, one of the radiotherapists I'd written to, now living in Melbourne. I'd rung straight away and arranged a meeting with him. Over the phone he sounded courteous, but wary.

Looking round to get my bearings, I spotted Eve, walking quickly, a pile of folders in her arms.

'Hi,' I said, catching up to her.

Eve glanced round. 'Oh,' she said.

'Mind if I talk to you for a minute?'

'I'm sorry. I don't really have the time.'

'I can walk with you if you're in a hurry.'

Eve hesitated, then began to move away.

'It's about the accelerators,' I said, keeping pace.

She took a quick left turn into a corridor with a wide green stripe painted down the middle.

'Have they given you any trouble in the time you've been here?'

Eve frowned. Someone called her name. She turned and her face relaxed a little as she waved at a fair-haired, good-looking young man.

Oh shit, I thought, just what I need. Another Dominic. But the young man grimaced, gesturing towards some double doors.

Eve quickened her pace.

'The accelerators?'

'I'm not allowed to talk to you.'

'Why not?'

Eve flushed, glancing in my direction but not catching my eye.

'I know about the overdose.'

She stopped and looked at me then, startled, but also passive, fatalistic.

'How often has the Ventac 2 been down in the last few months?'

'Please. I said I'm not allowed to talk about it.'

'What's wrong with the Ventac?'

'We have to get on with the job of treating cancer, that's what we're here for.'

'What did Dr Fenshaw tell you about Tanya Wishart?'

'Nothing,' Eve said with a grimace, biting her lip and raising her folders, holding them across her chest.

She disappeared through the next door, letting it swing shut behind her.

I retraced my steps, glad I had the green line to follow, thinking of the tension under Eve's skin, her small, bright frame, the impression she gave of living under siege.

. . .

A sharp voice made me swing around.

'What are you doing here?'

Having different-coloured eyes made it possible for Colin to appear concerned and disengaged at the same time, angry yet with a nervous desire to placate.

'Hi,' I said. 'One question. You were working with Tanya Wishart on the day of the accident. Why did you leave her alone in the control room?'

I watched a dozen different responses pass across Colin's face.

'Who have you been talking to?'

'Why did you leave Tanya alone?'

'Do you know how many patients we've treated here since we began, how many people are alive today because of what we do?'

'What's wrong with the Ventac? Why can't it be fixed?'

Colin looked from left to right, frowning, along corridors busy with the everyday comings and goings of staff, visitors and patients. His arms curved by his sides, and his hands, poking out of the too-short sleeves of his white coat, were clenched so tightly that the skin stretched across his knuckles looked transparent.

'I know your type,' he said. 'You're a parasite, feeding off other people's troubles. I met Moira Howley once. She was such a nice person. If you don't leave now I'm calling security.'

'Call them. Hospital security's important. There's the physical side. That's obviously important. Then there's the electronic side, that's important too, though perhaps not quite so well looked after as it should be.'

Colin reached for his beeper.

I gave him a goodbye smile, found the entrance I'd come in, and headed out across hectares of sodden car park, the rain a gentle but relentless poc-poc on the working side of my umbrella.

. . .

I rang Brook from my car.

'That hospital's a snake pit,' he said cheerfully.

For Brook to be interviewing doctors about cancer treatment and radiotherapy machines was a strange turnaround, a joke he would not have dared to script. Somehow, we seemed to be sharing the joke without having made it.

'Oh, the legal system's very useful when it works their way,' he told me. 'Their lawyer found out we were applying for another warrant. He met me with a court order blocking it.'

'So you weren't able to get the accident report?'

'I will.'

. . .

Eamonn called to complain that the police had been all over the hospital.

'What did you tell them about me?' he asked in a tone of voice I hadn't heard before, petulant with an undercurrent of hysteria.

'Did someone threaten you?'

Eamonn didn't answer.

'Tell Detective-Sergeant Brook that Fenshaw threatened you.'

'I tried to warn Niall,' Eamonn said. 'I did try to be a friend to him.'

'I'm sure you did.'

I thought of Moira Howley waiting for her son to offer her some sign, a sign that she, in her fear and anxiety and courage, longed to make herself. There was the shock, and after that came the unravelling.

Nineteen

It was a spring day such as only Melbourne could turn on, the sort I remembered being young in, when months of rain and wind and fog seemed atoned for and forgiven. Southern winters aged a person, seeming to go on forever. But then, one day in September or October, you woke up and everything was different.

It was Zhou Yang Zhu's day off and he'd invited me to his home for lunch. He lived in Hawthorn, in a pleasant, leafy street with a few houses and a lot of flats. It was close to a busy intersection, but as I hurried along looking for number twenty-five, the noise of traffic receded and I could hear blackbirds in the gardens.

I found the right entrance and began to climb the stairs.

A young man came to the door in answer to my knock, wiping his hands on a paper towel. He looked no more than seventeen, with fine straight black hair falling in his eyes, a wide attractive face and braces on his teeth.

I smiled and held out my hand as I introduced myself, thinking that this must be Zhou Yang's younger brother.

He explained to me while he served lunch – I don't know what I'd expected, but it wasn't a three course meal cooked specially for me – that his parents had been living with him, but they'd gone back to Hong Kong, that he was the youngest of the family. Depending on what happened now the handover was completed, he might return as well.

My curiosity got the better of me and I asked about the braces. Zhou Yang's answer was simple. He'd only recently been able to afford them.

All of this was very pleasant, but it wasn't telling me anything about linear accelerators, or Niall Howley. On the phone, I'd told Zhou Yang that Niall's mother had hired me to look into his death.

His dining table stood in front of a large window. I leant back in my chair, savouring the pleasure of looking down over the city. Few Canberrans, among my acquaintance anyway, lived in houses with stairs. The sun warmed Zhou Yang's perfect olive skin. His braces flashed a reminder. I bit my lip, trying to work out how to introduce the Ventac – whether the indirect approach was best, or should I come straight out with it?

When I finally asked a question, his reply was brief.

He knew there'd been an overdose, of course. He gave me a look I was familiar with, gauging how much I'd already learnt, how much he could get away with *not* telling me, a look only partly disguised by his good manners and evident willingness to help.

He pushed a dish of spicy beef towards me. 'Take some more.'

'Thank you,' I murmured, beginning to wonder if I shouldn't have insisted on meeting somewhere neutral. On his home turf, he was too much in control, and had the perfect excuse to duck out to the kitchen when he wanted to think about a question, or preferred not to answer it.

'Why did you leave Canberra?' I asked, thinking to try another tack.

He stared at me without replying.

'What made you leave?' I prompted.

'It was not a good place for me.'

'Why not?'

'In the beginning,' Zhou Yang pushed his chair back and looked at me, deciding to repay my directness with his own, but uncomfortable about it, 'it was not too bad. And it was my first job since graduating, you understand, so I had nothing to compare. And I was so busy, I had so much to learn.'

I nodded, thinking of Eve. 'And then?'

'I ask myself – what should I expect?' Zhou Yang ran his lips over his braces, heaped food into his bowl and began to eat. Each of his movements now seemed a subtle way of distancing himself from me.

He swallowed and said, 'Work became difficult. There were jokes.'

'What kind of jokes?'

'Anti-Chinese. Racist jokes.' His skin darkened, the memory bringing back an angry flush.

'Like what?'

'At first I try to ignore and do my job, that is all.'

'Who told these jokes?'

'Colin Rasmussen.'

'Did he tell them in front of the others? How did they react?'

Zhou Yang bent his head once more over his bowl of food. I gave him a moment, then asked, 'What did you do?'

'I tell Dr Fenshaw.'

'What did he do?'

'Nothing.'

'And?'

'I talk to Niall one day when he is my partner.'

'What did Niall do?'

'Colin call Niall a – a pansy.'

'What happened after that?'

'Niall tell me to complain. He tell me people to write to.'

'And did you? Complain?'

Zhou Yang shook his head.

'What do you think caused the accident?'

'I think Tanya must have typed incorrect dose rate.'

'Who told you she'd done that?'

'We all talk about it.'

'Who said it was Tanya's fault?'

'Colin was with Tanya in the control room.'

'If Colin saw Tanya making a mistake, why didn't he point it out to her? Why didn't she correct it?'

'I think Colin has to leave.'

'Why?'

'I don't know.'

There we are, I thought. Zhou Yang had been humiliated and all he'd wanted was to finish out his time and leave. He did not challenge Colin's version of events, even though it was Colin who'd humiliated him. And here I was reminding him of it, expecting truthfulness in return.

'When you were entering treatment data,' I said, 'did you ever get a message that you didn't understand?'

'Once I get – it says Malfunction 12.'

'Malfunction 12? That's all?'

He nodded.

'What did you do?'

'I check, and Brian, who is with me, he checks too. Then we call Dr Fenshaw. He tell us we must have make mistake and start again.'

'Did Fenshaw come and see the message for himself?'

'Dr Fenshaw is angry at anything that delays treatment.'

'So what did he do?'

'He authorise to go ahead with treatment.'

'And everything was all right? Your data was correct and the patient was successfully treated?'

'Yes.'

'If you wouldn't mind helping me with one more thing,' I said. 'What was the date you left?'

'May the eighteenth.'

I pulled out a fresh copy of the numbers and glanced at it, even though I already knew the combination wasn't there.

I watched Zhou Yang closely as I handed him the list and explained where it had been found.

'Why do you think Niall Howley recorded Tanya's date of departure, but not yours?'

Zhou Yang stared at the numbers, as I'd so often done.

'Could it be,' I said, 'because these here –' I pointed to the combination after 1602, 'refer to another overdose, a second accident which couldn't be Tanya's fault because she was no longer there?'

Zhou Yang nodded again, this time almost imperceptibly.

'So we have two overdoses, 8000 rads and 15,000 rads. On the twentieth of January and the eighth of April. What happened to the patient?'

'Mrs Slater was her name. She did not die straight away.'

'When did she die?'

'A few weeks later. She was going to die anyway.'

'Who got the blame? Did you?'

A quick flash of rebellious anger in Zhou Yang's dark eyes suggested I might have been mistaken about him. He said reproachfully, 'Shirley. It was Shirley.'

'Were you Shirley's partner?'

'No, Niall is Shirley's partner.'

Zhou Yang claimed he didn't know a lot about the second overdose, though he was able to confirm the date. Nobody had talked about it the way they had about Tanya's. It had happened only three weeks before he was due to leave the hospital.

'When Niall talked to you, did he seem depressed?'

'Oh no. Niall was not, was never –' Zhou Yang paused, searching for the right word. 'A quiet guy, but not –'

'Do you think Niall believed himself responsible for the second overdose? That it was his fault?'

'I think Niall tell Shirley not to proceed with treatment, but Shirley is worried about what Dr Fenshaw will say.'

'Did Niall argue with Fenshaw?'

Zhou Yang nodded, then said he didn't want to talk about it any more. The remains of the large meal, the dishes we had barely touched, looked back at us reproachfully.

. . .

I rang Brook from the airport. 'There was a second overdose. After Tanya left, so it couldn't have been her. Zhou Yang, the guy I've just been talking to, said that Niall was operating the Ventac when it happened. His partner's name was Shirley Henderson. I've an address for her in Perth.'

'Will this Zhou Yang sign a statement? Testify in court?'

'He might. What's happening with the court order?'

'We're appealing. I'll get back over to the hospital.'

. . .

On my way to Eamonn's that night I thought how strange it was that it had never occurred to me to front up there before. I'd been to Tanya Wishart's flat and Zhou Yang's, I'd flown thousands of kilometres to visit Sorley Fallon, but I'd never even asked myself where Eamonn lived.

Lights were on and his car was in the driveway. 13 Beechwood Avenue Kingston was a large house with a spacious, well-kept garden.

Luxurious for a man living on his own on a nurse's salary. Even after looking up the address, I'd still half believed that 13 Beechwood Avenue must be a block of flats.

I thought I'd try the back door first. If I was lucky, it might just be open. I parked in a side street and looked to see if there was a back gate leading to a laneway. No luck. A path down the side of the house led me to the back door, which was well and truly locked. Close up, I could hear music. Curtains were drawn in the front rooms, and lights on in two of them. What was Eamonn doing? I'd rung the hospital before setting out and learnt that he'd worked an early shift that day, and was scheduled to start early again in the morning.

Blinds were pulled at the back, over locked windows which I assumed belonged to the kitchen and laundry. I could try to force one of them, but Eamonn might hear me in spite of the music. Ivan hadn't wanted me to go at all. I half expected Brook to appear in a squad car with a couple of constables, in response to Ivan telling him where I was. Ivan couldn't leave the kids to follow me himself, but I knew I mightn't have much time.

I knocked on the front door. In less than two seconds, I heard movement, footsteps behind it. The door had an eyepiece. I made sure I was standing where Eamonn could see me.

'What do you want?'

'Some answers. If you let me in, I give you my word that they won't go further than me. If not, I'm going straight to the police to tell them you knew where Niall was going on the night he died.'

I held my breath while Eamonn digested this in silence.

When he opened the door, I pushed past him and headed for the living room.

Eamonn switched the CD player off and turned to face me.

'I didn't know where he was going. He wouldn't tell me. If he had I would have followed him. I wouldn't have let him keep such a mad appointment on his own. I should have followed him anyway. Don't think I haven't blamed myself for that every day for the last four months. You know what I did? I came home, listened to music and went to bed. I was *asleep* while he was –'

'Who did he meet?'

'He wouldn't tell me, wouldn't name names.'

'But you guessed?'

'I'm sure it was Fenshaw.'

'Why?'

'Because he and Niall were locked in battle, and Niall had met him, I mean met him outside the hospital before.'

'Where?'

'Not the tower. Regatta Point. Niall told me about it afterwards. He was *elated* that Fenshaw had agreed to meet him.'

'Regatta Point was his idea?'

'No. I mean I don't think so. But setting up a meeting away from the hospital was. Niall's big mistake was believing that if he could only get Fenshaw on his own, he could convince him to get rid of the Ventac. Niall was seduced by mystery, cloak and dagger bullshit. Regatta Point? Why not. Telstra Tower? Even better. As soon as Fenshaw dug his heels in over the Ventac, Niall should have gone to the police or press, or both. But he was in awe of Fenshaw. Not in love with him, though he probably wouldn't have said no. To his credit, I don't think Fenshaw ever put that on him. Everything else but. Niall kept believing that Fenshaw would come round to his point of view. I knew better. I knew what he was really like.'

'What did you know?'

'He caught me with a patient once. A boy. It wasn't anything, but he could have made it into something any time he wanted. And he made sure I never forgot.'

'What were you doing?'

'I was holding him. His name was Michael. He was very sick. I took care of him for weeks, then he – his mother took him home to die. He was fifteen. One afternoon, I was holding him, hugging him. His head was on my shoulder. I looked up and there was Fenshaw standing in the doorway with that smile on his face.'

'Did he threaten you directly?'

'He knew he didn't have to. I love nursing and he knows that too. Nursing's my whole life.'

'I know about the second overdose,' I said.

Eamonn nodded. 'Niall was struggling to get the hospital board to undertake a full inquiry. One that went further than exchanging clichés about what the Ventacs could and couldn't do, and then getting bogged down in arguments about human error. You see, Fenshaw claimed that in both overdoses, human error was the cause. And the board accepted that because, when they were exhaustively tested, no one could replicate the Ventac's error, nobody could find a technical fault. It was driving Niall mad. He didn't give up though. He kept on writing letters. He'd convinced about half the board. He didn't want bad publicity any more than Fenshaw did, but he was terrified that the next time it happened, someone would be killed.'

'But wasn't Barry and the second patient, Mrs Slater –'

'Their tumours were both so far advanced that it was very unlikely either of them would have lived, but Niall had nightmares about a young person, somebody they could have saved. A week or so before his death, he realised that he couldn't go on waiting and hoping any longer. He decided that he'd have to go public.'

'And when Fenshaw asked to meet him at the tower, he thought it meant Fenshaw had given in, or was about to.'

'That's what I think must have happened.'

'Why did you agree to meet me at the hospital? You knew that we'd be seen together.'

'I guess I was testing myself,' Eamonn said. 'I've always known I was a coward. Physically. I wanted to – I know it was stupid.'

'You're not stupid. Or a coward. It was you who told Sorley Fallon Niall was dead, wasn't it?'

'Another bully he is, another bastard with blood on his hands.'

'What did he say?'

'That he was sorry. Can you believe that?'

'Did you reply?'

'Are you kidding?'

I thanked Eamonn. 'You've taken a big risk. That story about the boy stays with me. All the rest – I won't say where I got the information.'

Eamonn looked exhausted now, past caring. 'I loved him. I hope he knew it. I hope he never doubted it.'

. . .

Ivan and I sat up in bed to talk, Ivan wearing the doona like a cloak. The temperature outside was minus one. People who'd planted their tomatoes early would be shaking their heads, admonishing one another. I shivered and tried to make do with my one-sixth of the doona. Faces scrolled in front of me – Zhou Yang's and Eamonn's – young faces, elastic and opaque; Colin Rasmussen's different coloured eyes and Fallon's cold ones; Niall Howley's smile for the camera, his stubborn inward wilfulness that chose a path and stuck to it; Alex Fenshaw's warmth and generosity towards his patients, the steel inside that a patient couldn't guess.

'Niall was a game player,' I said. 'He played *Castle of Heroes* for years. He was Sorley Fallon's right-hand man.'

Ivan looked down at me and frowned. The bedside light accented his high cheekbones, making his eyes blacker.

'I don't like that look on your face Sandy. You're not thinking of another trip to Ireland?'

I laughed. 'A bit too late for that. Poor Eamonn, he's scared out of his wits.'

'I've been thinking about that. It's just his word against Fenshaw's isn't it?'

'Are you kidding? Glamour boy head of department against humble nurse? That department's the hospital's star attraction.'

'But Regatta Point? The middle of the night?'

'Fenshaw was preparing a case against Niall – a case for sacking him, I mean. He strikes me as the kind of boss who can't stand any opposition. You're either with him one hundred per cent or he treats you as an enemy.'

I sucked in my breath, feeling as though the solution was there, between my palate and my tonsils. I jumped out of bed. Ivan groaned, but padded down the corridor behind me.

'Your first thought about the numbers was the right one,' I said. 'They *are* a list of dates and dose rates, but they're something else as well.'

'I've tried –'

'What if Niall made up his own key? It's a matter of how his mind was working, and who he was hiding the information for.'

'You reckon whatever the kid was hiding he was hiding it for Fallon?'

'Or himself. Fallon had condemned him for something that he hadn't done. They'd quarrelled. The night he was killed he was heading towards what he hoped was a victory. But the Telstra Tower? He must have known he was taking an incredible risk. Even if he believed Fenshaw had come round. I think he hid his files before he left, or else when Blacksnake started threatening him.'

'Fallon's not going to give us anything.'

'Maybe he doesn't need to.'

I got out the diagram while Ivan dialled up Fallon's website.

'He's changed it,' I said. 'He's got rid of the castle.'

The same photograph of a beautiful young Irishman smiled at the viewer, but gone were the mists of the Antrim coast and the shadow of Dunluce behind him. The updated homepage showed Fallon in his jewellery shop entwined in Celtic silver. Pleased I'd printed out the homepage when I first came across it, I found my hard copy and set it down beside the diagram with its named and numbered rooms.

'He's got rid of the directions for accessing the MUD as well. Here they are.'

Ivan booted up Niall's computer, which he'd borrowed again the day he'd searched Niall's room.

He typed GOTO 2. Nothing happened. I pointed out that, in Niall's diagram, the numbers were in brackets. He typed GOTO(2) and said, 'Oh shit.'

The diagram Ivan had found in Niall's room appeared on the screen momentarily, then was replaced by part of the operating log from the Ventac 2 for 8 April 1997.

It began with the treatment data for a patient, with numbers and groups of numbers against the following headings: SITE, DIRECTION, APPLICATOR, SSD (cm), FIELD ALIGNMENT, FILTER, TOTAL INCIDENT DOSE, which was listed as 150 rads. The time recorded at the top right-hand side was 2:10 pm.

On a line by itself, after the treatment data, was the single letter P. I recalled, from my conversation with Tanya, that P was the command to proceed with treatment.

Then on the next line, by itself, was the message NO DOSE.

Someone had re-entered all the treatment data. The log showed an exact repetition of the headings – SITE, DIRECTION and so on – with the same numbers against them.

Then P again, followed by a second NO DOSE.

Each line of the log had the time recorded against it. Between the first NO DOSE message and the repeat of the treatment data was a gap of nineteen minutes. The remainder of the log showed no such gaps.

Was the gap in time the reason Niall had gone to the trouble of saving and then hiding this section of the Ventac's log?

I pictured the operator sitting in that tight, windowless control room in the hospital, staring at NO DOSE.

Zhou Yang had told me Shirley Henderson was the operator responsible for the second accident, and that Niall had been her partner, but this section of log contained no names, neither Niall's nor Shirley's, and no comments, just the data, P command, and NO DOSE. The gap in time had to be the reason Niall had saved it.

I imagined Niall apologising to the patient for the delay, then leaving the treatment room to talk to Shirley, possibly to insist that they cancel the treatment and tell the patient to go home. I pictured Shirley ringing Fenshaw from the control room. What had happened then? Had Shirley made contact with Fenshaw? Had Fenshaw given the go-ahead to proceed with the treatment? How had he interpreted the NO DOSE message? Had he dismissed it, as Tanya claimed he'd dismissed her Error 53, instructed Shirley to override it without further delay?

If Shirley had spent that time checking with Fenshaw, possibly arguing with him, what had Niall spent those minutes doing?

Shivering beside me in his boxer shorts, Ivan typed GOTO(1).

Shirley Henderson's statement read as though Niall had transcribed it from a tape. It began with her name and Niall's, and the date and time of treatment. Then there was a description of the steps she had taken leading up to the first NO DOSE.

I felt a small twinge of satisfaction that the gap in time in the operating log turned out to be almost exactly as I'd predicted, with one important twist.

Shirley had phoned Fenshaw immediately the command appeared. Colin Rasmussen had answered the phone. Shirley had explained the problem and Colin had advised her to go ahead with the treatment.

Shirley had insisted on checking with Fenshaw personally. She and Colin had argued. Niall had also argued with Colin. Eventually, Shirley had got through to Fenshaw, who had given her the go-ahead.

She had then re-entered all the data, pressed P, and the Ventac 2 had delivered a dose of 15,000 rads, not 150 as prescribed.

'Bugger this,' said Ivan, and ran back to the bedroom for his tracksuit. At last I found myself looking at a statement by Niall himself.

Niall had documented as accurately as he could the number of times the Ventac 2 had thrown up a rogue message. It had happened to each of the operators, including himself, at least twice in two years. Before the first accident and her dismissal, Tanya had recorded five. On no occasion before Error 53 had the message resulted in an overdose.

Niall had also recorded the responses of the Wilton engineers who'd tested the Ventac 2 and stated that it was not possible for the machine to overdose a patient. When Niall had asked them whether they were aware of other reports of radiation exposure using the Ventac 2, they had replied that they were not.

Niall said that there was no way of ascertaining what the messages meant. Some of them had been repeated. Malfunction 12 had appeared a number of times. The messages were not explained in any of the manuals that came with the Ventac and the hospital's engineers were at a loss to explain them. In Niall's opinion, the Ventac 2 should be shut down until the fault could be found and remedied. If it could not, the machine should not be used again.

His statement went into more detail about Shirley's phone call to Fenshaw, and Colin Rasmussen's response to it on 8 April.

The policy Alex Fenshaw had adopted was to override the message and proceed with treatment. Niall stated his opposition to this and his belief that, when Shirley had been unable to locate Dr Fenshaw immediately, Colin, acting as Fenshaw's assistant, should have suspended the treatment.

According to Niall, Colin had reacted aggressively to this suggestion, threatening both him and Shirley. There was no justification for this. Colin had no authority to order the operators to proceed with treatment. Niall had made a complaint under the hospital's complaints procedures. There was a cross-reference number.

I took over the keyboard and typed GOTO(8). In front of me were a number of diary entries, the first for 2 May.

He's there again. Bridget thinks I'm exaggerating. Wish I could believe her. Blacksnake keeps his distance when Sgartha's there, but that doesn't mean he's given up and gone.

8 May
Alex would rather get rid of people than have to put up with their weaknesses, or worse, confront someone who's foolish enough to dare to point out his own.

15 May
Bridget says she'll stick by me if it comes to a showdown. I wonder if I believe that. I don't want to put it to the test. I need the Castle. It's my home. No outsider would believe that if I told them. Why would I want to crash his MUD? It's not as though I haven't got enough worries without creating more for myself. Why can't I make him see that it must be someone else?

25 May
Blacksnake has entry. He found me in the stables. I love the smell of horses. I could smell him too. I can *feel* him following me.
He's moved up six levels. He asked for a CHAT. I told him the stables were fine for that. He said he had things to say to me that he didn't want anybody else to hear. He asked for my assistance and told me how he'd won his shield. I said I was impressed.
He asked when I was expecting the next raiding party. I said I didn't know. Innocent questions, but they're *not*. That's how I recognise him. Before Blacksnake, he was Soltar. Different character, same mind. Soltar asked the same questions. Laughing at me behind his hand, following me around. Is he someone I once killed? Was he in a British raiding party? Is that the grudge he bears me? Seeing me surrounded by my guards and shields? I won them.
Will I have to quit the Castle? What will be left for me? I think I know who Blacksnake is, but I'm afraid of certainty. Doesn't he realise

that I long to give him the benefit of the doubt? Perhaps I am a coward. My father's right. Perhaps that's all there is to it.

Eamonn's ready to give up on me. He's worried, but that's about as useful as attacking the Ventac with a spanner. Tells me to quit the MUD, get a new job, take a holiday. He wants me to go on holiday with *him*. I tried ringing Sorley again. His line's always busy.

6 June

Tried to get Alex on his own. Can't believe he can't see for himself how urgent the situation is. He blows in and out like a whirlwind. Never has time for anyone any more, not even Colin.

Today Colin and I found ourselves standing in the corridor watching him disappear along it. 'Oh my paws and whiskers the duchess'. I almost said it, might have if it had been anyone but Colin.

Colin's not speaking to me, which makes it easier. Each of us could pretend he was alone. If I had said anything, he would have ignored me, or come out with one of his famous put-downs.

15 June

Waited in the car park. Should have known he'd be late. It was cold. I kept myself warm by walking round the car. For some reason I couldn't bear to wait inside it. I've never been down there at night before. The lights were beautiful around the lake, and then the gaps where the trees come right down to the water. When he finally appeared it was a shock, though I'd been waiting for what seemed like hours. He held out his hands to me, that messianic gesture I used to think could change the world.

'Niall. You're freezing. Let's walk.'

'Take it out of commission,' I told him.

He said, 'You are right, and everybody else is wrong?'

Everybody else? He meant himself.

'Decommission it,' I said.

'It's not just my decision.'

'If you say so, your word will carry the day.'

'Do you remember Sally?' he asked. 'Her mother brought her to see me today. She's looking fine and her mother is a different person.'

Of course I remember Sally. I don't know if he could see my nod in the dark. When I think about it, he didn't look at me the whole time we were talking. The feeling between us, the closeness, the respect, all that's left of that is in our antagonism. Is that why he wanted to meet me there, because he knew I'd have trouble reading his expression? It's never worried him before.

'The old Ventac would have saved Sally,' I told him.

'Our success rate's gone up twenty per cent.'

'It's a machine,' I told him. 'A machine with something wrong with it. Next time it might kill a child.'

He opened his hands again, not to me, but perhaps the gesture hadn't been for me the first time either, any of the other times.

He took my arm. I could feel his warm breath on my cheek. I shook him off. It's not much of a resistance I know, but I'm glad I did it.

'I won't go on waiting for a tragedy to happen,' I shot back over my shoulder. 'I've written my own report and I'm going to publish it.'

He let me get ahead of him. I hurried. He was soon out of sight.

. . .

I blinked and shook my head. It was hard to believe that there were people living in my street whose biggest worry that night was whether a late frost would kill their tomatoes. Ivan's worn tracksuit smelt of sun and soap powder. Our office curtains were open on a dark backyard, a hills hoist. A blackbird began to sing.

'His mistake,' said Ivan, 'was thinking he could fix things on his own.'

'That's what Eamonn said.'

How alike Niall and Fallon must have been. And how different. I imagined the pleasure, the small Celtic jewel of pleasure, perhaps the last of his life, Niall had got from modelling his hiding place, the way it must have brought them closer, in his mind at least, even as Fallon was condemning and rejecting him. I had a flash of Bridget Connell, alias Sgartha, in the middle of the factory, in front of the bird car, her spiky hair, enormous claim on her own and other people's fantasies. Had she seen herself as Niall's protector? How did she shoulder her share of the responsibility, alone, in the middle of the night?

On impulse, I forwarded all of Niall's files to Sorley Fallon.

Twenty

We dozed for a few hours, then I checked my mail. No reply from Fallon.

I rang Brook, who said that he thought he had enough for a warrant for Fenshaw, and that it would probably take about twenty-four hours to get.

'Sorry to wake you so early.'

'That's okay. I've got my second wind.'

'Second winds,' I told him, 'are blowing right through Canberra.'

The phone rang while we were having breakfast. It was Robert Ferris from the Telstra Tower.

He said the police had been back to the tower interviewing everyone. 'We all thought that business was over and done with.'

'Is there something you think the police should know?'

'I saw you there one night,' Ferris said. 'You had your kids with you. I've a grand-daughter about the same age as your little girl.'

'How did you know it was me?'

'Olga Birtus told me what you looked like.'

'Can we meet for coffee?'

Ferris didn't reply straight away, and I thought he was going to refuse, but eventually I got him to agree to meet me at the Botanical Gardens in the early afternoon. It was his day off, he was looking after his four-year-old grandson, and had already arranged to take the boy there. His wife would call by later and pick the boy up to take him shopping. I listened to these family arrangements, understanding that they were Ferris's attempt to impose normality on an abnormal situation, wondering what had happened to make him seek me out.

I fetched my photocopy of the coronial report to check what it said about him. Hans Rowholt had been in charge of security the evening Niall Howley died, and Ferris had been with him. A third man was mentioned, Ian McFarlane, who'd been on duty at the security entrance. The police did not seem to have taken a statement from McFarlane.

According to his testimony, Ferris had not heard or seen anything unusual. No visitor had been reported behaving suspiciously. He did not remember having seen Niall Howley. There'd been no one on any of the outside galleries when he and Rowholt had locked up at ten o'clock.

. . .

The Botanical Gardens consisted entirely of Australian native plants. They made me feel, contrarily, as though I was both inside a green-house, and wide open to the air. I remembered this feeling as soon as I stepped out of the car, recalling my visits to the gardens with Peter when he was a small boy.

The air smelt cared for. It used to make me feel better just to walk along gravel paths between eucalypts and acacias with such air around me. While Peter ran up and down, I'd stand at the edge of the rain-forest watching. One of his favourite games had been to run along the steep paths waiting for the sprinklers to come on. It didn't always happen, but when it did he'd yell with delight, flinging his arms wide as though to catch the water.

From the car park, you could see the line where the gardens ended and ordinary bush took over, the Telstra Tower's needle point above the mountain.

Ferris had arranged to meet me at the duck pond. It wasn't really a duck pond, but when he suggested it I knew immediately where he meant. Duck pond suggested grassy English banks. This stretch of water, surrounded by large untidy casuarinas, was nearly always in shadow, and the black ducks, being wild and not domestic, were some-times not to be found at all.

When they were there, they quacked appropriately and ate the bread that children threw. The water was edged with mud and slippery rocks, but there was a wooden seat for parents. In the spring, if you were lucky, duck parents paraded their offspring and kept children entertained.

I saw Ferris as soon as I rounded the corner of the car park. He was sitting on the wooden bench. It had to be him. There was no other grandparently figure in sight, and a boy in a red parka running madly up and down the grass was clearly in his care. I recognised him as the guard who'd appeared at the security door, while I stood at the lift well watching, the night Ivan and I had gone to the tower.

He looked up and I waved. He didn't wave back, but got to his feet and called the boy over to him.

I smiled at the boy, who didn't smile back, but stared up at me through a thick blond fringe. He was a comfortable-looking child. His parka was spotless, and his dark green tracksuit pants looked ironed.

'James and I thought we might walk down to the swamp.'

'Fine. That's fine.' I smiled again, to show that none of this was meant to be an ordeal. 'Lead the way.'

And lead the way they did. Walking, the family resemblance between the man and boy became more apparent. They both had the same square-shaped head on solid, rolling bodies. Though Ferris's hair was grey, it was thick and plentiful. I imagined it as once having been a bright mop like his grandson's, who gave a skip, then ran ahead along the path.

'How long have you been working at the tower?' I asked, glancing up again, wondering if he found its presence overbearing.

'Seventeen years.'

'How long have you been using your current computer system?'

Ferris shot me a look, but he answered readily enough. 'About two years.'

'Was it hard to get used to?'

'In many ways it's easier. Saves duplication and a lot of stuffing around. But well, you know, computers. Half the time they're down.'

We reached the swamp. Our gravel path followed the edge of it, and there were a couple of small bridges. James was kneeling in the middle of one, peering into the water.

I liked the swamp. With no large trees blocking the sun, it was one of the warmest spots in the gardens. On winter days, when it was too cold to play tag with the sprinklers in the rainforest, I used to bring Peter there. Once we'd seen a lizard solemnly eating daisies. Peter had talked about it for months afterwards. We'd gone back looking for it, but had never been able to find it again.

Ferris said, 'We had a bit of weather the night Howley died.'

'What kind of weather?'

'Spot of lightning. God moving the furniture around up top.'

'How long were the computers down for?'

He didn't answer me directly, and avoided meeting my eyes. 'We're used to storms up there. Can't shut up shop just because of a bit of weather. There's a UPS – uninterruptible power supply to you. Cuts in when something happens to the main power supply.'

'What happened that night?'

'Computers were jammed. That's what the technical blokes said. They couldn't figure it out. Got their knickers seriously tangled.'

'What time was this?'

'Still working on it by the time I went home. Then next morning that kid's body was found.'

'Why didn't the police take a statement from Ian McFarlane?'

Ferris sat down on a wooden bench facing the swamp. His face looked heavy suddenly, and miserable.

'Hans Rowholt and I have worked together for a long time. Then with Ian – Ian's a much younger bloke – we kind of made a team. We started out as government employees. About eighteen months ago, security was handed over to a private company.'

'To Swift.'

Ferris nodded. Even while intent on what he was saying, he kept his eyes on James.

'They cut costs, cut the number of guards, relied more on computers running the system. For security to work properly you need backup, and I don't just mean electricity. That night we were short-staffed. It was the middle of winter. People were sick. There was no one to replace Ian when he went off duty. He told Hans he thought we should close, send everybody home. Computers were going arse over turkey, excuse the expression. Hans was inclined to agree with him. He rang Sydney and they said, what's the problem? Couldn't see it. Told Hans he had a job to do and just get on with it. Ian said his wife was sick and there was no way he was working a double shift. He walked out.'

'Leaving no one on duty at the security entrance?'

'Hans told me to take over.'

'And the doors leading to the broadcasting platform?'

'Ian left them in the default position.'

'How long were they like that?'

'About fifteen minutes.'

'Why didn't McFarlane tell the police? If he'd lost his job, what did he have to lose?'

Ferris raised his chin aggressively. 'Ian may have told the Swift bosses to get stuffed. But he wants to go on working in security. Why shouldn't he? He's a good bloke, knows his job and honest with it.'

'They came to an agreement?'

'I don't know what was said. All I know is that Ian resigned and moved straight into another job.'

'And the technicians?'

'Should be fired for incompetence tomorrow. I mean who shut themselves in the basement for hours on end?'

'What about the outside galleries?'

'Hans said the kid must have already been out there.'

'But you know differently.'

There was a long moment before Ferris answered.

'Someone had been in the technician's lab, the one behind the broadcasting platform. Some of the furniture was moved.'

'Who told you?'

'One of the technicians. He said he had to tell someone, and he knows my opinion of Litowski.'

'I'm surprised no one blew the whistle earlier.'

'Hans was "retired". It was suddenly *his* fault that we were understaffed. Litowski was given the top job and we were told to take our cue from him. We were also warned what would happen if we didn't. I mean, how's it going to look for Swift next time they tender for a job? Oh, they're the company that let a nutter into a secure area of the Telstra Tower, so he could jump off and break his silly neck.'

'What were you told to say?'

'The kid had climbed over the fence and jumped.'

'What did you think?'

'At the time I didn't have any idea that he'd been somewhere else.'

'What about the storm?'

'It reduced visibility and made a lot of noise.'

'And the computers?'

'A minor problem. Had it fixed in no time. We kept quiet because we didn't want to lose our jobs. And frankly, at the time I couldn't see that it made much difference. The kid was dead whichever platform he'd jumped off. But if someone *pushed* him –'

James chose this moment to lean too far over the water for his grandfather's comfort. Ferris walked smartly to the bridge, but he didn't yank at the boy as I might have done if I was tense and upset. He knelt down beside him and spoke softly.

I walked across and showed him photographs of Fenshaw and Colin Rasmussen. Ferris said that the police had been back at the tower asking about them. He didn't recognise either man.

I left him to finish his outing with his grandson.

I rang Brook from my car. He'd got the warrant for Fenshaw in record time.

'Isn't talking but. He's got a lawyer with attitude.'

I relayed what Robert Ferris had told me, wondering why I hadn't pursued the one fact that had been staring me in the face that first morning at the tower. Mikhail Litowski had been promoted after Niall's death.

'More warrants,' Brook said dryly, 'though nicking some of those security cowboys will be fun.'

. . .

At home, I made myself a sandwich and checked my mail again. Fallon had sent me a memo, written by Alex Fenshaw to the hospital board, arguing that Niall was mentally unstable. The bizarre manner of his death proved this. Niall's testimony could not be considered that of a sane person. A further inquiry into the Ventac 2 was unnecessary. It would be an unwarranted cost in time and money. Earlier inquiries had been exhaustive and conclusive.

I rang Ivan at work. 'Fallon's got into the hospital records.'

'The sneaky bugger.'

'He's a better hacker than either of us.'

'Oh, I don't know about *that*.'

······

Twenty-one

It was almost three o'clock. I walked across to Lyneham shops, thinking to buy a treat from the bakery for afternoon tea, and meet Peter at the school.

There were a number of small rituals associated with picking children up from school, which, as a new parent five years ago, I'd quickly learnt. Parents of the younger children waited in a straggle around the playground equipment. In high summer they stood in the scant shade offered by school buildings, in winter hugged uninviting bricks for warmth and shelter against the rain that slanted off the Brindabellas.

Parents who waited at the senior entrance did so less obviously than those at the junior section. Many had driven, and remained in their cars. Those on foot stood a little way back from the doors and seldom looked at them. They chatted to each other, or stared into space.

It was blowy and warm. Sun bit through the new prunus leaves that lined the walkway to the school's main entrance. I always knew when the bell was about to ring, but still it was a shock. Momentarily deafened parents watched their kids pour out the doors, a mass of blue shorts and yellow T-shirts.

The second wave pushed through the doors, the third, and finally the stragglers. I turned around thinking I must have missed Peter. But surely he would have seen me.

I went right up to the doors and stared through them, unable to see much more than my own reflection. Maybe Peter's teacher had kept him in. With another backward glance, I pushed past a group of laughing girls and hurried along the corridor to Peter's classroom.

It was empty apart from his teacher, who was standing at her desk piling folders on top of one another.

'Mrs Hyles? Have you seen Peter? He wasn't at the front.'

'Oh,' she said. 'I think he left with the others.'

'Did you see which way he went?'

She was sorry but she hadn't noticed. 'Let's check to see if his bag's still there.'

The rack was empty except for a single yellow sweatshirt.

'He probably went out the back doors. You know what kids are like.'

There were four, if you counted the toilets five, doors Peter could have used. I'd only been a couple of minutes in his classroom, but by the time I got to the back of the school, the yard was practically deserted.

Four boys were dribbling a basketball. Some girls sat in a huddle on the steps, poring over a piece of paper. I demanded to know if they'd seen Peter.

They looked up at me with the dull contempt of children used to adults asking stupid questions. One said, 'Who's he?'

I realised they were year six and that my son was beneath their notice.

I didn't stop to explain, but rushed up to the boys, who shook their heads. Next I overtook a couple of girls who lived around the corner, one a tall blonde with the shy, superior air of girls who develop early. She thought for a moment then said no. I was almost at the high school now. I spotted a yellow T-shirt in the distance, heading for Mouat Street. I chased it for twenty metres before admitting to myself what should have been obvious.

I ran to where I had a clear view of my front garden. Peter would be waiting there, school bag tossed up on the porch. He would be round the back.

I pulled at the latch and shoved the back gate open, calling out his name. I ran round the side of the house. The backyard was empty.

'Fred?' I called out. 'Fred!'

Could he be sick or hurt? I checked the kennel, then walked around the yard looking in all the places he liked to lie, up by the back fence next to the rose bushes, underneath the fig tree. I pushed aside branches, stamped in the long grass. Fred was gone. Peter was missing and he'd taken his dog with him.

I choked on my breath. The air was impossibly dry and full of grit. I checked the nail on the wall of the garden shed where Peter kept

Fred's lead. It wasn't there. Why hadn't I noticed earlier that Fred was gone?

After school, Peter generally preferred his dog's company, or his own. Sam was the leader of the group he ate his lunch with. If Sam had invited him over, Peter might have been so keen to impress that he'd rushed out of school the back way, collected Fred, and left again without waiting to speak to me.

I rang Sam, congratulating myself that I'd had the foresight to copy his number into my address book. This piece of clear thinking raised my spirits and I expected to find Peter at the other end, with some laughably simple explanation of why he'd taken Fred with him to Sam's.

Sam answered the phone himself. No, Peter wasn't there. Sam thought he'd left the classroom with everybody else. He gave me the number of another boy. When I rang it, a woman answered and said her son was at basketball practice. It didn't sound as if she knew who Peter was.

I clicked on the answering machine, then ran next door and knocked, praying that my neighbour, Sylvia, had seen Peter go off with Fred.

Sylvia was often at home during the day. She came to the door after my second knock, dressed ready to go out. She'd been talking to her sister on the phone at three, she told me, rather a long call because her sister's husband had just had an operation. She was going over to the hospital now. She was afraid she hadn't seen Peter come home.

Most of the houses in our street were empty, their owners still at work. I ran from one to the next. Of the few people who did come to their doors, none had seen Peter or Fred.

I scanned the small horizons that bounded all the good safe places. I called Peter's name until the two sweet syllables crumbled to a bit of old dry wood.

I headed towards Southwell Park. Would Fred have willingly got into a car with a stranger? If the stranger had offered him food, I was afraid the answer was yes.

I stumbled over a tree root and looked down. The root was immense, growing with the slow confidence that finds its way through stone. Each blade of grass around it was singular and lovely, the brown pine needles that had come to rest between them, the light shining through the branches of the trees, oblique afternoon light that I'd always found restful, walking outside just to stand in it.

The road and traffic gave way to scrubby eucalypts and casuarinas. This was the way we'd always come, first when Peter was very small, then with Fred to show him fresh rabbit droppings, the best spots to dig. It didn't seem to matter to Peter that Fred took no notice of these treats, but simply ran from one garbage bin to the next, and when there were no more, when the playing fields ended and the overgrown bit around the creek began, turned round as if to say, there's no point going on. No one will have dropped a sandwich here.

I walked close to the trees that lined the creek, but even there it would have been hard for anyone to hide. The only place Peter could be, if he was for some reason hiding from me, was an overgrown copse that bordered the golf course on one side and the creek on the other.

I saw yellow everywhere. A leaf catching the sun was the corner of his T-shirt. I heard a dog bark and my legs gave way underneath me. A fluffy, impossibly happy golden retriever ran out of the trees on the other side of the creek. I could have shot it and its owner just for being there.

Under the thick trees, in the undergrowth, the air was cool and damp. I stood still, waiting for my eyes to adjust. There was the tree Peter liked to climb, while Fred stood at the bottom barking as though his master was some large, ungainly cat. There was the glen – funny unAustralian word, not appropriate at all, but it was what we called it – where we'd brought a picnic once during the school holidays. Fred had to be tied up so we could spread our food out on a blue and white cloth. The grass looked flattened as I walked across it, ducking my head to avoid low branches. Could Fred and Peter have been here, rested here?

The ground was soft. I looked around for open bits where foot-prints might show, but though a little way further on there were plenty of these, both human and dog, they were too big or too small, the wrong shape, not my son's or his dog's. My insides turned over as though all was pulpy there, and no outline could hold.

I called Peter's name, and Fred's, thinking there might be a chance that, if Fred wasn't on the lead, he would come when he heard me. But all that came back in response to my voice were the ducks on the golf course pond, and small birds rustling in the holly bushes that formed a barrier between the golf course and the copse. I had no sense of anybody hiding, watching me. Still I stumbled on, looking up into the trees, though how Peter would have kept Fred quiet while he climbed one, I couldn't guess. My feet were muddy, my legs wet from the long grass. I stopped again and for a few seconds there was complete, pure silence, and then my legs, which kept threatening to fail me, did, and I crumpled down by the trunk of a casuarina and began to cry.

. . .

I rang Ivan, and left urgent messages for Brook and Derek, who was out of Canberra at a conference. I looked through my kitchen window without being able to make a connection between myself and what was out there.

Ivan walked in holding Katya, his face hard as an early Cubist painting. I wanted to grab my daughter from him, take my remaining child and run.

I switched on my computer. There was another email from Sorley Fallon.

Overcoming time and distance was an image of a castle and a cliff beneath it, cruel rocks, a boy who, in spite of his twisted posture, might possibly be sleeping. But instead of long pale hair, a black shirt, the figure lying on the rocks was a true boy, no more than ten years old, dressed in blue shorts and a Lyneham T-shirt.

I must have cried out, screamed.

Ivan was beside me with Katya in his arms. A footfall in the corridor had me running to the door. It was Brook, who used my phone to ring his station commander. A couple of Belfast-based officers could be at Fallon's shop within three hours.

In spite of following through the hospital inquiries in his own way, stubbornly, methodically, Brook had never let go his suspicion of Fallon, or of what, in his mind, Fallon represented.

He examined Fred's kennel. I showed him the hook on the shed wall.

'Is anything else missing?'

'I don't think so.'

Dorothy Johnston

'Would Fred let a stranger into the backyard?'
'If he was offered food,' I said, thinking that I should have asked Sylvia whether she had heard him barking.

Brook left then, to put together a media release. He took a recent photograph and a full description of what Peter had been wearing.

'We'll start broadcasting at seven if he isn't found by then.'

. . .

Ivan fed Katya. His body bent over her highchair looked ridiculously big, her favourite small gold spoon all but invisible in his hand. When she'd had enough, he made sandwiches, offering me one. I shook my head, but decided I would wash the dishes.

The sink seemed filled with the discarded paraphernalia of illness – syringes, used gauze bandages, empty bottles and pink cotton wool. A slow leaching down through all these layers was no more, at that moment, than the pastel layers of hope, fading as I watched them. I shook my head to clear away the vision, but my eyes continued to betray me.

We watched Brook interviewed on television. Whoever had taken Peter knew that the one chance he had of making sure he came quietly was to take Fred, and then get word to Peter – during school? A note in his bag? Unless Peter did what he wanted, he would never see his dog again.

I saw this part with perfect clarity. The note. Peter too frightened to tell his teacher – wanting to run home and see if Fred was there, but then dismissing this as too risky. The horrible afternoon, the final bell. Peter working out which door he had to make for. And me waiting like a dumb fool as the minutes ticked by.

How could it be Fallon, or someone acting on Fallon's instructions? Fallon didn't even know of Peter's existence, let alone Fred's. He hadn't asked me anything about my life in Australia.

Night bells. Bells tolling the watches of the night, so that one person might say, it's over now, my shift. Some time, it could have been a few minutes after the news finished, it could have been hours, I let myself out the front door, locking it behind me.

The pine trees on the oval looked the same. I knew them well, where each branch went, the ones that had been amputated to make a cycle path.

I came to the path and turned left along it. The cream-brown wounds of the trees' lost arms shone under lamps that seemed placed at random, though they weren't. Weak light cut the darkness. The trees were neutral. The path, pine needles and grass had had their afternoon beauty and would have it again.

Thunder rolled off Black Mountain as I crossed the road back to the house. A sword of lightning cut the sky in half.

Twenty-two

Detective-Constable Freda Jansz met me on the grass at the front of the school at eight o'clock next morning. She was fair-haired, narrow-waisted. She shot warning glances at me, her blue eyes so dark they were almost black. I knew she could sense that a scream was there, just underneath the surface. It was as though we could both see it, this scream of mine, which would sweep away the effort I was making.

A number of people had rung in response to the news bulletins, reporting sightings of boys who resembled Peter, wearing the Lyneham uniform. Each of these calls was being followed up. In a case like this, Jansz reminded me, there were bound to be any number of false leads. Dozens of boys roughly answering Peter's description had been making their various ways home from school yesterday afternoon.

'With a man and a dog?'

'We're not certain of that, Mrs Mahoney.'

I wanted to start quizzing Peter's classmates, working my way through them one by one. I knew from the way Jansz looked at me that she didn't want me there, thought I should leave interviewing to the people who were trained to do it. She wanted me to see that she knew I was being indulged.

By the end of the morning, my head was buzzing with the sound of the same questions over and over, the answers coming back monotonous, repetitive. Three children I'd spoken to had seen Peter leaving through a side door. I interrogated these three as though they'd committed crimes themselves. Where had Peter been going? They didn't know. What door? The one near the library. Who had been with him? No one. What about once he got outside? They didn't know.

Two boys and a girl. They'd seen Peter leave the building alone, through a door the students weren't supposed to use, which led across a patch of grass to the street. The reason no one had seen Peter outside was almost certainly that no child had been between that door and the street. If Peter had turned in either direction, towards the front of the school where I'd waited, or to the back, the ovals, someone would have seen him. The only possible explanation was that he'd got into a car.

Police constables had already interviewed the shop owners and assistants in the shopping centre across the road from the school. They spent the morning tracking down and interviewing parents who regularly parked outside, plus everybody with a connection to Niall Howley.

. . .

'Hello, hello!' I shouted down the phone.

'I'm at the Downer shops.' Brook sounded out of breath. 'Get over here.'

I ran a late orange light on Northbourne Avenue, deaf to the long annoyance of a semitrailer's horn. I changed lanes like a demented rally driver.

Was Brook on his own? If the news was bad, then surely he wouldn't be ringing me from a shopping centre. I'd already spoken to him twice that day. He'd spent part of it interviewing Fenshaw, who'd been at a fundraising dinner the night before, and had about a hundred witnesses to prove it. Fenshaw had gone straight to the dinner from the hospital. It was just possible that he'd grabbed Peter from school and hidden him somewhere. There was an hour during the afternoon when he said he'd gone home to have a rest. None of his neighbours had seen him arriving at his house, or leaving. It was Colin Rasmussen's day off and nobody, including Fenshaw, knew where Colin was.

A brick arch spanned the small concrete square of Downer shops. There were two police cars in the car park. Brook was standing stiffly to attention underneath the arch, next to an empty fountain. As I ran up, he turned and nodded towards a small supermarket. His face was white, and the jacket of his suit hung on him as though on a wire coat-hanger.

It was only a short distance to the supermarket, across the barren square. As we covered it, Brook explained that he'd decided to take another look at Colin's flat, even though a constable had visited it last evening and found it empty.

The flat had once again appeared deserted as Brook approached it, blinds drawn, junk mail in the letterbox. He'd knocked on an adjacent door and found a surly, uncooperative tenant who said no, he hadn't seen Colin in the last twenty-four hours. A young policeman had already asked him that.

Brook said to the balding man behind the supermarket cash register, 'Here's Mrs Mahoney. Could you just tell her what you told me?'

The man blinked and pursed his lips. 'We're a small place here, as you can see. I know most of my customers, people from the flats like. They drop by on their way home from work to pick up milk and bread. I know that Colin fellow because he used to smoke. We used to joke about it as the price of cigs went up, the warning signs got bigger. I'm a smoker too, still am off duty. Then one day Colin, he comes in and gets his usual wholemeal sliced loaf, litre milk. No cigarettes. "I've quit," he said. "Don't talk to me about it. My willpower's about that big."'

The balding man held up his thumb and forefinger so close that they were almost touching. 'Last night Colin came in. He bought his milk and bread, a packet of rice bubbles and a coupla tins of dog food.'

'He doesn't have a dog?'

'Not allowed in the flats.'

'Did you ask about it?'

'He seemed to be in a hurry. As a matter of fact I had a few customers waiting.'

'Did he have a child with him?'

'Came in by himself. I would of told you if he didn't.'

'Where did he go after he left here?'

'Didn't see. Like I said, had some customers to serve.'

. . .

Colin's block of flats was surrounded by a double cordon of police cars. Brook explained as we walked towards them – I wanted to fly over the cars and men in uniform – that Colin's flat was at the back. He stopped me at the first row of cars, pointed out a van, said Frank was inside and may have already made contact. A man wearing close-fitting black climbed the steps to the van and disappeared inside it.

While Brook was busy with the duty officer, I called Ivan, who'd been sitting outside with Katya when Brook rang, left another message for Derek, who was on his way, then went over to the van.

From the outside, it looked like an ordinary white van. Through open doors, I glimpsed a floor to ceiling panel behind the driver's seat, covered with communication equipment. Narrow benches lined two sides of the interior. A man with short black hair, shiny as a panther's coat, was sitting with headphones on and his back to me. Was he talking to Colin? Was it Colin on the other end? Could it be Peter? If the duty officer hadn't pulled me back, I would have run up the steps.

I sat in a car with the duty officer and told him all I knew about Colin, packing as much into every sentence as I could.

A loud hailer on the car's back seat looked over-large, impossibly remote and smooth. I looked up at the sound of a door slamming. Derek's voice cracked through a thin bit of plywood that had been nailed inside me, holding me together. I watched him run first towards the van and then, diverted, to the car where I was sitting. He shouted at me through the window, banging on it with his fists. A young red-haired policeman dragged him off. I watched him go with no emotion, unable to connect him to my son.

Ivan arrived and sat with me. He'd left Katya with Sylvia, but he obviously wished he hadn't. I leant against him and listened to his heartbeat. His face was grey and craggy. I would have used it as a mask, to blot out the mocking frontage of the flats.

Darkness fell. People came and went across my line of vision. Bill McCallum walked like a man who'd once enjoyed authority, but had set it down somewhere along the way, and had not gone back for it. His shoulders were hunched and he did without a neck. It occurred to me that the body recalled effortlessly what the mind would just as soon set down and not return for.

I went for a walk. I watched McCallum and Brook talking. In the brackish light, they were trees of the same shape, same species, trained by the same winds. If Brook belonged anywhere it was with McCallum and these other men, whose shapes made patterns between the rows of cars. Brook's mind moved between barriers like these. His heart? That could be offered variously. What bound us – Brook, Ivan and myself?

Not marriage, not blood or work that was enduring, not, as we were here now, genuflecting to the illusion of control.

I was allowed to move around behind the cars. Colin had switched on every light in his flat. I knew what he was doing, what he was saying with the lights. You've made sure I've no way of leaving without being seen, but I don't care. I'm going to sit here with my lights on and you can watch my shadow on the blinds.

I found Brook, who said the duty officer was about to respond by turning off the power to the whole block. One second I was looking up at a phalanx of lights, the next a shadowy wall. I thought of the thick boles of trees on Lyneham oval, their amputated arms, how the physical world was at the same time precisely tuned to terror and indifferent.

'They won't let it go on past midnight Sandra.'

'How do you know?'

'I know the officer in charge. If he hasn't got them out by eleven, eleven-thirty, he'll get set to move.'

'What's Colin asking for? What's he want?'

'He's not making much sense. Got it fixed in his head that there's a conspiracy to stop him doing his job. Keeps ranting about machines that save lives and people who destroy them.'

'Is he using Peter as a hostage? Why doesn't he – ?' My voice cracked.

'Where would Rasmussen go if he *did* get out? He says Peter won't come to any harm if he's left alone to perform his duty. There's a heap of swearing and abuse, but that's the guts of it.'

I knew Brook was holding out on me. 'He's threatened to kill Peter hasn't he? *Hasn't he?*'

'If they don't get a result in the next half hour, they're going in.'

'What if it's too late?'

'Listen to me Sandra. If he was planning to kill Peter, he would have. He's boasting about how he threw Niall Howley off the Telstra Tower and fooled the lot of us.'

Brook was called away, and a constable dragged me back to what I thought of as my car. I held on to the steering wheel. Colin was crazy and might do anything to Peter. Throw him out the window. With a start of shame, I realised that I'd wet my pants.

Freda Jansz brought me a thermos and a sandwich. She didn't say anything about the smell of urine, or offer any reassurance, and I was grateful for this. I drank something from a cup. It had no flavour of tea or coffee, but was sweet.

There was movement on the roof of the flats. Men dressed in black, with black helmets and guns, merged with the darkness, moving with ease across the sloping roof.

An enormous noise filled the night, not one gunshot but ten. Another and another. My stomach heaved. Up came the tea and bread and I was running, screaming, kicking and punching at arms, legs, bodies that would hold me back.

I stumbled. The entrance to Colin's flat was a dark noisy tunnel. A man was coming through a doorway at the end of it with a bundle in his arms.

Peter was staring at me, eyes huge as though the pupils would never again get sufficient light. I squashed him to me as though my body, ill-practised when it came to danger, had only just now realised what was required of it.

The man who'd been carrying Peter let me take him and led both of us back to the entrance to the flats.

Derek rushed forward, his face framed above Peter's head in car headlights and the outside lights of the flats, so bright they blinded us.

An ambulance had backed up. I craned my neck, looking for Ivan. Where was Colin? What had the police done with him?

Someone was shouting behind us. Colin appeared, half carried by the special operations men. As they passed us, Colin swung his head and spat, hard and accurately, in my face.

Ivan and I managed a few words while Peter was being settled in the ambulance. He wouldn't come to the hospital with us. He wanted to fetch Katya and go home. The sight of his big head bobbing over others round the side of the ambulance, disappearing between paramedics in their red and white, told me it was over.

Twenty-three

'Come on,' Ivan said, 'a family hug.'

Peter grinned and held his arms out to his sister. He yawned – he'd only just woken up – then giggled, his face against Ivan's chest and my right arm.

Katya laughed. I squeezed Ivan's other hand and answered his raised eyebrows with a nod.

I'd cleaned myself up in the bathroom next to Peter's ward, and Derek and I had sat with him until dawn. Bill McCallum had looked in briefly. He'd told us that as soon as the team had broken down the door to Colin's flat, Colin had let Peter go. He'd shouted abuse, but he hadn't used Peter to defend himself. As soon as they got him to the city station, he'd said he wanted to sign a statement confessing to Niall Howley's murder.

Why had Colin hidden Peter overnight, then taken him to his flat? Had he planned to kill Peter, but found himself unable to go through with it?

This was the horror Derek had held over me, after McCallum left, as we talked in low voices while our son slept. Peter was safe now, no thanks to me. His life had been hanging in the balance for the last thirty-six hours. It was my fault, no one else's. I was an unfit mother. He wanted Peter to live with him and Valerie.

Had Colin meant to use Peter as a hostage to demand a safe passage for himself, out of Australia somewhere? But then, why hadn't he pressed his demand once the police had his flat surrounded? On the other hand, why was I expecting Colin to behave logically, make logical demands?

'Mum?' said Peter. 'Did you ask them about Fred?'

Fred had been sedated for most of the time since their abduction. It was Brook who'd found him, and for this Brook had gone up a thousand fold in Peter's estimation. Peter wasn't able to forgive me yet for going with him in the ambulance, rather than staying behind to look for Fred myself.

Brook had sought out the manager of the flats, and asked if he'd heard or seen anything of a dog. The manager hadn't, and kept repeating that there were no pets allowed in the flats, as though this was proof enough. But Brook had persevered, and eventually learnt of a basement room adjoining the laundry by a door only the manager had the key to.

Here, after braving the manager's protests that no tenant could possibly get into the room, let alone hide a dog there, Brook had found Fred, tied up behind a tall steel cupboard, lying on the concrete floor beside an empty water bowl and a pile of dried vomit. Brook had taken him straight to a vet in Limestone Avenue. He'd been doped so severely that the vet said it was a small miracle he'd survived.

It was the recurring theme of Peter's story, how Colin had taken Fred away and hidden him, how Colin had said that if Peter made any noise at all, if he didn't do exactly what Colin told him, he'd never see his dog again. The terror of Fred's death had hung over him every hour of his captivity, and was mixed up now with details of where he'd been taken, what Colin had said and done and threatened to do.

After Colin had picked Peter up outside the school, they'd driven out of Canberra. 'A long way,' said Peter, 'in the bush.'

He described how Colin had let him sit in the back with Fred, eat a leftover sandwich from his lunchbox, and have a drink. It wasn't until after he started feeling sick, especially after he was separated from Fred, that his real fear started.

He recalled a river, going along beside it for a while, then turning off onto a dirt road. They'd pulled up in front of a hut. Colin had tied Fred up at the back of the hut, but that was still okay, Peter said, because even though he was made to go inside the hut and stay there, he could look out a small window and see Fred, and could hear him whining.

There was no toilet. Colin made Peter go to the toilet in the bush, while he stood right next to him. Peter pressed his lips together as he told this part.

They'd spent all of that night and the next morning in the hut.

Colin had a gas stove and had heated up some soup. 'It tasted awful, Mum.'

Colin made hot chocolate and forced Peter to drink some of that as well. Then he'd gone to sleep.

The first thing he did when he woke up was run to the window to look for Fred. Fred was lying down where he'd been tied up. He didn't move when Peter called his name.

That was when Colin had turned really mean. Peter had to go to the toilet again, with Colin standing over him, and then was told to get back into the car. Colin said he wasn't to make a sound. If he did, that would be the end of Fred, a threat made more compelling by the fact that Peter discovered, when Colin lifted Fred into the car, that he wasn't really asleep, not normally asleep. His breathing was shallow and laboured.

'Like this,' Peter said, 'Uh-hng, uh-hng! I got really scared then. And Mum, I had such a bad headache.'

Peter leant against three great white pillows, the hospital blanket rucked up around his knees. His already pale skin was greenish-grey and his lips had become a thin line, but he didn't cry.

At Colin's flat he'd been locked in a room with the blinds drawn, while Colin took Fred away. When he came back, he wouldn't say where he'd taken Fred, but he had a grocery bag with him, and Peter noticed with joy that it contained two tins of dog food.

'I asked him, and he told me to be quiet or I'd get Fred in trouble. And Mum, he started acting really weird. He made me get under this blanket and he wouldn't even let me have my head out, but I did, I peeked, and he was just standing at the window.'

It had been much worse than the shack because he and Fred were completely separated, and he had no idea where Fred was, but also because he'd been forced to stay in one corner. And Colin had been worse.

'Weird,' said Peter. 'Really crazy. No one could hear me whispering, but I wasn't even allowed to do that. And you know what, all the time he was talking on the phone, he got so angry and he couldn't hit the guy he was talking to, so I thought he was going to hit me. Then when I heard that banging I thought, if I don't get out of here in two minutes I'll be dead.'

A nurse came, took Peter's temperature and pulse, and suggested that he use the bathroom and get ready for breakfast. To give him some time alone with Ivan and his sister, I went downstairs to visit Brook.

The accoutrements of Canberra Hospital were all arrayed before me as I followed the signs to the lifts and then ward 101, from chrome bed frames and railings glimpsed through open bathroom doors, to the curved night sister's desk with its serviceable lamp. Disposed in soldier lines, all those bright things that make a hospital. I thought about the time I'd sat in the Monaro cafeteria with Eamonn, the day I'd chased Eve up and down corridors toting a dripping, wrecked umbrella. Now the real heat, the flat, breath-squashing inland heat had at last arrived, the rain and those long September winds seemed not only to belong to another season, but another time frame altogether.

Brook had collapsed as soon as he'd delivered Fred to the vet. I'd looked in on him twice during the night. Both times he'd been asleep.

I sat down in a chair beside his bed. His arms were outside the cotton blankets, a drip attached to his left wrist. In a weak voice he asked how Peter was.

'Fine,' I answered, moving my chair closer. 'They told him if he's good he can come and see you. You should hear all the please and thank yous.'

Brook smiled.

'How are you feeling?'

'They've taken a bone marrow sample.' The parched edges of his voice summed up all the other times that marrow had been sampled. 'In the meantime I've been told to rest.'

'You've been doing too much.'

'I've been living.'

'I should have noticed.'

'What?'

'You getting thin again.'

'Fashionably.'

'I didn't say anything.'

'You didn't need to. I can tell what you're thinking by looking at you.'

'That's why I'll never make a detective?'

'One of the reasons. Come here.'

I squashed my face against Brook's chest, wanting to bury it, shut out the light. His chest was too thin to bury anything in, even a small gift, a mouse's heart. His chest was thin and brittle and resistant, and a little further up was where his dry voice came from.

'Has Bill apologised for doubting you?'

'Bill? Apologise?'

'But it's okay between you?'

Brook didn't answer.

'Thank you,' I said.

'I'm sorry you had to go through that –'

'Not me. Peter.'

After a moment, Brook said, 'When I saw that damn dog lying there, it could have been me.'

'Don't.'

'You think I never imagined dying in a hole?'

He started to speak again, coughed, then blinked as though the words were somehow trapped behind his eyes. Then his face cleared and for a moment he looked calm, unwrinkled, a man who accepted himself, who had no great wish, just then, for deliverance.

......

Twenty-four

Sitting in her garden, Moira Howley listened to my account in silence. I looked at her and thought how summaries must always be unsatisfying, and how, as so often, the important things were not being said.

The old Moira, the Moira I'd met at the beginning of September, would have been tense and concentrated with the effort of what she wanted to say next, of not losing the thread of her intentions, of what she must impress upon me. Now she seemed drained of responses and emotions.

We talked about Colin Rasmussen, who'd made a full confession. On 21 June, Colin had sent Niall an email pretending to be Fenshaw, and asking Niall to meet him at the tower the following night. Niall had emailed straight back saying yes. Colin had intended getting Niall onto the public gallery, then overpowering him and throwing him over the fence. He hadn't reckoned on the weather being so bad. He'd got there early and walked around, keeping out of sight of the guards, confronted by the practical problems his plan presented. He'd over-heard the two technicians talking. They'd been so absorbed they hadn't noticed him. When he saw them disappear into the basement, he'd tried the security door and found it open.

He'd met Niall, explained that Fenshaw hadn't been able to make it, but that he and Fenshaw had decided they could see no problem with a new inquiry into the Ventac. They'd reconsidered and come round to Niall's point of view.

Colin then told Niall that there was something going on and nobody appeared to be paying much attention to security. 'Why don't we sneak a look at their fancy equipment?' Niall had agreed. Once inside, Colin had pushed him over the edge.

Colin's sarcasm came strongly though this part of his statement, as though the fact that Niall hadn't run away, or called for help, made him easier, and therefore more contemptible, prey.

Colin had stalked Niall on the MUD and, masquerading as Ferdia, caused trouble between Niall and Sorley Fallon, threatening to steal the game's source code and bringing Fallon's wrath down on Niall's head. Fallon's counter threat had been perfect from Colin's point of view. He hadn't thought of murder until then, but when Fallon made his threat known on the MUD, the idea came to him of the Telstra Tower, and a way of getting rid of Niall for good.

Colin had picked Peter up from school and then sent me that spiteful picture. Re-routing it so that it appeared to come from Fallon's computer, and timing it so that it arrived after Peter was missing, had been easy for someone with his skills.

In his confession, I could find no hint of remorse for kidnapping Peter, or for killing Niall, but he did state that he'd had no intention of harming my son. His aim had been to punish me, and to draw attention to the evil that I represented. People like myself and Niall were 'parasites whose aim in life was to spoil everything' and 'the scum of the earth'.

I'd risked Peter's safety, wilfully brought him into danger. Derek would never forgive me. I doubted if Brook would either.

Ivan was reluctant to let Katya out of his sight. He'd rung the creche and told them we'd be keeping her at home till the start of school next year. I knew he was within a hair's breadth of chucking in his job at the ANU, so he could be with her all day and not have to leave her with me.

How much of Colin's confession was calculated to sound insane, and how much genuinely so? The whole of his vendetta against Niall was crazy. Most chilling of all was that Colin seemed completely convinced that what he'd done was right. Anyone who challenged him or got in his way deserved to be eliminated. The Ventac saved lives. People would always make mistakes, and were expendable.

But I couldn't help wondering if Colin had *wanted* to be caught. When his carefully constructed fantasy about Niall started to unravel, and the police began turning up again at the hospital, when it was clear that Fenshaw was under serious investigation, Colin had grabbed Peter and, when caught, confessed immediately to Niall's murder. Was it too far-fetched to see the kidnapping as a desperate, last ditch bid to save Fenshaw and draw all blame, all responsibility down on his own head?

Fenshaw had played a part in attempting to discredit Niall, and, that night at Regatta Point, it was *Fenshaw* Niall had told about his decision to go public. I knew that if Colin went ahead and pleaded guilty, as he was intending, I'd have a next to impossible time trying to convince anyone that Fenshaw was at least partly to blame.

Colin had found Niall's body at the base of the tower that night, and, wearing gloves, removed his wallet and keys. He'd waited several hours, then gone to the Howleys, where he'd let himself in with Niall's key, loaded the castle scene and deleted everything else. As a parting gesture he'd emailed it to Sorley Fallon. Then he'd packed up all of Niall's letters and papers and left again, but not before Moira had heard him. One last trip to the tower car park to replace Niall's keys. Even using the bad weather as a cover, it had been an audacious plan.

Moira lifted her face to the smell of the roses. Her thick grey and brown hair was pulled back off her face with combs. Exposed, her face spoke of a knowledge and a sadness that would always hold her apart from other parents.

Bernard had moved into a flat in Braddon. Their house was up for sale.

'What will you do?' I asked her.

'Oh,' she said, with a touch of her old dismissiveness, 'I have money of my own.'

I could have thanked her for paying me handsomely, which she had. She would have thanked me for my thanks, and that would have kept us afloat over shallow ground.

She said suddenly, 'I've written to some of my Irish relatives.'

'Did you write to Fallon too?'

Moira smiled. 'He wrote back. A nice letter.'

There was no breath of wind. In an hour, or less, it would be too hot to sit outside. Just so the summer had arrived, cold one day, hot the next. The wisteria blossoms were long gone. The vines were covered with a mass of healthy, dark green leaves.

'It will be winter over there,' I said. 'He'll take you to see Dunluce castle in the snow.'

Moira's smile faded, but she didn't contradict me. Before she could leave Australia, she had police interviews to get through, court appearances.

I left her in a garden that had not been able to help itself turn green. Whenever I wished to, I could think about that, and how Moira might go on breathing in and out, might make it through the next day and the next.

Pictures can tell a simple story. Perhaps we don't give them enough credit for that. The Telstra Tower and Fallon's castle were connected in a dozen different ways, each an edifice behind which games were played, of threat and counter-threat, played in the mind and on the nerve ends. But were human motives simpler when you boiled them down – pride and fear together? Where did love come in? Once the play-acting began, did love enjoy the view? Or did love become its own dance down a mountain, not stopping for the gum trees? Who had understood this best? Sorley Fallon? Alex Fenshaw? Colin Rasmussen?

If Fallon's existence on that Antrim coast was proof of anything, then it was proof that unexpected contacts might be made. What would Moira Howley find when she visited his jewellery shop? Would she be the only visitor? When Fallon took her walking on the cliff path, would she look up, or down?

. . .

To walk into Brook's house was to experience seasons coming at me in waves of different coloured air, light and heavy, cold and hot. Brook hated being stuck in bed. The women in his life took up positions round the sick room, along with Bill McCallum, Ivan too. We who cared for him stood round about and waited, while seasons rumbled at each other through rooms that had lost their heart. Brook sat up in bed and complained at our attempts to wait on him. His eyes, when they were open, said he could not bluff anybody any longer.

I brought Katya over in the afternoons, when I knew that Sophie, who worked part-time for an insurance company, wouldn't be there. Sophie had asked for reduced hours in order to do her share of the nursing. I did not mind meeting her on my way out. We could be civil then, each of our meetings recalling, in a sadder way, that one on the steps of the city station, on a day of furious retrograde winter, day of happiness, a woman in a good suit and high, high heels walking up some steps to meet her man.

When Brook was awake and had the energy, he liked holding Katya, or letting her crawl up and down the bed, making a tent for her out of the sheet, which she hid in, shrieked and laughed, understanding perfectly, and all at once, the intense duality of pleasure in hiding and anticipating being found.

Other days, I watched Brook breathing with his eyes closed, and shrank into myself, and wished my daughter would be quiet, and felt too tense to read or look about me while I waited for him to wake up, if indeed he was asleep, and hated myself for feeling relieved when I left to pick Peter up from school.

We talked about Colin Rasmussen and Fenshaw, Sorley Fallon and Niall Howley. Our talk had an air of unreality about it, the same air that moved, too compressed, too mixed-up, through the house. Yet Brook wanted to talk. Wondering aloud about these men, one dead, one awaiting trial, one being questioned by British and Australian police officers, one so far escaping culpability, made Brook feel his mind had not closed down. His voice gained some of its laconic confidence, though always with a shadow underneath.

'Do you think you would've liked him?'

'Fallon?' Brook said, thinking this was who I meant.

'Niall.'

'Probably not. I don't know what kids are coming to these days.'

I bit my tongue. Here was another warning that I should look after mine.

'Niall was brave,' I said.

'But crazy. That Fallon's crazy too, if you ask me. And Rasmussen. Jesus.'

'Colin had an older, calculating mind behind him.'

We'd reached a stalemate over Fenshaw's involvement, which Colin was denying vehemently.

Katya had been tired that afternoon. While we were talking, she'd dozed off in my arms. She was at the stage of resisting an afternoon sleep, but I'd sat her on my knee with an open cardboard book, the kind she liked to pat and hold a conversation with. I didn't want to move in case I woke her.

Brook closed his eyes. While I waited for him to gather the energy to continue talking, or let me know he'd had enough, I watched the progress of the afternoon across a back lawn Ivan had mowed the previous weekend. Mowed seemed to precise a word for the scrawly lines across thick grass he'd managed to incise.

The year was nearly over. Soon the school holidays would begin. Peter would be home all day. Soon these long afternoons, their anxiety and moments of companionship, would be interrupted by a Christmas nobody seemed ready for. Through Brook's bedroom window, the hot, settled air approached midafternoon.

I heard a noise and turned round.

Sophie stood just inside the door, a plastic bag of groceries in each hand. Her expression said what mine must have too, that for once our system of avoiding each other hadn't worked. The bags looked heavy and her face was flushed. There was a line of sweat around her hairline and along her upper lip. I pictured her emptying the bags, tidying their contents into cupboards, taking care of her face and hair in Brook's small bathroom mirror. Then what? Sitting as I had just been doing, while the shadows lengthened?

Words stuck on the roof of my mouth. Katya wriggled in my arms and made a short, sharp sound.

'Come into the kitchen.'

I shut the door behind us, and sat down again with Katya on my knee. Sophie had not acknowledged my daughter, not so much as glanced in her direction.

'It's bad isn't it?'

Sophie stood with her hands hanging loosely by her sides, a woman who despised empty hands.

'They're talking about a bone marrow transplant.'

'I thought he was too old for that.'

Sophie moved her head and shoulders, half a nod and half a shrug of helplessness.

'It's less effective the older you are, but –'

'What about more chemo?'

'It's an alternative.'

'How much longer would it give him?'

'The doctor wouldn't say.'

'I wish –'

Sophie did not want to hear my wish. 'He needed to keep well for you. And your daughter. He wasn't going to let anything spoil that. He wouldn't have more tests. I tried to make him and he just got angry. He said he wasn't a patient any longer, wouldn't be a patient.'

She raised her hands again, this time vigorously, a person who's suddenly decided to do something after a long period of inactivity. There were the groceries to put away. There was Brook's afternoon tea.

Katya made a fist of one hand, raised it to my cheek and gurgled.

I said, 'I need to get my bag.'

Brook's eyes were still closed, and he was lying in the same position I had left him in. I bent for the cardboard book and put it in my bag. Then I leant again, over the bed this time, and kissed him gently on the forehead. Katya was staring into my face, her black eyes wide and, perfect mimic, she pursed her lips exactly as I'd just done, and kissed the air.

· · ·

Over the phone, I told Bernard Howley that there was no record of Sorley Fallon ever having been in Australia.

'In spirit maybe, but that's all.'

There was a silence which felt like Bernard was searching for a way to contradict me. I'd already told him that the friendship society had been thoroughly checked out, and it was no more, or less, than what it appeared to be, a fundraising organisation. There was no record of money having found its way into bombs or guns. I told Bernard that Detective-Sergeant Bill McCallum would be happy to talk to him about it any time he wished, and to go through the results of the investigation. I was pretty sure that he would not take up the offer. For Bernard, it was enough that Moira had gone behind his back and sold those concert tickets, continued an association that he disapproved of, and encouraged Niall to do the same.

Bernard wasn't in a position to challenge anything I said, but that didn't make him like it, or approve of me. I hadn't expected him to thank me, but a slight unbending in his manner would have been welcome.

In a reflective mood, I called Sorley Fallon and thanked him for sending me Fenshaw's memo to the hospital board. I apologised on behalf of Brook and his colleagues for the sudden arrival of a carload of police demanding to know about the kidnapping of a ten-year-old boy.

Fallon said he was sorry for what Peter had been through. 'Give him my best wishes.'

'I will.'

I heard a young male voice in the background. Of course, it could be a customer. It was the middle of a working day in Ireland, but I'd never seen much evidence that Fallon bothered himself with ordinary work.

He mentioned Moira Howley and said he was glad that she'd made contact with him. When I referred to the possibility of her visiting Ireland, he surprised me by saying, 'If business picks up, I might even make it to Australia next year.'

'We don't have any ruined castles. Plenty of natural attractions though.'

Fallon laughed. Again I heard a voice, or voices, though I couldn't make out any words.

'I'd like to see where Niall lived.'

He didn't need to add, and where he died. The image of the tower was strong between us. I said I'd look forward to meeting him again, and then goodbye.

I rang Bridget next, clocking up a phone bill. At this rate, I'd use up all of Moira's last cheque. But I needed to hear Bridget's voice, as I'd needed to hear Fallon's, that Irish sibilance, a way of saying 'Sandra' that they had in common. I needed to keep convincing myself that there was more to them than sleight of hand, ciphers on a screen.

I told Bridget, thinking that she'd probably already got the news from Fallon, that Colin Rasmussen had confessed to Niall's murder, and that when it came time to enter a plea he would be pleading guilty. I said I was afraid that no one would get to the bottom, the extent of Dr Fenshaw's responsibility. I asked Bridget if she was still giving tours of the factory, and she replied that her father had finally put his foot down. She didn't sound disappointed, and I recalled her telling me that she was getting bored with it. I had no doubt she'd find another game, another bit of acting to amuse her for a while, even another MUD, or some kind of net impersonation. The possibilities, after all, were endless, and the attraction always there. She didn't share Sorley Fallon's guilt. She'd taken Niall's side, supported him as much as she was able to. Somehow with Bridget though, I had the feeling that guilt would never cut deep, or dissuade her from a course of action that she'd set her heart on.

· · ·

By the weekend, when Ivan and I headed off for a few days at the coast, I'd seen Brook's doctor and discussed his treatment. They were going ahead with the bone marrow transplant. When the doctor spoke to me, it was always with a slight frown between his eyebrows, not knowing where to place me. Clearly I wasn't family, yet I persisted in asking questions that only family members had the right to ask. Just as clearly, there was no wife around to ask them. There was Sophie, and there was me.

I couldn't pester Brook to contact his ex-wife and children. He'd made it clear in the past that he didn't want to. But I pestered McCallum on Brook's behalf. I was determined to track them down, one way or another. I didn't discuss this plan with anyone except McCallum. It had arrived perfectly clear and fully formed, and I knew it would succeed.

I watched Fred and Peter running in the surf. Peter was determined that Fred could learn to catch waves. Never mind that Peter couldn't catch a wave himself. Fred was the cleverest dog, and he would learn.

It hadn't been easy finding a place that would take dogs, but eventually we did – a small Bed and Breakfast the other side of Moruya. Too far south for the main tourist trade, and a couple of kilometres inland, it was a farm rather than a beach house. Fred had to stay shut up in a small yard when we were at the house, but we headed off to the beach early each morning and, luckily for us, the weather held.

Ivan spent as much time as he could under the umbrella, set up as close as possible to the water line so Katya could dig in the damp sand. What Katya loved most was for her father to dig holes, so she could watch the water seeping in.

We had the beach practically to ourselves. I divided my time between lying in my crescent of shade, squinting at the roistering dark shapes in the water that were my son and his dog, looking for shells along the tide line, and short bursts of swimming. After one of these quick swims, I flopped down on my towel next to Ivan, listening to the soft sounds of spade and hands as he dug yet another hole.

'There's planning that goes with an ability to take advantage of circumstances,' I said. 'Surely that was Fenshaw's kind.'

Ivan looked up from his digging reluctantly. 'You're still insisting he told Rasmussen what to do?'

I thought of Sorley Fallon, and the extent to which a man should be considered responsible for his followers, the lengths such a man would go to repudiate them, if and when those followers became a nuisance.

'"Will no one rid me of this turbulent priest?"' I said. 'It's odd how, in the play, you're waiting for those words, you know they're coming, yet they're still a shock.'

'What's a shock?'

'The coldness I suppose, the inhumanity.'

Peter took a tumble and came up blinded by swirling sandy water. I called out. Peter rubbed his eyes and, still half blinded, managed a wobbly wave.

I smiled at Katya, sitting perfectly straight and steady between us, talking to herself as she patted down the sand.

'What do you think? In a minute it might be time to pack up and have lunch?'

I called out to Peter to tell him we were going. He pretended not to hear me. After Christmas he was going to stay with Derek for a month. Derek was having his backyard dog-proofed and he'd bought a kennel. He was taking the whole of January off. Peter had permission to drop in to see his sister any time. She would miss him more than he could guess.

I shook sand out of my towel and folded it. I clenched my teeth as I collapsed the beach umbrella. Our umbrella was old and vicious, and either refused to dismantle itself at all, or did so with such force and speed that I'd frequently had my fingers jammed.

Peter came running up from the water's edge with Fred, and both of them shook cold salty water over us.

I laughed and handed him his towel. I hoisted the swimming bag over one arm and picked up the umbrella, which had for once behaved itself. I enjoyed the tramp back to the clump of trees where we'd parked the car, the trappings and slowings of parenthood. Even Fred's nose pressed against the backs of my knees, announcing that it was dinner-time, didn't bother me. In fact I found myself wishing we could spend the rest of our lives, or at least the summer, on a beach.

I saw the frightened way Peter hugged Fred to him, in this expanse of sea and yellow light. I saw the way his eyes went blank sometimes when I spoke to him. We would be going back to Canberra all too soon for Peter, city of white towers and dark plunging verticals, a town built for men caught on a trajectory of love and duty, young men who had to learn to jump, and then to keep on jumping.

`. . . . . .`

The White Tower

Dorothy Johnston grew up in Geelong, Victoria, and has lived in Canberra since 1979. Her debut crime novel, *The Trojan Dog*, which introduced crime consultant Sandra Mahoney, was joint winner, ACT book of the year 2001, and runner-up in the Davitt Award for the best crime novel published by a woman in 2000. The *Age* included the novel in its Best of 2000, crime section. Dorothy has twice been short-listed for the Miles Franklin Award, for *Ruth* and *One For The Master*.

Dorothy Johnston has a website at www.webone.com.au/~dorothy.